# DISTURBANCE-LOVING SPECIES

BOOKS BY PETER CHILSON

*Riding the Demon: On the Road in West Africa*

*Disturbance-Loving Species*

# DISTURBANCE-LOVING
## SPECIES  *A Novella and Stories*

## PETER CHILSON

A MARINER ORIGINAL ♦ HOUGHTON MIFFLIN COMPANY
Boston   New York   2007

For information about permission to reproduce selections from
this book, write to Permissions, Houghton Mifflin Company,
215 Park Avenue South, New York, New York 10003.

Visit our Web site: www.houghtonmifflinbooks.com.

*Library of Congress Cataloging-in-Publication Data*
Chilson, Peter.
    Disturbance-loving species : a novella and stories / Peter Chilson.
        p.  cm.
    "A Mariner Original."
    ISBN-13: 978-0-618-85870-5
    ISBN-10: 0-618-85870-9
    1. Niger — Fiction.  2. Americans — Africa — Fiction.
3. West Africans — United States — Fiction. I. Title.
    PS3603.H565D57 2007
    813'.6 — dc22    2007004210

*Book design by Melissa Lotfy*

PRINTED IN THE UNITED STATES OF AMERICA

MP 10 9 8 7 6 5 4 3 2 1

Some of these stories have appeared, in slightly different form,
in the following publications: "Disturbance-Loving Species" was
first published in *Clackamas Literary Review;* "Freelancing" was
first published in *Ascent;* "American Food" was first published
in *Gulf Coast.* "Toumani Ogun" was first published in *The Long
Story.* A section of the novella, *Tea with Soldiers,* was also published in *Ascent.*

For Abdoulaye Mamani
and Oumarou Badini

# CONTENTS

# FOREWORD

These powerful stories are distinguished by moments in which their characters find themselves confronted by the contrast between North America and Africa — instances of startling and life-altering collision. In their candor, even bluntness, the stories are about politics, but they are not mere set pieces or diatribes; nor do they romanticize Africa, although they are haunted by its landscape and its people. Instead, Peter Chilson uses the intersections of the two worlds to remind us of our human limitations, illustrating, over and over, the startling connections and disconnections between peoples and places.

In "American Food," Keita Traore, a West African soil specialist living in Oregon, receives a visit from a sheriff's deputy and considers the possibility of arrest. In "Toumani Ogun," the narrator, an American political science professor, encounters a ghost from twenty years past, an African army major who shot an innocent man before his eyes. While each piece in the collection brings out the richness of such geographical and cultural juxtapositions, Chilson explores these themes at greatest complexity in the novella, *Tea with Soldiers*, which follows a few weeks in the life of David Carter, volunteer English teacher at the Lycée Centrale in the northwest African country of Niger. It is 1993, the third year of a war between the military government and Tuareg rebels, and the people of Niger are subjected to growing oppression and terror by their government.

In the young American David Carter, Chilson introduces a naive protagonist whose desires appear innocuous enough, even well
intentioned. When asked by his friend and colleague Salif why he
has come to Africa, Carter replies, "I'm young, I want to travel. I'm
here to broaden myself." Carter had envisioned Hemingway's and
Dinesen's "images of great and beautiful landscapes," remember-
ing his college's Africa Night celebration, with a blond student
reciting poetry.

His position of privilege shelters Carter from the political reality of the country he supposedly seeks to know. Even his clothing
marks him as someone who exposes himself only selectively to his
surroundings. Salif calls him *Mai Kaya Dayowa*, "Owner of Many
Things," and a "toureest," explaining that Africans apply this term
to the earliest soldiers and explorers, the administrators and scientists, the missionaries and now the diplomats, aid workers, and
"volunteers." However good Carter's intentions, he has come to
Africa for his own sake, and his travel to fulfill personal goals becomes increasingly absurd when juxtaposed with the terror and
violence in his country of destination.

The novella underlines the questionable morality of Carter's
position. Foreigners experience Africa, as Salif says, "like travelers
in perfect cubes of ice." But as the weeks go by, it becomes clear
that even the most naive and protected "toureest" is not immune
to suffering. Carter's assumption that it is possible for him to
"leave the issue of the Tuaregs alone" is ultimately self-deceptive:
violence not only escalates but reaches closer and closer to home.

In our times, it is acceptable to focus on the universality and fa-
miliarity of all human experience — to brush over the great forces
that create our differences. Yet our best fiction also seeks to bring
us face to face with the reality of what we cannot know. Readers
of the stories in *Disturbance-Loving Species* may be troubled by
the complex questions that are raised in this powerful collection,
but also inspired by the desire for friendship and fairness that is
shared by many of the book's diverse characters.

LAN SAMANTHA CHANG

# TEA WITH SOLDIERS *A NOVELLA*

# WEEK ONE

## Monday

CARTER HEARD THE SOLDIERS just before sunrise, knew them by the sound of weapons slung over shoulders and clicking against belts as the men walked from the prison up the road past his apartment, a room with a balcony and French windows above a dusty street. As they emerged from the half-light, he leaned back in his chair, sipping from a mug of coffee and counting the prisoners, who formed a line between soldiers ahead and soldiers behind. The captives, barefoot in blue T-shirts and shorts, were linked with a rope tied at the waist. The soldiers wore faded fatigues and berets. Some wore sandals and others, boots.

"Bastards," he said.

He bit his lip and tapped his pen on the wooden table he kept on the balcony with a steel lawn chair. He'd been awake since five, drinking coffee and studying the darkness, his routine before the heat set in. In his notebook, he wrote a couple of lines under the heading "The Morning Count": *Six soldiers and eight prisoners after first light this morning, half past five...* The prisoners shouldered shovels and hoes or hefted bags of cement on their heads, on the way, Carter imagined, to repair a wall or culvert or to perform a task at some official's home.

From the opposite direction, he saw six men ride up the street on bicycles, carrying cartons of vegetables from gardens along the river. Tomatoes, squash, carrots, and potatoes. This was Niamey, the capital city, which Carter thought of as a giant village. Two riders transported great wads of lettuce, like giant flowers, wrapped in wire netting and tied to the cargo board over the rear wheel. At night they stowed wooden tables for their produce in the courtyard of the apartment building and every morning set them back on the dirt beside the road. Now, with soldiers and prisoners marching by and vegetable sellers dismounting from their bicycles, Carter felt darkness fade. Wisps of cloud, like old scars against the sky, brightened from red to pink over land that had seen little rain in three years. Some days the air itself—given the right chemistry of sunlight and red dust—gave a reddish glow to the land beyond the city, fields of pockmarked volcanic rock that emerged where wind had taken the topsoil. He thought of the monsoon storms that would come in a few weeks, wind ahead of rain, stirring dust high in the atmosphere, billowing as if the earth were being sucked into the heavens.

A prisoner looked up toward the balcony and shouted. *"Bonjour, le blanc. Mes respects,"* he said, waving and smiling.

Carter waved back. *"Bonjour, mon ami,"* he said, adding in Hausa, *"Sanu da aiki"*—My respect for your work.

The man stumbled as a soldier pushed him along, striking his shoulders with open hands. A few days earlier, from his balcony, Carter watched a soldier stab the barrel of his gun hard into the back of a prisoner who wasn't moving fast enough. He'd scribbled the incident in his notebook. *Afraid the gun would go off,* he wrote. Soldiers, he thought, were more visible than ever in the city. Students and civil servants had staged protests against the army, and he'd heard talk of mass arrests. Nine students had been shot to death in the street outside the Ministry of Defense the week before. Students made a weekly event of marching in silence down the Boulevard of the Republic, but every week fewer of them showed up for the walk. Carter sometimes saw soldiers and prisoners from another barracks cutting across the grounds of Lycée Centrale, where he taught English.

He switched on his shortwave to listen to the BBC. He turned the volume low to keep an intimacy with the broadcast, which led with news confirming a rumor that had been spreading in the city for days:

> The French newspaper *Paris Soir* reports that two months ago soldiers in the West African country of Niger killed more than one hundred Tuareg nomads in the town of Tchin-Tabaradene in the Sahara . . . Soldiers opened fire when refugees rioted during distribution of food aid. The newspaper cites witnesses who fled across the border to Algeria. Most of the dead are said to be women and children. The news comes as Tuareg guerrilla bands struggle to set up an independent Saharan state.

The street was filling now with cars and donkey carts, with people shouting and bartering, with animals and engines moving in various states of protest. Carter witnessed this every day in Niamey, awed by the furious spontaneity after sunrise. Bicycles and scooters streamed both ways, weaving among other vehicles and people on foot, between herds of goats and the occasional camel. A thousand near misses every minute. He was smiling as he went inside for more coffee, pouring water from a kettle on a small gas stove into his cup and adding instant coffee. Off a shelf, he picked up three green lesson notebooks and returned to the balcony to work. After a few minutes he heard the sound of lilting French, calling to him from the street.

"*Ahh, l'Américain,* above the world, sitting on his lovely balcony. *Comment ça va?*"

Carter looked down at the source of that clear baritone voice—"*L'Américain chez nous. Tout va bien?*" Salif, his colleague, a French and math teacher, waited, with lesson books in a plastic folder under his arm. He wore a white cotton robe and leggings, with skullcap and sandals.

"Monsieur Daveed, representative of the world's most powerful country, here, among us, in Afreecaaaa. *Ça va?*" Salif pronounced Carter's first name, David, with a distinct French cadence.

Carter stuffed his lessons and a water bottle into a canvas shoulder bag and met Salif on the street. The American felt a little embarrassed, as he always did in response to Salif's early-morning wit. Carter's clothes — sturdy hiking sandals, khaki trousers, and a short-sleeved cotton shirt — contrasted with those of his African friend. Also, Carter never went out without a straw hat and sunglasses.

"Yes, Amereeeecaaa, God's chosen government, the policeman of the world."

Carter shook his head. "Come on, Salif. Let's go."

Salif raised an index finger and smiled. His teeth were yellow and perfectly even.

"Yes, it is true. That is how God made it, you know. But one day, God may change his mind."

Carter smiled, wondering if soldiers would hassle them on the way to work this morning. Soldiers walked the streets in threes. "Ghosts" in plainclothes rode buses and frequented bars, marketplaces, and offices. The president's photograph hung in every home and workplace and above the windshield in public buses. One photo showed his profile, looking stern in uniform, with peaked cap and khaki tunic. But the most popular image portrayed the president at prayer in the Great Mosque, wearing a white robe and skullcap, his hands before his face, palms turned inward, eyes closed.

Carter's expatriate friends joked that if you looked the wrong way at the photo, a "ghost" would flash a green-and-white Commission of Truth and Solidarity identity card and arrest you. Bad nerves fed the jest. A war was on, nearly three years old now. From November to March, when the northeasterly harmattan wind shrouded the land in dust, Tuareg rebels ambushed aid convoys and stole cars; they attacked army patrols, lobbed mortar shells at government outposts, and kidnapped tourists. They held a team of Dutch botanists for a ransom of food and medical supplies. People quipped that inflation was bad because the president had to manufacture the money to pay his security police, but only expatriates made such jokes. Carter knew the Africans said something different — that the security police could make themselves invisible and appear anywhere, in any guise. Foreigners who spent extended time in country ignored such talk. They worried about complications, about being sucked in. So they kept to themselves, alone or in their clubs and embassies, telling their jokes. They took in the country, as Salif said, "like travelers in perfect cubes of ice."

This city, this entire country, in Carter's mind, seemed awash in uniforms: a blue Land Rover and soldiers on every third or fourth street. Soldiers were a constant here, like the dust. That, too, was something Salif told him. Mornings, on the mile-long walk to the school, Carter learned to measure the level of paranoia by counting checkpoints. The two men tried to bypass them, but checkpoints were unavoidable. Carter kept a chart in a notebook he carried in his bag. Usually he and Salif passed through five or six checkpoints on the way to school, though one day he counted eleven. Often soldiers set up random roadblocks by stretching a cord knee-high across the road. Sometimes the barrier was just made of rags tied together and looped around wooden posts pounded in the dirt. Here, soldiers from a tribe of farmers and merchants, identified by three inch-long vertical scars high on each cheek, confronted lighter-skinned men with braided hair and the leggings, tunic, and conical hat of a nomadic tribe, their faces marked by smaller scars around the eyes and corners of the mouth. And the struggle at the checkpoint reflected the suspicion that existed between a man whose heritage lay in tilling the fields and another whose ancestors had roamed the land in search of grass for their animals, respecting no boundaries.

Carter and Salif stayed tight to the roadside, weaving in and out of throngs of people and keeping an eye out for camels, donkeys, cars, and motorcycles. Carter liked the confident way his African friend looked and moved, this tall, thin man, all muscle and bone, with sharp cheekbones framing the wide smile that greeted any-one he met. Salif walked with deliberate smooth strides, swing-ing his arms high, the lessons folder clutched in one hand. He placed his feet with certainty, as if he knew every spot where they would land. He walked as if mimicking a soldier on parade, Carter thought.

"Daveed, are you ready for our friends at the checkpoints?"

Carter walked with his arms folded. "They're assholes, Salif. It's not possible to be ready."

"Daveed, you must relax."

"Okay."

Soldiers stopped them after three blocks, half a mile from the school. The men—kids, really—wore fatigues too large for their thin bodies and sunglasses taken from travelers. They snapped their fingers to demand identity papers. Carter and Salif handed their cards to a young soldier who studied them with a blank expression. (Carter had learned to keep his card ready in his breast pocket; women kept them tucked in their wraps or headscarves.) Every week they dealt with soldiers at this corner, some new and some they'd seen many times. This soldier squinted at Carter's identity card. His face was puffy and his fatigues were wrinkled and dusty as if he'd slept in the dirt by the road that night. He peeked at the lesson books and water bottle in Carter's bag. "Teecha man," he said, smiling, as he handed the card back. There'd been a time when Carter glared at soldiers, baiting them by refusing to hand over his card. He'd enjoyed the shouting matches, but now he wore an air of detachment, as if he didn't care—as if the soldiers were irrelevant. Indifference, he'd learned, was a more efficient way to deny them power.

Two other soldiers leaned against a Land Rover, smoking and laughing, with rifles slung across their backs. From a distance, Carter thought the gun barrels resembled extended limbs, and the men looked like an entomological curiosity, perhaps an outsize breed of mantis. One soldier he'd seen many times kept wads of West African francs tucked under his beret over his right temple. The notes fanned out from under the headband like an earflap, advertising a fact: *to pass, you must pay.* From time to time the soldier yanked the bills out, counted them, and put them back in the same way. Another carried a wooden replica of a rifle, painted black, with a leather strap hooked from the barrel to the shoulder stock. Sometimes he pointed the weapon in the air and shouted, "Boom, boom, boom," jerking the rifle as if it kicked on each firing. People on the street would scatter and duck. The soldiers would laugh.

The one with the puffy face took Salif's card between his thumb and index finger, looking back and forth between the photo and

Salif. He shook his head and turned around. Holding Salif's card in his hand, he walked to the roadside and, without a word, dropped it in a metal box. Salif began to protest amiably, smiling and addressing the soldier as *"mon frère."* He approached him with open hands raised in a questioning manner. The soldier slapped him. Salif's head jerked sideways, though he did not stumble. Another soldier ordered Salif to sit by the roadside. Carter started shouting.

*"Qu'est-ce qu'il y a?"*—Why do you hit him?

Carter pleaded as the soldiers pushed him back. He responded in kind, shoving a soldier against the chest. The soldier gripped Carter by the back of his neck, aided by another soldier, who held him by the shoulder. Salif, squatting on the roadside, put a finger to his lips. Carter relaxed a little, realizing his anger might cause more problems. He raised his hands in a gesture of surrender and smiled.

*"Bon, ça va, ça va."*

The soldiers backed off, and Carter walked to the opposite side of the road and waited, arms folded, watching over Salif while the soldiers eyed both of them. Carter's shirt stuck to his back, and his neck itched from a fresh coating of dust. After a few minutes, the soldiers led Salif and two other men to a blue Land Rover. Carter kept an eye on their actions, and when the vehicle began moving he ran alongside, pounding the engine hood.

"Where are you taking him?"

As the Land Rover sped away, two soldiers grabbed Carter by the shoulders and hustled him down the street. After a few hundred yards they let go of him. One soldier explained that Salif would be released in a few hours after he got a new identity card.

Carter thought of trying to find Salif, but he couldn't be sure which barracks they'd take him to. He turned to the soldiers and pointed at them. "That man is my friend. Where are you taking him?" he shouted again. "If I don't see him again today, I'll be back."

The soldiers said nothing and walked to the roadblock.

This was Carter's twenty-third month in country. He was going home in a month. As he walked down the road, he looked back at the crowds waiting to be checked or taken away, as if through some cosmic doorway. Poof! Gone.

Carter began to run.

## September

"WHAT ARE YOU DOING HERE?" Salif asked Carter, as Salif shook rinse water from a tea glass. He fixed his eyes on his new American friend. "Why did you come to Africa?"

"I want to get rich, Salif."

The joke died. Carter laughed anyway.

Salif smiled. "Yes, but why Africa?"

Carter sat cross-legged with his hands in his lap and said nothing for a minute. He wiped his lips with his fingers and shrugged.

"I'm young, I want to travel. I'm here to broaden myself."

Salif dropped sugar cubes one by one into the teakettle. He crushed them with a spoon.

"Mmm, yes, to travel just for oneself and nothing else. It's an American idea, I think. To travel for pleasure?" Salif smacked his lips, savoring the tea. He grinned at Carter. Then he said a few words in English.

"Oh, yes, the American way of life . . . Monsieur Daveed, you're a tourist." Salif raised the pitch of his voice. "Toureest, toureest."

## Monday

CARTER HURRIED through the streets, intent on seeing the headmaster before classes started. At checkpoints, soldiers barely glanced at his identity card, embossed on the cover with an open book beneath a blue United Nations globe, the emblem of the UN World Education Program. He knew they would check his card again at the school gate, as they did at the university and all other schools. They even demanded identity cards of children. Yet the ease with which Carter entered and left checkpoints annoyed him, as if his skin color made him invisible, tribeless. He hurried through knots of Africans, citizens of this land detained for one reason or another. Many had no papers. Taxis, minibuses, and small Peugeot pickup trucks lined the roadside. People — students, clerks, merchants, women carrying buckets of water on their heads, and farmers with hoes hooked over their shoulders — stood or sat on the dirt. Carter walked through this every day and always felt relieved to arrive at the school, not so much to get away from checkpoints as to enjoy the open space.

In the two years they'd been friends, Salif had been absent from work many times, though never more than a few days at a time, but this morning marked the first time Carter had witnessed the soldiers taking his friend away. Soon after Carter started teaching at the school, Salif was away for two days. The second time, two months later, he was gone almost a week. When he showed up again, he had a broken finger and an injured eye. There were more disappearances. A day here, three or four days there. Carter recorded each in his notebook, with dates.

Salif waved off Carter's queries. "Misunderstandings," he'd say. Sometimes, when he got back, Salif would joke, "Oh, it was only a short official vacation."

At a jog, Carter approached the school gate, which stood on a side street, away from the city's busy thoroughfares. He heard the clatter of shutters as the groundskeeper threw open French windows across campus. In the street, students gathered in small groups. A low cement wall and leafy neem trees enclosed the lycée grounds, a few hundred acres of hard-packed sand and gravel. Long cinderblock classroom buildings covered with white stucco accommodated six hundred students, with four classrooms to each building; a large playing field ran alongside. A flagpole stood in the center of campus, where mornings, just before classes, students and faculty waited at attention for the raising of the flag and the singing of the national song.

Students shouted at Carter as he passed. "Good mawning, sah. Good mawning, Meestaa Daveed. How ahh yuuu?"

Carter smiled and returned the greetings, but he did not stop as usual. He walked by the soldier at the school gate, ignoring him even though the soldier snapped his fingers and shouted, *"Monsieur, s'il vous plaît, votre carte, votre carte!"* But the soldier had seen the American before and let him go.

In the administration building at the center of campus Carter found the headmaster at his desk, under a broken ceiling fan. He was bent over paperwork, wearing a red fez tipped slightly forward, and a billowing light-blue cotton robe called a boubou. His round face shone with sweat. Twice before, Carter had spoken to the headmaster about Salif's absences and was told not to worry, that Salif would soon be back. Now, Carter stood before him again, trying to calm his own breathing.

"Monsieur David," the headmaster said, without looking up. "You need something?"

"Soldiers took Salif this morning. I saw it happen."

The headmaster kept his eyes on his paperwork. "Don't worry about Salif. He is fine. They want to ask him a few questions. He'll probably be transferred to another school."

Between breaths, Carter said, "Tell me about 'they.' Tell me about the people who need to ask Salif questions. Who are they? Maybe I can talk to them."

The headmaster put down his pen and sighed. "Monsieur David," he said, leaning into his desk, hands spread over his papers, "I don't want you talking to people about this. Questions are dangerous and Salif has enough troubles." He paused. "These matters aren't your concern."

Sweat stung Carter's eyes and he blinked. He felt like picking a fight. "He's your countryman," he said. "Do you care if Salif is still alive?"

The headmaster allowed a few seconds of silence to pass. Finally, he spoke in measured words. "You think no one cares? We are all suffering, monsieur. My own brother is in prison and I don't know why. They won't tell me where he is."

The statement startled Carter. He took a breath. "Look, I'm sorry about your brother, but that only makes me more concerned. Your own family and staff are being arrested and you sit here doing paperwork. What's the matter with you?"

The headmaster glared and spoke quickly. "I received word from the police a week ago that Salif is suspected of sedition and that he would be arrested and held, perhaps for a longer period this time. I have no idea of the specifics and I don't know where he is. The serious cases they send to the military camp at Dirkou, in the desert. But that cannot be Salif's situation. He's just a teacher who talks too much. I'm certain they will release him soon."

"Dirkou? That's a week's journey by road," Carter said. He faced the headmaster with his arms akimbo.

The headmaster picked up his pen and tapped the ballpoint on the desk. He shook his head and put the pen down. "You know, you people, I don't understand what you people are doing here . . . You are a volunteer." He snorted and sat back in his chair. "What is that? What am I supposed to do with you?"

They eyed each other across the desk, each expecting an answer. The headmaster folded his arms. "Monsieur David, we have an inspection tomorrow morning. The minister of education himself will be visiting each class. You must be in your classroom at seven and be certain your students are prepared."

"Prepared for what?" Carter asked.

The headmaster returned to his paperwork.

Carter pleaded with him. "Look, you know Salif is harmless. You know he's not a Tuareg, you know his tribal identity. You can intervene for him?"

The man looked up sharply. "Don't tell me what I know and don't know. You understand nothing about this country. You know nothing of our lives."

Carter drew a breath as if to speak, but he could not respond. He shook his head and walked out, frustrated and angry. He knew the headmaster was right. Salif had told him as much.

He paused at the bottom of the steps to gather his thoughts. Students and teachers hurried to classrooms, to await the call to the flag ceremony. Carter recalled Salif's words — an accusation — that Carter never took the time to really learn about the country and its people ("Daveed, get out of Niamey and see how we live"). Yet Carter felt it was enough of a challenge to adapt to life in the city and at the school. He lowered his head and ran his hands through his sweaty hair, feeling nauseated and thirsty. He'd never seen anyone take Salif, until now. He had wondered how it was done—did the soldiers surprise him on the street or go to his home? After being released, did he report to someone on a schedule, like a parole officer of sorts?

Carter took out his notebook and pen and scribbled a few words: *Day One of Salif's eleventh "official vacation" since I've known him.* Carter put the notebook away and began walking to his classroom, thinking that this time, when Salif returned, he would have to explain everything. Carter spoke the thought aloud in English, to hear himself say it: "Tell me the whole story now, Salif. I'm part of it. I'm involved."

## April

CARTER FIRST VISITED Salif's home a year earlier, during one of his friend's disappearances. Salif rarely discussed his wife and children, nor did he invite his American friend to his home, so Carter had to ask around discreetly to learn that Salif and his family lived behind a high mud wall in a concrete bungalow up a narrow dirt pathway two miles from the school. The corrugated iron door to the compound was padlocked. Carter pounded the metal with the flat of his hand, shouting Salif's name. A group of old men, relaxing on grass mats outside the wall, stopped talking and stared at him. Carter stood on tiptoe, with his hands on top of the mud wall, pulling himself up to peer over at the house.

One old man smiled at Carter. He cradled a wooden cane in his arms and was fingering prayer beads with his right hand. He raised his voice and spoke in French.

"What do you want, friend?"

Carter let go of the wall and smiled, trying to look unconcerned.

"I'm sorry. I do not mean to disturb you. I'm looking for my friend, Salif Moustapha, and his family."

The old man nodded and studied Carter for a long minute. Finally, he told him that Salif's family had gone to his wife's village a few miles from the capital.

Carter squatted with the men, keeping his head down and

avoiding eye contact, out of respect. He made small talk about the drought and hard times.

"It is very hot. I think it is a good sign. The rains will be good this year."

The men nodded and repeated the phrase *"Insha Allah,"* granting that yes, the signs were good, but everything was up to the will of God.

Carter made little circles in the sand with his fingertips before asking more questions.

"Do you happen to know the name of that village? Maybe I can visit him there."

The old man looked at his companions and then back at Carter, shaking his head.

"I am sorry."

The next morning, Carter left his apartment to walk to school and there was Salif, waiting in the street and smiling as if he'd never left. He mimicked the greetings of Carter's students: "Good mawwwning, Meestaa Daveed. How ahh yuu?" The flesh around Salif's left eye was cut and swollen, as if a marble had been inserted under the skin at his temple. His right index and middle fingers — his smoking fingers — were bound together in white medical tape, so one finger could act as a splint for the other, which was broken. But the first thing Carter noticed was that his friend was very thin, as if he'd not eaten for days. He slouched, smoking with his left hand. Carter looked at Salif's eye and his bandages.

"Are you sure you want to risk being seen walking with me?" asked Carter. "I'm worried someone may be suspicious of the time you spend with an American."

Salif smiled and shrugged his shoulders.

"What happened?"

Salif reached for the kola nut Carter offered from his shirt pocket. The nuts were thumb-sized, with green skin. Carter carried them especially for Salif, who chewed them for the juice, which produced a sharp caffeine high. Salif said nothing of his eye, and Carter knew better than to press his friend. They walked to school without speaking.

Late that afternoon, Salif entered Carter's classroom while Carter graded exams. The students were gone. Salif leaned against the door frame, with his arms hanging loose at his sides, his face hollow and drawn.

"Daveed, I need money for medicine."

Carter put his hands on the armrests of his chair and pushed himself to his feet. He fumbled in his trouser pockets for money and in his mind for something thoughtful to say. He gave Salif all he had, two thousand West African francs, about nine dollars, and watched him fold the bills in half and slip them into his breast pocket. Salif's set his lips and blinking look expressed a certain resentment, which made Carter nervous. Carter thrust his hands in his pockets.

"You should boil your water. Be sure your wife cooks your food longer."

Salif wiped his mouth on the back of his wrist and squatted in the doorway, resting his arms on his knees. Carter continued grading exams. He could hear Salif breathing through his nose and turned to face him.

"What happened to your eye, Salif?"

The two men studied each other. A few seconds passed.

"Every day, Daveed, you eat what and where you like. Have you ever eaten with us? Have you tasted African food with African people? You Americans, you come here, you stay a while, and you fly away."

Carter looked away, feeling a twinge of anger.

"What are you trying to say, Salif?"

Salif's eyes wandered past Carter, over his head. He didn't answer.

"Salif, you visit my apartment almost every day, but you won't even let me see your home or tell me what is happening to you."

With two fingers, Salif plucked a cigarette from a loose bunch in his breast pocket and put it in his mouth. From the same pocket he pulled a wooden match, which he scraped on the floor to light the cigarette. He squatted with his back against the wall, sucking deeply, with the cigarette between his thumb and forefinger, savoring every drag and licking his lips.

"You haven't seen enough, Daveed. You know nothing of what's happening in this country. Why don't you get out of the city? You'll see something then."

"Go there with me, Salif. We can visit your village."

Salif laughed. "The funny thing, Mr. Daveed, is that this is my country, but you have more freedom than I do. I can't leave this city very often, and I don't want to. I don't have money and there are too many soldiers on the road. They are more of a problem for me than for you. They don't care about white foreigners."

Carter leaned forward in his chair, elbows on his knees, hands open. At times he thought Salif hated him for the ease of his life, his power to casually buy a cup of coffee, a pack of cigarettes, a pound of meat.

"What do you want me to do, Salif?"

They sat together, silent. After a while, Salif flicked the butt away and exhaled a thin cloud of smoke.

## June

FOR CARTER, the first months in country had seemed okay, considering he had arrived in a place so unfamiliar, a land of wind and dust and heat and also dread. In the West African Sahel, a savanna on the southern edge of the Sahara, heat makes movement oppressive; combined with the silence of vast, arid lands, heat can also fray reason. It was said to drive people mad. The French had a name for such madness— *l'africanité*. Aid workers called it "cultural exhaustion."

Political strife was equally inescapable, though a visitor might at first be blind to it. Foreigners, when they arrived, had ignorance on their side—no frame of reference for this type of conflict. When people spoke of civil war and insecurity, of random attacks by nomads, Carter could cling to the notion that the worst fighting occurred deep in the desert, hundreds of miles away. As far as anyone knew, it had been going on forever. He came to Africa having read a few books, without experience that could provide a context for what he found. When told that drought had killed much of the nation's livestock, two million head of cattle, goats, and camels, Carter saw no evidence of this disaster in the city, where animals filled the streets.

Besides, more immediate worries occupied his mind — a new language to learn, a harsh climate to adjust to. He had to be sure that his drinking water was clean; that his food was burnt, boiled, or soaked in iodine; that he remembered the schedule for taking malaria pills; that flies and scorpions didn't breed in his laundry; and that his identity papers were in order each time he went out. The slightest illness left him worried about hepatitis or malaria or some other awful tropical disease. A woman he knew at the German embassy complained that she'd looked in the mirror one morning and found a worm wiggling under her eyelid. She was going to fly to Paris for treatment. In fact, such worries could be a welcome distraction. Being the outsider, the foreigner, was safe; it convinced Carter that what was happening in the streets, in the desert, and in the lives of people around him was not his problem.

He didn't choose Africa. South America would have pleased him as well, or Bangladesh, Jamaica, wherever. He'd gone to college in upstate New York — the same small liberal arts college that generations of his family had attended. He'd read about Africa's droughts and military rule, about civil wars, but his imagination couldn't be convinced of their magnitude. Instead, his mind teemed with the continent's noble and beautiful landscapes, with the music of hi-life beat and talking drums, with images of simple village life. He couldn't get past the romance wrought by Isak Dinesen, Ernest Hemingway, *National Geographic,* and even the annual Africa Night staged at his college. The students filled a ballroom with a buffet of goat meat stew, dishes flavored with peanut sauce, and sorghum cakes, and they performed music and poetry. Carter heard a white student from an African studies class recite his poetry barefoot on stage. He wore a pastel blue African robe, and his blond hair spilled out from under a red fez.

Africa, Africa,
Land of beauty, source of life . . .

After living in Africa awhile, Carter winced at such images, while recognizing that they still reflected part of what he expected of the place—he hoped for a vague sensual experience, choosing what he liked and wanted to understand, leaving the rest alone.

Once in country, for example, he decided to sidestep any debate about the Tuaregs. He knew no Tuaregs, even though the men walked the streets openly in high turbans and long robes, some wearing a sword at the waist. He knew a little about them, such as the fact that Tuareg women sold vegetables and jewelry in the markets, managing their incomes independent of men. It intrigued him that Tuareg women had that power, as well as authority to divorce or seek partners outside marriage, a fact that had perplexed Arab missionaries for centuries. Rebellion against another group's customs or rules, Carter came to understand, was a Tuareg way of life.

Carter's only memorable encounter with a Tuareg occurred on his first New Year's Eve in country, while camping in the desert with German and Dutch health workers. They drove—a dozen white people in four gleaming white Land Cruisers with food, gas stoves, beer, wine, champagne, blankets, sleeping bags, and lawn chairs—one hundred miles northwest of the capital to a field of dunes near the border with Mali. They camped at the base of a high crescent dune, arranging their vehicles in a half-circle as a shield against the wind. Sand blew from the top of the dune, blurring the land into the sky. They cooked steaks, drank, and danced to Bob Marley. Near midnight the sky was clear and the air cool and windy. They climbed the dune and toasted the New Year and Africa and the beauty of the Sahara. A few, including Carter, slept atop the dune that night, beneath stars that glowed with a sharpness unlike anything he'd seen. He recorded a few details in his notebook: *The dune has suffocated everything around it. We see no plants, but the dune itself is alive, moving with the wind. Sand moves in little tempests so that from a distance the dune looks as if it is growing hair.*

The sun burst over the horizon, striking hard. Carter and his friends awakened instantly. Laughing, they rolled and leaped off the dune, through the loose sand, to have breakfast in its shade, away from the wind. They were tired but delighted by the desert's terrible loveliness.

Suddenly everyone fell silent. With coffee cups and plates of eggs in their hands, they stared at the silhouette of a man atop the dune. He stood still, arms at his sides. His turban made his head look wide, round, and sinister, and his robes blew gently in the wind. Dieter, a German doctor, said, "Keep eating, everyone. If he comes over here, offer him food."

Abruptly, the man was gone. While the others finished breakfast and talked among themselves, Carter went to his bag and retrieved a book he'd brought from the states, *Veiled Men, Red Tents, and Black Mountains,* by an archaeologist named Alonzo Pond, who traveled among the Tuaregs in the 1920s. Leafing through the pages, Carter found the passage he wanted.

> I'll not forget their impressive dignity. Their turbans were neatly wound about their heads. A blue-black veil covered each man's ears and hung down over his forehead to the bridge of his nose . . . Only a slit between upper and lower folds of the veil allowed a view of the direct, piercing black eyes . . . Their long strides carried them swiftly over the sand, their strange garments billowed out by the ever-present breeze.

Carter wanted to read the words aloud, but the festive mood was gone, and he thought better of it. His party packed and returned to the capital in a tight convoy, driving across the desert's hardpan soil, which was at some places covered with gravel and at others smooth like clay. They drove past villages, square mud compounds that may have stood for centuries, for all they knew. Eventually they followed an old colonial track worn deep in the ground by decades of French camel and horse patrols — mounted officers in white uniforms leading African *tirailleurs,* riflemen on foot in blue coats and wide red pantaloons. These were the border makers, as Carter thought of them, the first of the colonial producers of boundary lines, and, as Salif told him, they made their cartographic marks by means of torch, bullet, and saber. These men forced villagers to carry and crush stone to build roads, packing it hard with their feet. They shot village chiefs who couldn't provide labor.

In this region, a century had passed since a French officer accused a Hausa farming village of harboring Tuareg warriors and thus ordered the massacre of its 150 residents. The French had reason to be afraid. In the Saharan winter, when winds draped the land in grainy spumes of dust, Tuareg raiders used the dust clouds as cover and attacked patrols. The captain's evidence against the village was the presence of a single Tuareg camel trader. The Frenchman's orders were explicit: use bayonets, not bullets. Spare no one. Force the trader to watch the slaughter. The *tirailleurs* from villages on the Senegalese coast did the killing, and when it was finished, the officer, a captain of the marines, a son of Normandy dairy farmers, used his sword to decapitate the bodies. He told his men to collect the heads and throw them in the village well. Then he had two soldiers remove the Tuareg's turban and use the length of cloth to hang him from a baobab tree. Seven other French officers watched, astride their horses on a sandy ridge above the scene.

The partygoers drove fast and in silence, many sensing for the first time that this land didn't wholeheartedly welcome them. Carter knew—because he'd read of it and because Salif told him the story—that the captain who'd ordered the massacre was shot to death by an African soldier who couldn't live with what he'd done in the name of France. As the captain surveyed the aftermath of the killing, the soldier fired his rifle into the man's chest. Afterward, the soldier stood for some time at the edge of the well, staring into its bloodied depths stuffed with heads, before he knelt, drew a pistol, and shot himself in the back of the head. The bullet's force tumbled his body forward into the hole. The rest of the soldiers put themselves under the command of the remaining officers, who'd witnessed the suicide as they had the massacre—quietly, on horseback, from a distance. The captain was buried where he fell, somewhere among dried brush and these same rocks. With relief, Carter and his friends pulled onto the asphalt of the north-south highway and fled back to the city.

A few days later, Carter wrote this:

The capital is heavy with rumors of Tuareg intrigues. A teacher at the lycée says they are plotting to bomb the marketplace. He said he heard this in the streets. It's unusual to see Tuareg men in the city. They stay close to home or workplace. People say Tuaregs carry Kalashnikov rifles beneath their robes, ready to strike when the order comes. Bystanders and merchants beat a Tuareg in the central market a few days ago over what was thought to be a gun. The story appeared in the government newspaper. The man made and sold leather goods in a small wooden stall. Someone, according to the newspaper, saw a black object beneath the belt around his robes and shouted that he had a gun. The words drew a crowd. People tore his clothes, beat him with their fists, and kicked him to the ground. They ripped his stall apart, carried off the table on which he displayed his work, and took his tools and leather goods. Soldiers intervened and carried the victim to a police station. No one found a pistol or any weapon, not even a knife. Instead they found a leather pouch on his belt. His identity card and money were inside.

## November

"ARE YOU NOT FRIGHTENED, DAVEED?"

"What do you mean?"

Salif sipped his tea with loud slurps and set his glass on the metal tray.

"I mean, well . . . this is a foreign country to you, so when you walk the streets, everything is different, the language, the people, their dress, the food, the checkpoints. All of it. Are you not afraid?"

"Of course not."

"But you must be nervous. They sent you here to Africa without our words. How strange. You come here to teach the English, which is really just bringing more words from someplace else. Not a great deal of use to us, you know."

Salif bowed his head for a few seconds and then looked up.

"Haven't you learned? We Africans have more languages than we ourselves can speak. You speak French, but you don't know *our* languages. You are a man who comes here speaking in a borrowed tongue. Here in Africa that is not good, my friend. That means you have no history. This is French West Africa. In this place the French language carries its own history."

Carter sat with his arms folded. He shook his head. "What do you want from me, Salif? I just got here. I need time."

Salif looked at him.

"Yes, time."


## October

THE AFRICANS CALLED white foreigners "tourists." Carter understood that. He knew the word applied even to the earliest soldiers and explorers, the administrators and scientists, the missionaries and now the diplomats, aid workers, and "volunteers." The "experts" in soils and crop planning, tourists all of them, even the people who could "predict" harvests with remote sensing satellite radar and computer models, and others who worked in "debt management," in health, or, like David Carter, in "curriculum development" and "pedagogy."

"*Notre nouveau touriste,*" Salif said of him at school.

Salif Moustapha, Carter's friend and colleague, his political muse and tutor of culture and the tea ritual. Carter kept a photograph of Salif that showed him squatting in the shade of a tree in front of a teakettle being heated on a bed of coals in the sand. He held a shot glass of Chinese green tea — a brand called Gunpowder — in one hand and a cigarette in the other. He faced the camera, not smiling. Carter knew Salif mostly in the context of Lycée Centrale, where the curriculum was a cross between what was taught at American junior college and high school. The students were creatures of the capital, from civil service or merchant families. A few walked in every day from villages in the countryside, as far away as ten miles. A smaller number went on to university. Most became teachers, clerks, foresters, and soldiers. Carter encountered Salif as someone who loved argument and asked questions that halted the march of a man's words. He was twenty-eight, six years older than Carter, with a wife, a baby boy, and two daughters, ages three and four. Before he married, he'd spent a summer studying German on scholarship at the University of Tübingen. He spoke fair German and, of course, French, Arabic, Hausa, and his native Tamachek, the language of the Tuaregs. Salif was not a Tuareg, though. He was Bouzou, but Carter was never certain about all the implications of that tribal name. He was never certain of anything in Africa.

Except for tea. Three rounds of green tea brought the two men together every afternoon before late classes began at 4 P.M., when the heat began to break. They talked while sitting on grass mats spread in the shade of a leafy neem tree outside Salif's classroom. "The classic tree of our land," Salif called the neem, whose thin and sturdy trunk supported a dense canopy of oblong leaves. After each round, Salif would clean and rinse the glasses, which he kept on a metal tray in his classroom, with the kettle and box of tea. His cleaning motion was rhythmic and smooth. He worked with two glasses at a time — an enamel bowl of soapy water and another of rinse water in front of him — washing one glass with his right hand and rinsing another in his left, quickly and precisely, his fingers wiping inside each glass, without wasting a movement.

Salif delighted in brewing the tea. His whole body, thin and sinewy, took part in the task — shoulders hunching forward like those of a piano player, long bony fingers never making an error. As he worked, he relaxed his face, which was narrow, with deep-set eyes. He scooped spoonfuls of tea leaves, dried and ground like parsley flakes, into a small kettle on the bed of charcoal, and then dropped in a dozen or so cubes of sugar. Every round, he packed in fresh tea and sugar because, as he said, "To make weak tea is to rob the occasion of its flavor and energy." Salif made a show of raising the kettle high, holding it elegantly with his long fingers, and directing the hot stream of brown liquid into a shot glass on the tray, letting some splash over the rim. Next, he set the kettle down and with the other hand picked up the shot glass and poured the tea back into the kettle in the same dramatic manner, holding the glass high. "The tea must be softened," he explained, and so he performed the ritual several times, pouring the liquid from kettle to glass and back again. Carter loved to watch the hot ropes of tea moving back and forth.

Salif liked to lecture on the process: "You must let the tea breathe before you drink it."

The first round was an hour in the making, and then with a crisp nod Salif would hand Carter a glass of tea, giving thanks to God in Arabic: "*Bismilahi Allah!*" Or sometimes he shouted "*Santé*" or "*Prost*" or "*Layhiya,*" the Hausa word for "health."

Once, he raised his tea glass and spoke in clear but slow English, for he had to think carefully of the words: "Today, Daveed, I feel English. We Africans are a little of everything, true bastards of geography. French West Africans, British East Africans, Spanish Saharans, Belgian Congolese, Portuguese Angolans, and don't forget German Tanzanians and Togolese and, forgive me, Soviet Ethiopians. Now, there are Americans in Africa. Everywhere, Americans. We Africans are the children of white men's maps."

Salif raised his glass. "Good health!"

Carter smiled. He felt his face redden and grow warm, though he'd come to like Salif's irreverent banter. He raised his own glass halfway as Salif sipped loudly.

The tea sessions worked like cultural seminars, though Carter was often slow to catch on. Salif had to explain that students called Carter *Mai Kaya,* a Hausa expression that means "the owner of things." Early on, during one of those first weeks at the school, he was standing outside his classroom, talking to Salif, when the school groundskeeper, Ahmed, a lanky old farmer who spoke no French, walked up and addressed Carter.

"*Ahhh, barka, barka, Sarkin Kaya.*"

The old man grinned. Salif laughed. Carter smiled politely.

"Do you know what he is saying, Monsieur Daveed?"

Carter shoved his hands in his pockets, shaking his head.

"He offers you peace, *barka,* and he calls you *Sarkin Kaya,* 'Prince of Possessions.'"

Carter frowned. "What?"

The old man and Salif laughed together.

"We also like to call you *Mai Kaya Dayowa,* 'Owner of Many Things.'"

Salif put his hand on Ahmed's shoulder and continued in French, for Carter's benefit. "Monsieur Daveed hasn't learned much. He is always working. He is preparing his lessons inside his classroom or reading something and not noticing. So, Daveed, we must also call you *Sarkin Aiki,* 'Prince of Work,' or *Sarkin Livre,* 'Prince of Books.'" He paused and grinned broadly at Carter. "I suppose that means we can also call you *Sarkin Kudi,* 'Prince of Money.'"

A few students gathered to listen. Some laughed as Salif began to speak of Carter in the third person.

"When I first saw this man, Daveed Carter, I thought, ah huh, here is *Mai Kaya Dayowa.* He always wears his wide straw hat and glasses for the sun, and when he is inside, away from the sun, the glasses hang from a string around his neck. He has leather shoes so the skin of his feet never becomes dry and cracked like mine. He has a watch that lights up in the dark when he touches it, and he carries his books and things in a strong black bag that hangs from his shoulder."

The students laughed. Carter folded his arms and smiled weakly. He kicked at the dirt.

A student told him not to worry about what Salif said. "Monsieur Salif likes you."

At the school, Salif carried more personal authority than the headmaster did. The windows to all classrooms were always open, and Salif's running commentary, accompanied by students' laughter, played like a radio show for the entire school to hear in bits and pieces. Sometimes teachers stopped their lessons, merely to listen. Political discussions were forbidden, but in grammar lessons and lectures on algebra, Salif dropped in stray references to "those brave soldiers who point their guns and take our money every day." He once told his students, "Whenever they stop you, always thank them, compliment them on their work, especially if they strike you or take something from you. Tell them what fine people they are. Tell them how proud their families must be of what they do every day in the streets." Carter heard that last line himself, during a pause in a lesson, when he realized the concentration visible on his students' faces had nothing to do with the English lesson. Salif's words shot like embers from the windows of his classroom.

A student spoke softly, as if to himself: "He is dangerous, that one."

## Monday

CARTER CROSSED THE GROUNDS after leaving the headmaster's office, trying to calm his anger before he faced his students. He'd have to find a way to cope with Salif's arrest, and he knew anger would be of no help in the classroom, where his students represented seven distinct ethnic groups and languages. As he climbed the steps and entered the doorway, the students stood all at once, as was the custom. Fifteen boys and two girls greeted him in unison: "Good mawwning, sah. How aahh you?"

He set his books on the desk and turned to them, his face a stern mask. "Good morning, class. I'm fine." The students took their seats and Carter walked among the desks, fingering a piece of chalk and asking questions in English as a warm-up: "Moussa, what did you eat for breakfast this morning? Fatima, what will you do after school this afternoon?"

A young man named Cisse, a footballer — tall, strong, and confident, with an attitude — raised his hand and Carter pointed at him. "Yes, Cisse?"

Cisse spoke in French, a gesture of defiance. He said, "Is it true that white men eat babies?"

Carter stared at him, suppressing a smile. The question's irreverence forced him out of himself. "Well, of course we eat babies," Carter said, giving Cisse a frown. "What other questions do you have? And, this time, speak English."

The other students were quiet, but Cisse smiled and exchanged glances with another boy, who raised his hand and spoke in French. "Do you get extra money for teaching, aside from what the CIA pays you?"

Carter didn't let a moment go by. He shook his head and breathed an exaggerated sigh.

"No, no, the CIA pays poorly. I work for the Russians now."

This time the students laughed and Carter relaxed. But worry concerning the minister's inspection the next morning kept him focused. He drilled his students hard, firing questions at them in English about grammar and class readings.

"Know your lessons," he told them, "and this man, the minister, will leave us alone." Even as he spoke, he wondered if the minister might tell him where the soldiers had taken Salif.

## September

IN THE CLASSROOM at Lycée Centrale, telling students to be "prepared" made Carter feel a little ridiculous, even angry. How could they prepare well with the materials they had? The school lacked proper textbooks, and students shared the volumes they did have, such as the outdated readers written for English children thirty years before. Every September the students received one notebook and two ballpoint pens, which they protected fiercely, sometimes resorting to vicious fights. Students had no gym or science equipment and no access to medical care, except for the few whose families could afford private clinics. There were government medical dispensaries in every city district, dirty places staffed by poorly trained people who had little medicine to offer. People went to them to pick up food aid distributions and to die.

One day, when Carter had been in country almost a year, a student collapsed in his class. Carter stood over the boy, who lay on his back beside his desk, his whole body shivering. The boy's lips quivered, and spittle formed at the corners of his mouth. Carter looked at his students and the stricken boy; with no idea of what was happening, he felt a sudden panic. He knelt while students gathered round, wide-eyed and chattering. He attempted to mop sweat off the boy's face with a handkerchief, but the boy knocked his hand away. He just stared, not at Carter, not at anything. Carter noted that he didn't blink. He was a tall boy, thin, not strong. Carter held the back of his head in the palm of his hand because he kept knocking his skull against the floor, leaving a dim round sweat spot on the concrete. *Malaria, it's malaria,* Carter told himself. He grabbed a student by the arm and told him to fetch the water bottle from Carter's desk.

Carter asked the stricken boy his name (though he knew it) to see if he could respond. Some students laughed. A boy shouted in French, "You don't even know his name. He is called Hamza."

The boy curled up on the floor was Hamza Saidou. His knees were drawn tight to his chest as if he felt cold or anticipated a beating, and maybe he did. Carter squatted beside him, trying to get Hamza to take sips from his water bottle, but Hamza drew an arm across his face. Carter shouted at the students to get back. He stood up and told the biggest boy in class to help him carry Hamza to the dispensary a block from the lycée. But the eyes of everyone in the room looked past Carter, who turned in time to see Hamza leap out of one of the room's high, open French windows. The boy fell to his knees in the sand, then rose and ran, stumbling and rising again, across the school compound.

Carter didn't pursue him. He realized the indignity the boy had just suffered in front of his peers was worse in some ways than the malaria. He sent two boys to find him. After a few minutes they discovered Hamza huddled in the shade of a tree outside the school walls.

In fact, the boy's humiliation that day had begun half an hour before he fled the class, and Carter was its cause. When Carter began his lesson promptly at 7:40 A.M., after the flag raising, heat hung wet and heavy in the air. Hamza laid his head on the desk; so did two other students. Carter shouted at them in English.

"Hamza, Ibrahim, Fatima, wake up! It's time to begin," Carter yelled, clapping his hands twice. Then he spoke in French: *"Ohh, qu'est-ce que vous faites, là?"*

Students whispered and giggled. Hamza looked around but then leaned his head on the wall. His eyes were closed and his mouth was open. A stain of perspiration ran from his neck down the front of his long tunic, but this didn't seem unusual. Everyone was sweating. This was April, just before the onset of the rainy season, when no time of day offered relief from the heat. Hamza was sixteen years old, stood nearly six feet tall, and was dressed in a brown knee-length khaki tunic and leggings. He wore blue plastic sandals. Hair sprouted from his head in uneven orange tufts, a symptom, Carter knew from his first aid training, of long-term protein deficiency — a lifetime of not eating well. He saw the symptoms in city streets every time he left his apartment: the child with the skeletal frame, with hair like rust, a grossly distended belly, a wrinkled face, and the hard stare of someone very old. Carter had been told how to spot malaria, too, but he'd never actually witnessed someone afflicted with the disease. Carter noted only that Hamza's eyes seemed glassy, like those of a boy daydreaming, flickering from Carter to the blackboard and over the heads of his classmates. Minutes later, the shivering started and became so violent that Hamza's desk rattled. *Certainly the boy is clowning around,* Carter thought, *defying my authority. That little troublemaker Hamza.*

"*Tu dors dans ma classe?*"

The shaking stopped, and the boy did something strange. He slid from his chair and stretched out on his back on the concrete floor. He clutched at himself, shivering. From across the room Carter could see the boy's head vibrating.

Hamza Saidou died the next day.

Some days, in class, Carter was startled to see a clear image of the boy looking at him from the back of the room. At other times Hamza surfaced in Carter's mind as a dull feeling of depression, of unfinished business. Soon, he told himself, he'd walk to Mumbe, the boy's village, and set things right with the family, tell them about Hamza's last day and about what he, Carter, had done, and how sorry he was.

## Monday

CARTER LEFT THE SCHOOL late in the afternoon, reworking in his mind just how the Land Rover drove off with Salif that morning. It occurred to him that Salif had not looked back at Carter after he was shoved into the car. He sat between two soldiers, looking straight ahead, like a man afraid to acknowledge the world he'd just come from—life outside captivity—as he entered a different reality.

"Sedition charges," Carter said to himself, pronouncing the words aloud. They sounded menacing and final, like a death sentence. "Salif could never keep his mouth shut."

Carter had decided to attend an embassy reception late that afternoon for American aid workers and volunteers—anything for distraction, even an embassy party. Such events simmered with sexual tension. Too many people just passing through, he thought. People alone, away from families or the routines of life in D.C., Paris, or Nairobi. They tried to best one another, reciting the details of their benefits packages, their research bravado ("I'm studying the fat-tailed scorpion, the most deadly species; I wander the desert at night, poking under rocks, because these creatures glow in the dark, you know"), or their travels in war zones. Carter found sex an easy and at times predictable game in the capital, the center of a constantly evolving expatriate community whose population turned over every few months. People on short contracts and those on standard two-year tours, people on fact-finding trips, journalists on parachute visits, medical workers, missionaries committed to the country for years, and the food aid jocks, the NGO engineers, the diplomats, the Peace Corps volunteers, the French *bénévoles*, the academics and tourists, most of whom, Carter included, were hyperconscious, even paranoid, about their health, but very horny. Everyone carried condoms. Sex, it seemed to Carter, was usually antiseptically correct in this place, even if a "friendly fuck" was not hard to come by.

He cut through the central market, which offered a shorter route home. Weaving his way between the merchants' stalls he saw Cisse, the bold-mouthed soccer player, arguing with two soldiers. He was seventeen and confident, nearly ready for the military himself. Carter liked Cisse and thought of him as the image of what Hamza Saidou might, in different circumstances, have become—self-assured, tall, and strong, a natural leader. Hamza, too, was tall, but thin and weak. Carter admired Cisse's calm as he talked with the soldiers, towering over them. One held his identity card clipped between two fingers, like bait. Behind Cisse, another soldier leveled his rifle, pointing it at the boy's back. Carter was only a few meters away, pretending to browse through music cassettes. He could see Cisse talking and gesturing, but the young man's face was composed and friendly. He didn't show fear. The soldiers let him go after a few minutes.

Cisse disappeared into the crowds and the soldiers meandered on through the market, their brief encounter just another instance of the vast weirdness of Africa, which Carter found so unnerving. It was almost as strange as the government's decision to bulldoze the refugee camp that once stood along the river. The settlement, an assemblage of mud-brick huts and canvas and nylon tents, some green and others dirty white, had sat on the riverbank as if shoveled into place there, while the chocolate brown water flowed by, silent and blind. These dwellings were destroyed to make space for a luxury hotel, whose four hundred rooms, marble columns in the classical Greek style, and bulletproof windows now faced the water and were visible throughout the city. Carter could look up from any location and find the broad, rectangular expanse of that hotel feeding his anger. Hard angles and whitewashed stucco stood out starkly against blue sky, that endless blue, tarnished only by dust and, rarely, by clouds. Some European got the contract to build the hotel, and the army walked off with its cut. The behemoth stood nearly empty.

And one more incomprehensible aspect of life here — the utility officials who came to Carter's apartment every so often. They drank his tea, inquired after his family and work, and then threatened to evict him if he didn't pay the bills supposedly left outstanding by previous tenants. A welcoming gift from the government.

Carter caught a taxi to the embassy, wearing his teaching clothes — sandals, khaki pants, cotton shirt, and straw sun hat — a little sweaty and dusty from the day. He thought he might as well present himself as he was.

That's how he looked, standing with a bottle of beer in his hand at the hors d'oeuvres table, when he met an epidemiologist, a young woman who traveled the world, tracking malaria. She had an abrupt manner and didn't even stop to introduce herself, a social pattern Carter had become used to among people who lived in a world of short stays. That's how things worked. No time to lose.

"Do you live in country?" she asked. She was small and thin, and Carter noticed that she focused her eyes when she spoke, moving her body only when she had to. She had slightly unruly black hair, cut short. A lock of hair trickled down over each temple.

"Yes, couple of years," he said. "I'm an English teacher."

He asked her name.

"Amelia," she said.

Amelia held a drink wrapped in a white napkin, though she wasn't drinking. She complained about how hard it was to get statistics from rural medical workers. She spoke earnestly, as if expecting him to empathize like someone who knew her work as well as she did.

"The last time I came through—a year ago I think it was—I tried to set up an information network," she said. "I spent weeks traveling to villages, I talked to health workers and village chiefs, I left instructions. Nothing ever came of it." She shrugged and pursed her lips. "They're overwhelmed. I should have taken that into account." Her voice trailed off, as if she'd realized something for the first time, or maybe she feared revealing too much to a stranger.

Carter spoke a little too quickly. "Well, be patient," he said. He explained, by way of example, how he met Salif, "my good African friend," as he called him. "I entered his classroom one morning and asked to borrow some typing paper. Barely knew 'im. I didn't even say hello. He didn't say a thing for an entire minute." Carter tilted his head back and laughed. "He just looked at me. Then he said, 'Gooooood mawwwning,' you know, the words drawn out, the way you teach someone greetings in English." Carter smiled and shook his head. "Of course, his English is pretty good."

He sipped his beer, warming to his story. He told her how he apologized to Salif, winded by his own rudeness, and how this tall, thin, coal-skinned African with deep-set eyes from the north of the country had smiled and handed over the paper Carter wanted.

"We've been friends ever since," he said, trying to read Amelia's face. "Now I never talk to anyone without greeting them and asking about health and family. You must make that investment, you know. It's the traditional way."

Amelia lowered her head and smiled slightly, as if amused. Carter was too nervous to stop, to risk a few seconds of silence or raise a question that might reveal that she had spent more time in Africa than he had. Which was true. Anyway, he liked the way she dressed — leather sandals, a modest light-blue cotton dress, sleeveless, so practical for the climate. As he studied her, he kept talking, losing track of his ideas. She had strong, well-defined arms, like a field researcher, he thought, the restless kind who gathered her own material and didn't like laboratories. She held her glass in both hands, her thumb tips touching. Her eyes darted to the ground and then up at him.

"But how do you get anything done?" she said.

Amelia kept looking away from him, at the ground, though still with a trace of a smile. Carter wanted to sound as if he'd spent serious time in Africa and knew what he was talking about. "Look," he said, "the point is, the system emphasizes human beings over business. For me, it's like this — I feel like I needed to come here to Africa just to understand what an asshole I can be."

Suddenly — maybe it was his exaggerated tone or the look of her tightened brow — he was sharply conscious of his own voice, as if he could see the spray of his words covering her face. His mouth went dry.

Amelia touched her temple with two fingers and bit her lip as if trying to hold back a laugh. "Oh," she said, "you're so well-informed."

They began laughing at the same moment. After that, they talked more easily and not about their work. They talked about home and about the stiff silliness of embassy parties. Amelia began to enjoy her drink. The ambassador had a weight problem and they watched him mingle in a too-tight white suit. "He looks like a walrus," she said.

"I'm thinking polar bear," Carter replied. "I don't envy him." He looked at her. "Where are you staying?"

"At the Hotel Sahara, along the water." She shook her head. "It's pretty out there on the river, but the hotel windows don't open, and they're a little hard to see through. They say they're bulletproof. How strange."

Carter smiled. He said, "Yes, I know the place."

## September

"WHAT ARE YOU going to do about that boy, Hamza? We have all heard about him, you know."

Flies hovered around Salif's hands, which were sticky with tea as he sloshed rinse water on the tea tray. Then he flung the water onto the sand behind him.

Carter frowned. The tendons in his neck tightened. "What do you mean? He's dead, Salif. There's nothing I can do about him."

"You know what I mean, Daveed. He nearly died in your classroom, right in front of you. Are you not going to visit his village? You can tell his family you were Hamza's teacher and that he was a good boy. You can sing his praises, you can tell them stories about their son."

Carter folded his hands in his lap. "Yes, I should probably go. But Salif, that boy's last conscious experience on earth involved a white man screaming at him."

Salif nodded. "So, Daveed, you have a sense of tribal identity."

## Tuesday

EARLY THAT NEXT MORNING, Carter decided to make a notation on Salif every day until he returned. While Amelia was in the shower, he fished the notebook from his shoulder bag and added an entry: *Salif still gone.* He mouthed the words, "Salif still gone," like saying a prayer. He kept the note simple, as if brevity would shorten his friend's absence. He said nothing to Amelia about Salif's disappearance because he could not yet frame his emotions or the details of the story for someone he little knew.

Carter and Amelia parted happy, she for an appointment at the Ministry of Health and Carter for the school. Amelia was flying back to D.C. that night. They exchanged addresses and kisses between the marble columns on the broad front steps of the Hotel Sahara. Carter got her a taxi and insisted he'd walk. He wanted time to transition back to city life. He wanted to think. After all, the minister was coming to the school that very morning.

The awkward start to Carter's meeting with Amelia and the memory of his I-needed-to-come-to-Africa-just-to-understand-what-an-asshole-I-can-be wisdom still stung. *How,* he wondered, *do you explain Africa?* He'd wanted to tell Amelia about the fishing and farming families who once lived on the hotel land, about Salif, and about how the soldiers affected life in the city. He wanted to tell her about Hamza Saidou but feared that she might say, "You should have recognized malaria. They trained you to understand your students, didn't they?" It turned out she spoke fluent French and good Swahili. Amelia, in fact, had spent two years living in villages in Kenya to study dysentery, or infectious diarrhea, as she called it.

*Dysentery,* Carter thought. *My God. Two years.*

"Strange, I know," she said. "Somehow, I'm drawn to parasites. They're so efficient. You know, it's an accident that certain parasites and viruses do such harm to the human body. Think about it, David. They're only trying to survive on this planet as we are, inside whatever host will have them. I respect that."

They were in bed, Amelia on her back, looking at the ceiling as she spoke, and Carter on his side, stroking her hair, which was stringy and wet with sweat. With his finger, he lifted a strand behind her ear. "Amelia," he said, "you're the greatest scientific iconoclast since Darwin."

She laughed. "Thank you, but maybe Coleridge would be a better analogy." She laughed again. "Oh, my, what a pompous thing to say."

"I don't get it. Coleridge was a poet."

"Yes, but he was obsessed with disease." Amelia sat up and hugged her knees. "His poem *Rime of the Ancient Mariner* is about an English merchant ship blown off course to the icy waters near the South Pole before it makes its way back north, toward the other extreme of temperature at the equator. Coleridge's fear of fever is there in the hot and cold course of the ship, like the way malaria works, or yellow fever. It's a beautiful poem. I memorized the whole thing." She smiled and wrapped her arms tighter around her knees. "Eventually the crew all die. Coleridge writes about the 'bloody sun' and tongues 'withered at the root' and 'throats un-slaked with black lips baked.'" Amelia shook her head. "Some say it's all a metaphor for the ills colonialism forced on unsuspecting lands." She paused. "Like the effect fever has on the unwary body."

Carter lay there, watching her face. "What do you think?" he asked.

She rested her chin on her knees. "I read his letters at the British Library in London. Coleridge described how smallpox originated in the locust plagues of Ethiopia. He wrote that it crawled out of huge heaps of putrefying locusts." She sighed. "I have no idea what to think. Coleridge lived in a time when people were much closer to life, to what takes it and what gives it." Amelia stopped talking and smiled at Carter, resting her hand on his hip. Then she said, "If I get too high on myself as a MALARIA SCIENTIST"—she raised her voice on those two words, making quotation marks with her fingers—"then I remind myself that I used to study peo-ple's shit."

## February

SALIF SAT BACK on his knees, flicking water from his hands after washing the tea glasses. "You should know that the name Tuareg is an Arab word. It means 'abandoned of God.'"

Carter scratched the dirt with a stick, listening to Salif and the clicking of the teapot cover as the water boiled. He understood Sa-lif was Bouzou, which is to say he was the son of slaves to the Tua-regs. He also knew that Tuaregs were Berber nomads who had roamed the Sahara for a thousand years, herding camels and goats, raiding other tribes, taking slaves, and bleeding desert caravans. Carter, if he set slavery aside, loved the idea of an entire people be-holden only to the land, the wind, their animals, and themselves. The Tuaregs resisted Arab colonization and Islam centuries ago.

Salif boasted of this history, which confused Carter. "Tuaregs are slave traders, Salif. They bought and sold members of your own family. Even today they still own slaves, a few of them, anyway; you know that. Doesn't that bother you?"

"Yes, you're right. But the Tuaregs resist. That is what they do and I like that." Salif paused a moment, smiling to himself. "Did you know that in Tamachek the Tuaregs call themselves *imashaghen*, 'the noble and the free'?"

Carter shrugged. "That's a name, Salif. I'm named for David, the chosen of God, leader of the Hebrews." He smiled and shook his head. "I only know that because my parents never let me forget. Whenever I complained about anything, my mother would say, 'Remember who you are named for.' I hated that. David is just a name, and I am not a great leader." Carter raised his hands to emphasize the word *great*.

"You are a Jew?"

"No, Catholic, I'm Catholic by birth. My parents aren't religious. They wanted to name their son after a revolutionary. An activist. They were young students in the 1960s. They opposed the American war in Vietnam."

Salif nodded.

"My parents are attorneys now. Anyway, the David of biblical stories was a rebel. My parents liked rebels."

He learned from Salif that the Hausa called the Tuaregs *iska barawo*, which means "ghost thieves," or literally, "thieves of the wind," because Tuareg warriors astride their camels descended on their prey suddenly, appearing out of dust clouds raised by the wind. The Bouzou were, until the French arrived, the human bounty taken in those raids, from a variety of dark-skinned peoples across the Sahel — Hausa, Toubou, Djerma, Woluf, and many others.

Salif tutored Carter in the finer details. "The government thinks we Bouzou sympathize with the Tuareg rebellion. I don't remember slavery myself, and my father never speaks of it. He insists he was never a slave to anyone, though we are Bouzou and our family language is Tamachek."

Salif looked straight at Carter. "I am a black man, deep black. The desert tribes' bloodlines are tangled because raiders took slaves from so many tribes and because some Tuareg and slave families stayed together for generations. They intermarried, but perhaps my family did not. I do not know for certain. It's a little strange, all this. The French outlawed slavery. Some slaves dispersed to new lives as herders or farmers. After independence, suddenly there were political borders across the land and new countries. New governments forced the Tuaregs and the Bouzou to be citizens of one side of a border or another. Soldiers confiscated livestock. They forced nationalities and identity cards on us. There were massacres."

Salif fell silent.

## Tuesday

CARTER WALKED BRISKLY through the city, concentrating on the minister's upcoming "inspection" — an odd word, he thought, for an official visit to a school. The headmaster's word. Carter pictured his students lined up, as if they were soldiers waiting for an officer's review. Many teachers said the minister was a harsh man. And suddenly Carter intensely envied Amelia and the solitary independence of her life as a researcher, her freedom to wander like a free agent, chasing down diseases.

At the school gate soldiers inspected Carter's identity card, and as he entered the campus he saw tanks parked between classroom buildings. Soldiers waited in small groups. Some smoked. Others huddled over teapots set on beds of hot coals in the ground. Some soldiers waved and shouted greetings at him.

He had to be careful not to appear curious or resentful. Though he was used to being under scrutiny, Carter knew how easily words, gestures, or actions could be misconstrued, by either party. He was still adapting to African ways, some of which seemed strange. In the streets, children touched his arms to see what his skin was like. He felt the eyes of older people upon him, a powerful connection, as if they were absorbing part of him. If he acknowledged them, they'd hold up their right arms and shake their fists in a sign of welcome. They gave him spacious grins that revealed orange teeth and gums stained by kola nut juice. This expression of friendliness could feel oddly threatening. Carter knew the story of a French co-lonial governor during the 1920s in what was then called the Niger Military Zone. The officer decided to tour the countryside in an open car driven by an African orderly. They passed a farmer who raised his fist at the white man in the backseat. The Frenchman ordered the driver to stop. He got out, walked into the field, drew his pistol, and shot the farmer dead.

Carter often thought of the French governor and the farmer. What sort of historical memories stirred in his students when they looked at Carter? As soldiers waved at him, he thought of Hamza Saidou lying in a coma and wondered what his students thought of their teacher on the day he'd humiliated the boy who was guilty only of being ill, near death. And he imagined how he might have told the story to Amelia, had he the guts. How much would be colored with truth, or lies?

## September

IN HIS LOWER MOMENTS or when he'd had a few beers, Carter would refer to Hamza as "the student I killed." He didn't sincerely believe it, though a vague sense of guilt dogged him. What Carter really felt about that death was not regret that he couldn't save the boy's life. After all, Hamza's body—tormented by malaria, intestinal parasites, lack of food, and who knows what else—had reached the end. Quinine treatment at the dispensary had failed to save him. *This is Africa,* Carter told himself, *where disease and untimely death are a way of life.* But no, what really bothered him was awareness of his own lack of understanding and the fact that he had not made the effort to understand. That, and the guilt of having spoken harshly to this boy in his last moments among his mates. For Carter to respond differently, to investigate Hamza's condition rather than assume the boy was intentionally misbehaving, would have meant reaching across a chasm, trying to connect with an unfamiliar culture, taking a risk. It was Carter's habit to keep company with Salif and other teachers or stay in his apartment, reading and writing letters to avoid the humiliation and frustration, the stares and questions—the hard work of confronting new languages and another culture. In fact, when Hamza died, Carter had been teaching at that school five days a week for nearly a year, yet, absorbed in his own concerns, he had never closely considered the situation from the point of view of Hamza, or any other student.

The afternoon after Hamza ran from his classroom, guilt sent Carter to the neighborhood medical dispensary, an old white-washed cement building with a corrugated iron roof over a row of barracks-like rooms. A male nurse took him to a room with cots lining the walls beneath high French windows screened with mosquito netting. Over the years, the walls and roof had been patched with mud and painted over in white. Still, the roof leaked under monsoon rains, which poured through the repairs and streaked the walls with mud.

Hamza lay on his right side, his body arched in a crescent, like the shape of the parasite that was killing him. His right arm was tucked beneath him, and the other was bent behind his back at the waist. He'd crossed his feet and his mouth gaped open. He was drooling heavily. The white sheet he lay on was damp with sweat, and spittle bubbled on the boy's lips. The nurse said Hamza had been brought in unconscious.

Carter's training had included courses in first aid and tropical diseases. He suspected, based on what had happened in class and the way Hamza lay in a coma, his body contorted, that the boy was in the last stages of cerebral malaria. The Latin name, *Plasmodium falciparum,* sounded quaintly clinical to Carter, nothing like the war that had exploded in Hamza's blood and spread to his brain.

Carter knelt at the bedside. Behind him, he heard the nurse's voice. "The boy can't hear anything, monsieur."

Carter turned to the man, vaguely aware of coughs and murmurs from other patients in the ward.

"He's one of my students."

The nurse nodded. He wore a traditional white skullcap and long white medical smock, streaked by dust and dried blood.

"We gave him quinine."

Carter stared at the boy. "Where's his family? Shouldn't there be someone here with him?"

The nurse shrugged. "He comes from the village of Mumbe. It's outside the city, in the hills." He pointed northeast, out one of the windows. "He walks in to school, seven kilometers. He passes by here early every morning."

In the afternoon, when the heat climbed above 110 degrees, Hamza would return home, trudging back up a slope of sand and molten basalt that had dried in gentle, deep-brown ripples a million years before his time.

Carter nodded. He heard the nurse's sandals tap the concrete floor as he moved among the patients. The room was full of infected wounds, snakebites, dysentery, and fevers. Most patients also suffered from malaria.

Hamza's eyes were wet and empty. He wore dirty blue gym shorts. He had long, awkward legs, with big knees and not enough muscle tone. His ribs showed a little.

Hamza breathed shallowly, releasing a soft gasp. Carter picked up his hand. The fingers felt wet and warm, but stiff. He watched the boy's body twist in slow convulsions, legs moving back and forth, as if in terrible pain.

Carter couldn't watch anymore and left the ward. In the morning, when he went back, the cot was empty and the nurse told him of the boy's death. An ambulance had already transported the body back to Mumbe, where he would be buried immediately, the nurse said, according to Muslim tradition.

"Will you visit the village?"

Carter shook his head. "I don't know. I wouldn't be welcome there."

## Tuesday

CARTER KEPT HIS EYES on the ground, averted from the soldiers and tanks, as he crossed the last hundred yards to his classroom. A lanky soldier rose from a squat. He was drinking tea with his comrades. He wore green fatigues too small for his frame. "Meesta teecha," he shouted. The soldier raised his fist and smiled, showing off his schoolboy English. "Drink tea with us."

Carter waved back. "*À la prochaine*," he said. "I must go to work."

He was afraid of what might come out of his mouth if he sat with these men. Besides, his colleagues and students hated the army. Many were convinced Carter was CIA, sent to spy on behalf of the president, or that he lived abroad because he couldn't function in his own country. Suspicion swirled around foreigners. Many older people who'd experienced colonialism blamed the French for the drought, telling stories of a great conspiracy that poisoned both land and sky. One English teacher, a Ghanaian man, called Carter "Mister Ceee-Iyyy-Ayyy," the letters nicely drawn out.

When Carter first started teaching, students were curious about him. They'd test his poor command of Hausa and comment on it: "Your mouth is ill."

One day in class, a young woman spoke bluntly. "*Qu'est-ce que vous faites ici?* You must have done something really stupid to be sent here, to such a poor country. You can't really be here to teach English."

Like Cisse, the football player, she used French rather than English, a minor act of defiance, though she might have upped the ante by using her own tongue, Djerma. Carter's French was good, a small advantage, even if that means of communication, like English, had colonial overtones. Still, French was the "national language," spoken everywhere, enabling a person to cross ethnic boundaries in a place where the native language changes from village to village — though speaking the language of the colonists seemed to Carter an odd expression of neutrality.

The young woman smiled and cocked her head to the side. Her name was Mariatou, and she wore her hair in thin braids and was dressed in a shawl and a light-blue cotton wraparound cloth, like a long skirt. The word for such a cloth was *pagne,* and women used it to cover the head or to hang in a doorway to keep the flies and sun out. But Mariatou didn't wear a headscarf, as most women do in a Muslim nation.

She switched to English. "Are you a crazy man?"

Carter raised an eyebrow and pointed at his forehead. "Crazy as a donkey. I work for Colonel Khadafy."

Nervous laughter rippled across the room. Cisse was the only one to laugh heartily.

"Ahh, Meesta Daveed, the crazy man."

So that morning, on his way to the classroom after leaving Amelia and the Hotel Sahara, Carter passed up the soldier's invitation to tea. He feared the questions that would follow: "Why were you drinking with those beasts? What did you tell them?"

## March

"I HATE SOLDIERS, SALIF. You have so many here."

Salif busied himself with the second round of tea. "Daveed, what do you know about Africa? You've only just arrived. You don't have soldiers in Amereeeca?"

"I'm not afraid of them, Salif. I'm angry. Soldiers make me angry—"

Salif interrupted him. "Did you read Frantz Fanon at university?"

"I've read some."

"Fanon wrote something about soldiers. I know it by heart. He says, 'The colonial world is cut in two. The dividing lines, the frontiers, are shown by barracks and police stations. In the colonies, it is the policeman and the soldier who are the official instituted go-betweens, the spokesmen of the settler and his rule of oppression.'"

"But the colonials are gone."

Salif shook his head. "Not really. A new army replaced them. That army uses the same policies of brutality and exploitation. Don't you see? Soldiers make me angry, too. The Europeans left, but the soldiers are still here and so are the borders the Europeans left behind, dividing us against ourselves."

Salif looked at Carter, his eyes narrow and unblinking. "Daveed, the government is terrified of the Tuareg rebellion. The Tuaregs have challenged the borders, the very framework of power for all these new African countries. Just by rebelling they have declared the borders invalid. When you take many peoples like this — dozens of ethnicities with different languages and values — and then group them together in a country by fiat, you're going to have problems."

Salif paused. "It's hard to be president of a country that has sixteen different ethnic groups, no history as a national entity, and no legitimacy as a country in the eyes of its own people. Being president means you are paranoid all the time. You need soldiers so you can sleep at night." He smiled.

Carter said, "So you are challenging the validity of all these new countries? Mauritania, Mali, Burkina Faso, Niger, Chad, and so on?"

Salif nodded and leaned forward. "Soldiers seem to interest you so much, Daveed. Let me tell you something else about soldiers and how we live in Africa. Many years ago a young man from the village of Misago, near the border with Mali, wanted to join the army and become a big man among his people. He wanted power and respect. But somehow his ambitions went awry. Before he was to go off and join the army, he went at night to the village burial ground and secretly started to exhume the bones of an army officer, a hero of the village who had died many years earlier in a border fight with Malian soldiers. The elders said the officer's spirit protected them all and honored the name of the village. But the opened grave was discovered, and one of the elders hid near the burial ground at night to see who was abusing it. He fell asleep behind a tree and awoke to find the young man digging, with his bare hands, in the dead officer's grave. The old man slipped away and told the other men in the village.

"They went to the culprit's hut and found more bones in a pile on the floor. When the young man returned from digging up more bones from the grave, the men were waiting for him. The elders accused him of using the bones as fetishes to make him a great soldier and of practicing sorcery to harm the village. He confessed. Stumbling and whimpering, for he knew he was in trouble, he led the village men to the place behind his hut where he had reburied more bones as charms to protect his home. The elders worried that his actions would offend the officer's spirit and bring angry soldiers down on the village, and maybe even the wrath of the president himself."

Salif told the story in an even voice, without drama.

"The elders ordered the guilty man to bury the bones back in the original grave, but he told them he was frightened to touch the bones and begged them to let him go. So they beat him and forced him to comply; his own father handed the bones to him as the young man trembled and sobbed. He squatted in the officer's grave, placing each bone in the dirt as he was told. When the job was done, the men beat him to the ground with their fists and wooden clubs. They hit him until he no longer breathed. Then, with machetes, they hacked off his arms and feet, so his spirit would be powerless to pursue them for revenge. They carried him inside his hut, and covered his remains with stones and dirt, and then demolished the hut. People say the young man's own father delivered the blows that killed him."

## Tuesday

CARTER LOOKED UP from the blackboard, chalk in hand, alerted by the sound of engines. He glanced at his watch. It was 8 A.M. and the minister was arriving. Beyond the classroom windows to the north, blue Land Rovers, with khaki canvas shells, skidded to a dusty halt in front of the faculty building. Two more stopped outside Carter's classroom. He glanced out the south windows and saw similar vehicles pulling up at other campus buildings. Soldiers spilled out of jeeps and took positions at doors and windows. Weapons hung from canvas straps slung over their shoulders. For a couple of minutes Carter kept an eye on the soldiers, while his students stared straight at him, afraid to peer outside, as if a soldier might notice a face and never forget it. Carter looked around the room, taking it in as if for the first time, the badly chipped cement floor and the light-blue concrete walls awash in sunlight.

He continued the lesson, a reading about an English boy and his nanny in London; now and then he turned to look outside. The story was a favorite of the headmaster, who'd spent a few weeks in London on a cultural exchange and ordered for the English curriculum a reading series about an English family. "We have to give students a sense of where the language came from," he said. But Carter had come to hate the sound of English in this place and the ringing irrelevance of the content of the stories. The words seemed to bounce off his students' sweaty faces.

Now the soldiers were making a show of shouting and running around urgently as the minister walked the grounds. Carter labored through the reading, asking questions about pronunciation and vocabulary. After a while the minister entered the classroom, slapping his thigh with a tree branch. His boots echoed sharply on the concrete floor. The minister was a military man — a thick-muscled lieutenant colonel. Not tall, but big-boned, and his head and wide face were clean-shaven. He wore new khaki desert army boots, carefully pressed green camouflage with red shoulder boards, and a red beret tilted to the right. He wore sunglasses with mirror lenses, which he did not take off, and from his belt hung a shiny white-handled pistol. Carter thought of Hermann Göring, who paraded about in his spotless field marshal's uniform even as Germany crumbled. He was splendidly outfitted in a greatcoat with wide red lapels and held his gilded scepter the day he surrendered to American soldiers in Austria.

Other officers, in crisp fatigues and berets and wearing side arms, accompanied the minister. The headmaster followed in white robe and sandals, his face a shield of sweat as he tried to match the soldiers' grim expressions.

The minister moved among the desks, hands folded in the small of his back, one hand gripping the tree branch. His sunglasses flashed, reflecting the faces of students as he strode around the room. Carter looked on. How was it possible to start the day pleasantly after a night with Amelia, walk to school with purpose through the maze of tea tables, checkpoints, and street peddlers, and then suddenly be drawn into a rage in his own classroom? The anger was like the stomach problems that, out of nowhere, left Carter curled up in bed, with his arms folded over his abdomen. He glanced from the minister to the students, who sat straight, hands in their laps, as if this were a well-rehearsed drill. The minister opened notebooks with his stick, flipping a page, nodding, and proceeding to the next desk. He ignored Carter, who remained at the blackboard, with his arms folded across his chest and holding chalk in his moist hand. The minister picked up a student's workbook and snorted, thumbing through the pages, stopping here and there to read.

Then, his eyes still on the workbook, the minister asked in a low and measured voice, "Who is the best student?" A few seconds passed, and he looked blankly at the American, who glared back. Carter was thinking that if he walked up and slugged the minister, he'd be a legend, Che Guevara with an Anglo face. And he'd be dead. The corners of the minister's mouth turned up slightly, as if he was pleased by the anger in Carter's eyes. He dropped the student's workbook on the desk and repeated, slowly, "Who is the best student?"

"They are all my best students," Carter said. He smiled, and the minister's entourage chuckled softly, nervously. The students remained silent. Carter felt a jolt of triumph.

The headmaster stepped forward, taking his place beside Carter. He was holding several class file folders, and Carter knew that he'd anticipated just such an impasse. "Colonel, Monsieur Carter is a hardworking teacher," he said, putting a hand on Carter's shoulder. "Our records show his best student in this class is . . ." He pointed to a girl in the second row.

"Stand to be recognized," the minister said. She obeyed, her face expressionless, her eyes focused on the blackboard. Her fingertips lightly touched the desk. The minister frowned at the girl and turned to Carter. "Who is your worst student?"

Carter knew that question would follow, and he did not answer. He concentrated on the wall at the back of the room, unable to bring himself to meet his students' searching looks, which he could feel acutely. He turned his gaze to the minister and saw the playful malice he recognized well—it danced on the face of every soldier in the city. The headmaster licked his fingertips and paged through the contents of another folder.

"I don't know," Carter said. "I have no such student." Though, of course, he did, and without meaning to he glanced at him, a sixteen-year-old boy sitting next to a window. Carter did not announce his name, but the boy rose to his feet anyway, eyes cast downward, his body shaking. He sobbed quietly. Carter felt his own face go cold, stunned by his act of silent betrayal. The students sat at their desks, hands in front of them, eyes lowered.

The minister walked over to the boy. "Look at me," he said. He raised his stick to rest atop his shoulders and turned to Carter. "What is his name?" he asked in crisp French.

Carter said nothing, unaware he was sweating heavily and that his hands shook. Without thinking, he clasped his hands behind his back and stared above the faces, toward the back of the room. He wanted to ask the minister about Salif, to shout the question he constantly asked himself, so everyone could hear it: *Where's my friend, Salif Moustapha? He taught French and math in this school, to these students. He is loved here. What have you done with him?*

The headmaster cleared his throat. "Minister, I think Monsieur Carter is nervous. He does not remember the name, but I have it here. The boy's name is Ibrahim Moctar."

"Bottom of the class!" the minister shouted, turning back to the boy and enunciating every word with precision. "Is this true?" The boy had stopped sobbing but kept his head bowed. "You cry, but you can't speak. You coward!" On that last word — *lâche* in French — the minister exploded. "You disgrace this country before a foreigner!" He raised his stick but then lowered it to his thigh. The boy made no sound, no move to run or to raise a hand to protect himself. Carter's body grew tense, not with raw fear, but something worse, a feeling of vulnerability. He knew his true nature, his cowardice, couldn't be denied. Everyone could see it. The muscles in his neck ached, and he had trouble breathing. He looked up again, from the minister to Ibrahim, thinking he might still say something courageous.

The minister nodded to Carter. "Good," he said, turning to glance at Ibrahim. "Sit down!" He barked the words. He nodded to the headmaster and led his entourage out of the room.

Carter, standing at the blackboard, watched them leave. He looked down to find that the chalk in his hand had turned to paste, and then up at Ibrahim, who sat with his eyes straight ahead, hands in his lap. The class sat silently. Carter crossed the room to Ibrahim's desk.

"I'm sorry," Carter said.

A student laughed. "He's sorry," the boy said.

"Shut up," hissed another boy. "It's not his country."

Carter returned to his desk, wiping his sweaty hands with a wet cloth from the chalkboard. Softly, he said, "Take out your books and read."

*It's not his country.* The words knocked about his head. *Not my country, not my problem.* He began making notes for a new lesson. He tried to be cool, as if the minister's behavior no longer bothered him. He figured Salif would have handled it that way. Carter flipped through the reading text. No, he was not sure how Salif would have conducted himself — no one remembered the last time a minister had visited campus.

*The last time.* Carter pondered the phrase as he turned pages aimlessly. The words were a little melodramatic, heightening the significance of the situation they referred to. The last time, the last meal, the last hurrah, the last supper . . . the last thought before falling asleep, the last time Humphrey Bogart saw Ingrid Bergman in *Casablanca.* Carter had seen the movie many times and often replayed in his mind the final scene at the airfield, with the German officer dead on the ground and the former lovers standing on the edge of a new life. A border crossing.

Around Salif, Carter often felt an uneasy awareness that the two of them were approaching such a border. The broken finger, the swollen eye worried him. Was he witnessing his friend's last days? The notes he kept about Salif increased in details and urgency.

Had tea with Salif this afternoon. He seemed moody and didn't participate in conversation with his usual sharpness. He made tea, he listened, he studied people's faces, but he said nothing . . .

Salif let me sit in on his French class today. I've wanted to find out how he wins the students' respect. There's always laughter in his classes . . .

Later, he added a parenthetical note to the entry about the French class: *Approaching borderline.* Salif had moved among desks, firing off sentences in French and pointing randomly at individual students to recast them in the subjunctive, on the spot, a standard exercise, except that Salif spit the sentences like accusations. The class waited sullenly, hands on their desks, looking at Salif only when he pointed at someone to give an answer. He gazed with unusual intensity at the student. Carter sat in back, his head resting against the wall. The spirit of Salif's classroom, the humor and irreverence, was gone. The room seemed cold, even as the sun and the hot desert breeze burned through open windows. Carter shivered. Salif let students' errors stand without correction. He cut them off, rushing to the next student, *searching as if picking a jury,* Carter wrote later, *impatient to move on. The students noticed.*

"*Vous vous fâchez, monsieur.*"

Salif raised his eyebrows and frowned in mock surprise. He turned to the speaker, Cisse.

"Angry? Is that what you think I am? Angry?"

There was a long pause as Cisse and Salif looked at each other, Salif glaring and licking his lips. Carter could even hear him breathing. Cisse looked confused. At last Salif spoke.

"No, not anger — fear. What you see in me is fear."

Salif glanced around the room, but he didn't look at Carter. A few moments of silence passed, and the students shifted in their seats. Then Salif gave Carter a brief, stern nod and walked out of the classroom, down the steps, and across the school grounds. His sandals slapped the balls of his feet, as if announcing his escape, or something worse. Salif had left his books and lesson plan on his desk.

Carter waited a minute, wary about openly confronting Salif about what bothered him. Then Carter picked up the forgotten lesson plans and left the classroom to find Salif. Carter walked the campus, he asked around; he went to Salif's house and found the family gone, again. No one had seen him. Carter was certain that people were lying. His friend did not simply evaporate. Surely Salif had been taken, and Carter realized he had sensed the approach of another "official vacation." Then Salif showed up again four days later. But instead of feeling relieved, Carter felt his friend slipping farther away with each disappearance.

That was it. The border.

Carter raised his head from his desk and rubbed his eyes. He peered at the students' faces. Twenty minutes had passed since the minister and his people had gone. Carter felt thirsty and awfully tired. Most of the students were reading. Cisse and two others whispered together. Ibrahim Moctar sat at his desk, with his hands folded on his books, staring at the floor. He looked up abruptly and held his teacher's gaze. Carter looked away.

## October

SALIF SMILED as Carter sipped his tea, holding his head back to drain the last of it.

"You know, we have a saying in Tamachek. The tea, as you know, is served in stages. The first glass is bitter like life, the second is strong like love, and the third glass is sweet like death."

Carter squinted at his friend. "I thought a Frenchman wrote that, Salif. He's a desert naturalist, Théodore Monod. I can't remember where I read it, but I am sure he said that."

Salif frowned at first, then laughed. "Daveed, you know so little of the desert and its people. No Frenchman can be capable of those words. They are the words of desert people, my people."

Carter smiled and nodded, bowing his head deeply. "My mistake."

## Wednesday

"ARE YOU A MERCENARY?"

"What?"

"Do you work for the CIA or the French?"

Carter was walking to school. He was at the same checkpoint where the soldiers had taken Salif just two mornings before. He rolled his eyes and the soldier grinned. Carter decided to play the game.

"What do you think?"

The soldier kept on smiling. Carter smiled back and asked another question.

"Are you a Tuareg?"

The soldier laughed and gave him back the card.

Niger was not a country where Carter could travel casually, not a place where he could unobtrusively ask people, "I'm looking for my friend, Salif Moustapha. Have you seen or heard of him?" Still, the memory of soldiers driving off with Salif deepened his worry. Sometimes Carter thought Salif was dead, and sometimes he convinced himself that his friend had escaped. But such rationalizations didn't alleviate his sense of guilt and anger. Under the circumstances, Carter liked to think he was doing what he could.

He made gentle inquiries at school, with students and faculty. "Haven't seen Salif in a while," he'd say, fishing for a response.

His efforts drew shrugs, though Ahmed, the old groundskeeper, at least spoke in response. He clasped his hands and begged Carter to leave the matter to God and be patient. "*Sai hankuri,*" he said. "*Sai hankuri.*" Teachers and students came to avoid Carter outside class. He went out on the streets for tea. As each new day arrived and Carter found that Salif was not waiting for him outside his apartment, he believed more strongly that his friend had been murdered.

Finally, after four days, Carter walked into the headmaster's office and asked a blunt question.

"Do you know which police commissariat is holding Salif?"

The headmaster looked sad. He avoided Carter's eyes.

"I can't help you."

"Yes, you can."

There was a long silence. The headmaster sighed and leaned back in his chair. "I told you I don't know."

Carter looked out the window, pursed his lips, and nodded. He turned to go without saying anything, but stopped as the headmaster pushed his chair back and got up at his desk, speaking in a low, strong voice.

"Please, Monsieur Carter." The headmaster waited for Carter to turn around.

"They keep lists of detainees at the Ministry of the Interior. You can check there. But they will wonder who you are and why Salif is associating with you. You risk nothing for yourself by asking, but you risk everything for Salif. You must wait."

Carter did wait, sort of.

He opened a new notebook on Salif, unlabeled, and wrote notes in his own shorthand code, just in case someone with a little English decided to read the contents at a roadblock. He wrote down the rules of evidence as he remembered them from his scholarly training in history: *Direct evidence establishes an absolute connection to fact without interference or presumption. All other evidence is circumstantial, or indirect. When direct evidence is lacking, the remaining circumstantial evidence must be somehow clear, convincing, and conclusive.*

Carter walked by Salif's home that night, listening for voices, checking for the light of a lamp. He had a photograph of Salif at tea, but he couldn't simply stop people on the street and ask them about the man in the picture. Carter had no direct evidence of wrongdoing, either. What he did have was a whole world that behaved and wanted him to behave as if Salif had never lived. After a few weeks, Salif seemed like a surreal memory. Carter's agony lay in his ignorance of Salif's fate and his inability to find out more about it.

On Thursday night, Carter went back to Salif's house, where he found the old men who once greeted him outside the compound wall. When he addressed them directly, the men looked down and waved him away. He stood above them, his form barely illuminated by the light of a hurricane lamp. "You know where he is," he said. "Salif Moustapha is my friend. Please tell me what you know."

The eldest of the men, the one who cradled a cane in his lap and who months before had addressed Carter as "friend," was the only one to speak. "We have enough trouble," he said, his voice hushed. "Please go away from here."

Carter said, "I'm sorry." He left quietly.

## January

"YOU MUST HOLD the kettle high. Yes, that's right. The tea must travel some distance through the air. Remember, you must let it breathe."

Salif tried to suppress a smile as Carter spilled most of the first round. "It doesn't matter. You will make another pot, and another. The purpose is to make time, to extend time, and to talk. Spilled tea is not a bad thing."

Carter tried to brew a second round, watched by a dozen sets of eyes: Salif, a few teachers and students, and the groundskeeper, Ahmed. Even the headmaster sat with them awhile, but without accepting Carter's offer of a glass.

"Do not rush it, Daveed. Take your time, pay attention. You wait, and we wait, for the tea."

Carter spilled much of the second round, leaving enough tea for only one glass, which he handed to Ahmed, the eldest. He added water, sugar, and tea leaves for another round. He set the kettle back on the coals. Then he rinsed the glasses. The tea maker had to do all these things and entertain his guests while keeping an eye on the kettle, waiting for the lid to jiggle from the pressure of the steam.

Salif mimicked Carter, frowning in concentration, his lips set tightly. "*Kai, mai chai!* Daveed, you must talk with us while you work." Salif called Carter by the Hausa title *mai chai*, "tea master." "We are here to drink your tea and listen to your stories."

Carter's face reddened. He was unable to work and talk well at the same time.

"You know, Monsieur Daveed, in Germany they tell many stories about forests and the powers of spirits who live in them, the demons and dwarfs and monsters, just like we do in Africa. I learned this proverb that storytellers use at the end of a story: '*Und der das zuletzt erzählt hat, dem ist der Mund noch warm.*' It means, 'And the mouth of him who last told the story is still warm.' Daveed, your mouth is still cold."

There was laughter. Carter became more nervous, more intent

on the tea. The conversation lulled. After a while, Salif asked another question. "You have not been to visit that boy's village, have you?"

Carter sighed and ran his hands through his hair.

Salif leaned forward, his eyes unblinking. "My friend, have you already forgotten his name?"

Carter bit his lip. "His name is Hamza Saidou, and yes, you're right, Salif, I haven't been to his village. It's a long walk."

Sometimes guilt seized Carter and made him angry at himself. He wanted to shout at Salif, tell him to shut up and let him take care of this on his own. Instead, the words came out merely terse. "I understand what you're saying. Just let me handle this. This is my affair."

"Well, Daveed, when you do, you will have a story for us. You can come back and tell us all about it."

## Friday

EARLY IN THE EVENING Carter walked the three blocks from his apartment to the bar where he often took his dinner of goat meat, rice and beans, and beer. Sometimes he went to street tables where women prepared pounded yam. He liked the way they worked in pairs, driving heavy wooden pestles, like huge baseball bats, into a wide wooden mortar full of boiled yam — first one woman, then the other, working in an even rhythm marked by a satisfying hollow thump. Now and then they stopped, mixed in water or millet flour, and resumed. They served thick white yam smothered in spicy sauces. Carter would sit with other men on a long bench and eat out of a plastic bowl with his fingers, scooping yam into his mouth, sucking and licking each finger.

But tonight he'd go to the bar to take the edge off that classroom face-off between the minister and the boy, Ibrahim Moctar. Amelia was fading in Carter's mind, an encounter outside the current context. Not a dream, but an accidental interlude, wonderful but irrelevant. Carter found it easier to cope if he didn't think of her. On the street a soldier demanded his identity card, but Carter had no energy for argument. He wanted to drink. While the soldier examined the card, Carter saw a foot patrol waiting nearby, obscured by the night. Three soldiers guarded four young men whom he recognized as the vegetable sellers who set up shop in front of his apartment building every day. They sat together on the dirt just off the street. The soldier handed Carter his card and noticed the American looking at the prisoners.

"They have no papers," he said.

Carter looked from the officer to the young men sitting on the road. "But I know these men. They're here every day. They bother no one."

The soldier shrugged. "This doesn't concern you," he said. "We will only take them to get identity cards and let them go."

Carter jerked his head toward the tables piled with produce. "What about their vegetables and the tables?"

The soldier smiled. "We will protect their belongings. Don't worry." He gave an order to rouse the prisoners to their feet. Carter watched the patrol, with its harvest of captives, fade into the darkness. Then he hurried down the street to the bar.

Carter opened an iron door into a gravel courtyard surrounded by a six-foot mud wall, rounded at the top. Inside, white metal tables with plastic lawn chairs filled the space. Along one wall stood a boxy, whitewashed cinderblock building, where the barman, Brahima, kept a large refrigerator for meat and beer. A woman sat on a wooden stool in a corner before a fire, stirring pots of rice and beans and serving customers food on metal plates.

No one knew where Brahima lived. No one wanted to know. Salif said he'd once been a news announcer at the government radio station but had been fired. No one understood why, though everyone knew he talked too much. Rumor held that he came from a prominent family of Muslim teachers and scholars, which gave him a measure of protection from the soldiers. So he spoke his mind freely inside the high, thick walls of his bar.

Carter took a table near the wall. A few oil lamps lit the courtyard. Men in twos and threes were scattered among the tables, barely visible in the night. Brahima emerged from the building. He was a huge man who favored brightly colored cotton tunics and trousers and who traded in Nigerian pot. He kept his head shaven. Sweat beaded his face, though his clothes were fresh and dry. He was over six feet tall and weighed nearly three hundred pounds, yet he moved fluidly, his body more muscle than fat. At one time Carter bought pot from Brahima in half-liter coffee cans, though in a country where checkpoints and patrols owned the roads, these purchases worried Carter. He thought Brahima might be growing pot plants on the premises, right here in Niamey, and Carter was concerned that they both might be caught. The risk bothered him — especially in a city where the law was redefined at every turn — but not enough to make him stop. When Carter ran out of pot, he silently made another transaction at the bar, raising his index finger to indicate "one" as he handed Brahima a wad of francs to ostensibly pay for a beer. The next evening a taxi driver would arrive at Carter's apartment with one can.

Carter began smoking his first month at the lycée. A morning joint on the balcony, with his coffee, calmed him just enough. He smoked more every week to handle the stress of the street and the school. When classes ended, he rushed home to smoke. Before bed, he smoked in order to sleep. This went on for three months, until one morning, as Carter smoked on the balcony, he saw soldiers staring up at him as they escorted more prisoners past his apartment. So he quit for fear of being caught. He thought Brahima would say something, but like a good bartender, he never pressed the issue. Never got personal. Carter stuck with alcohol. That way he was still a paying customer.

Now Brahima took a seat across from Carter. "*Monsieur le professeur,*" he said, raising his index finger, "I must warn you. This is a Muslim country and we Muslims drink in hiding, in the dark, behind high walls. You must be careful." Then he burst out laughing.

Carter smiled. "It's good to see you, Brahima. Drink a beer with me."

Brahima patted his belly. "I cannot, my friend. Stomach problems tonight. Perhaps I'll lose weight and look like you, a mere stick. White people don't eat enough, that's your problem."

"I hope that's all it is. Bring me extra meat tonight, just to be safe."

Brahima leaned forward with his forearms on his knees. "What have you heard about Salif?"

"Sedition charges," Carter said softly. "The headmaster told me. No one knows where he is. What about you?"

Brahima shook his head. "In my work one does not make inquiries. One listens, and I have heard nothing." He paused and sighed. "Perhaps he'll finally quit smoking."

They laughed together.

Then, after a short silence, Carter said, "Brahima, I'm supposed to leave here in a few weeks. My visa expires the day after I fly out."

Brahima tapped the table and nodded his head. "Better for you, my friend, better for you." Then he stood up. "Let me get you another beer."

Carter watched him walk away and then heard a curious whispering and giggling. He turned his head toward the entrance of the bar, where the wall was not as high, and realized he had an audience. Children watched him, their hands clutching the top of the wall. Their heads bobbed as if about to roll away. A boy shouted a word for white people: *"Anasara, Anasara,"* an Arabic term that can be roughly translated as "Christian person." Other children joined in. The voices sounded oddly fuzzy to Carter, and when he smiled and waved, the children laughed, and their heads wobbled before dropping out of sight.

Brahima returned with another beer and the two men sat and talked. Carter was not an aggressive drunk. Alcohol settled him, which was the point. Carter drank in order to sleep.

Late in the night, Carter looked in the direction of the other patrons and then at Brahima. He said, "Don't you worry that there are police here?" He spoke softly and slowly because the beer had muddled his head.

Brahima folded his arms and stared at the ground for a few moments. "My friend, I am a bad Muslim, but I *am* a Muslim and that means my fate is in God's hands." As if to make that point, he said in a voice loud enough to be heard across the bar: "Of course, any man knows that if I find out he's a 'ghost,' I'll kill him." He paused. "Unless he gets to me first." Brahima laughed softly.

Near midnight Carter smiled and hung his head. "I'm drunk, my friend. I'd better go."

## May

SALIF LIKED TO SAY, "I am a man of my vices." At other times he'd say, "I am not a good Muslim." He said that often, to which Brahima would explode, "My friend, you are an awful Muslim," and shake with laughter.

Salif drank some, he chain-smoked Gauloise cigarettes, and he ate little. His loose cotton tunics and leggings made him look thinner. Sometimes in the evenings Carter joined Salif at the bar with Brahima and a few teachers. Salif would drink from a large bottle of beer and set it down to suck on a cigarette. He kept kola nuts in the breast pocket of his tunic. Between a beer and a cigarette, he'd pry open a nut with his thumbs and chew on half of it, sucking the juice before spitting out the masticated remains a few minutes later.

Salif never got drunk. He argued, he told stories, and he provoked his friends and his enemies, just as he did under the influence of tea.

"Do you believe in God?" Salif looked at the faces around him and answered his own question. "I don't believe in anything."

One night another teacher grew nervous. "Shut up, Salif. You put us all at risk. You, too, Brahima. Think of your families."

Salif lit a fresh cigarette and leaned back in his chair, staring at the sky for a few seconds. Finally, he leaned forward, pointing at Carter. "You know, our American visitor does not understand the fear you are talking about. Perhaps I should explain it to him."

He dropped his unsmoked cigarette in the dirt between his feet and turned to Carter, who looked up too quickly, betraying his unease. Salif raised his voice loud enough to be heard above the group. "Welcome to Africa, my American friend, where you must worry about your every word because once you release words they become like birds, free to roam where they like and to be used against you."

The other teachers quietly left the bar, but Salif ignored them, his eyes on Carter, who listened with his arms folded. Brahima put a hand on Carter's shoulder and raised his head in Salif's direction, as if to say, "Listen to him."

Salif's tongue fell hard on every consonant, shaping and releasing words individually. He thrust two fingers at Carter over the table. "The power we Africans know is eternal and dangerous. That is why African leaders fear words more than anything. More than rebellion. More than cholera and locust plagues. More than famine. You have to understand that."

He paused.

"And you have to be careful, Daveed. *You* give them words. That is what they have trained you to do."

Carter tried to think of something to say. He felt as if he was being ambushed. "I teach English, Salif. That's all I do. I give them words in English. So be it."

## June

CARTER WAS TRAINED near the capital at a wooded encampment where, in air-conditioned concrete buildings, foreign volunteers learned to be teachers, health workers, and foresters. They worked for churches, universities, governments, and organizations whose names promised more than they could ever deliver: Catholic World Relief, World Bank, Mercy Corps, Peace Corps, CARE, and the United Nations. The names implied the existence of infinite resources and power to cast nets of money and "experts" around the globe.

One evening, a government official arrived to announce that the trainees could expect sirens early the next morning, signaling the passing of the president's motorcade on the road below the encampment, a half-mile away. This was the east-west highway, which, visible from the compound, cut through a village of mud homes that spread gently from both sides of the asphalt. The trainees awoke before dawn and shuffled to the cafeteria. This was Carter's favorite time of day, when the desert air was cool and new light spread over the land as if radiating from the ground itself. Monsoon season was beginning. Carter sipped coffee and studied the sky. He loved to watch storms develop. Clouds would pile on the horizon, first gray and then dark blue, which eventually turned yellow and brown as the winds gained strength and raised dust, which turned day into night. Then rain would rake the land, sometimes gently, sometimes with a violence that flooded villages and destroyed crops. Water rushed over hardpan in pursuit of anything that could be dissolved. Carter had seen some violent monsoon rains, but that morning at the compound there were no clouds. Dawn began red and faded to pink, a pattern that awakened the land every day.

Across this land, foreigners ran projects intended to save soil gone red, what experts called laterite, full of iron and aluminum and kaolinite but stripped of the elements needed to grow crops and grasses. The experts told villagers that laterite develops when the rains stop, trees are cut, and the ground is exposed to too much sun, heat, and wind. People from Holland dug wells, using mechanized pumps to bring water up from very deep in the earth. Canadian engineers rebuilt roads to withstand the rains. German meteorologists studied the movement of dust and advised that tree lines be planted to stop erosion. Economists from all over tracked markets for onions, peanuts, and grain. Biologists laid out study plots, using photographs made by satellites equipped with infrared cameras, prickly oblong contraptions that hurtled through space, thirty miles above, with lenses that swept the earth for vegetation patterns, soil moisture, livestock movements, even the growth of sand dunes. The biologists in the field huddled over the photographs, writing in notebooks. They dug holes. They dropped samples of red soil in test tubes. They left white paint on a rock beside each hole and moved on. Eventually they returned to offices in the capital and abroad, where they used the data from Africa to "grow crops in computers."

That men took away bits of soil and spoke of taking directions from some mechanism in the sky scared people in the countryside. Villagers who grew millet and sorghum in the sand watched these men from a distance. Sometimes they asked questions of the scientists or fretted among themselves about what the newcomers were doing to the ground. Mostly, they left the scientists alone, but one day an entire village chased them away. Men, women, and children shouted and made an awful noise by clapping their hands and pounding on pots and pans — that's how they scared off hordes of locusts or herds of elephants. Some carried clubs. They chased the scientists to their cars; villagers broke the windows of some vehicles. They shouted, "You are bringing us drought. You put bad things in the soil. Why do you do this?" Others filled in holes or collected the painted stones and buried them far from the village.

That dawn at the training center, Carter had taken a hunk of bread and a cup of coffee, gone out to sit on the ground, and stared at the sunrise and the ribbon of highway that flung itself at the horizon. The narrow road, traversing such a broad land, seemed tentative, as if it had occurred by accident. Then Carter turned his head and saw, in the soft light, six tanks like great mushrooms in a row, facing down the rocky slope that rose to the south above the compound. The color of desert khaki, they had large wheels, and their cannons pointed toward the horizon. No longer hidden in darkness, soldiers in red berets sat atop their tanks and cheered at Carter as he ate his breakfast. Others from the training camp walked over with their coffee to look at the tanks and the happy soldiers.

Then sirens blared. The motorcade approached, and the soldiers scrambled to form neat rows in front of their tanks, with one man standing at attention atop each machine. Carter heard clapping and singing in the village down the road. Farmers and their families could be heard shouting the president's name, while the soldiers saluted and the experts in training sipped coffee. With this welcome, the president passed.

Carter had other training. In college, he'd spent a summer researching an obscure chapter of the American Revolution for his senior thesis. He was drawn to the subject by a roadside plaque about the massacre of an entire Iroquois village as well as a visit to the Seneca Reservation.

One summer, Carter hiked north from Wyoming, Pennsylvania, back across the New York border, camping in forests and farm fields. He worked here and there on state-park trail crews to pay his way, all the while taking notes and putting the facts together about the summer and fall of 1779, when thirty-five hundred farmers and Continental army regulars burned, looted, and slaughtered their way north, up the Susquehanna River Valley, to deprive the British of their Indian allies. He titled his thesis *George Washington and the Iroquois Genocide.*

That August, Carter had visited the Seneca tribal museum, a sullen room in the reservation headquarters, where artifacts lay in glass cases. On the walls, paintings by a local artist told the story of the Susquehanna campaign, atrocity by atrocity. Soldiers burned Seneca families in their homes, destroyed crops, and dragged women into the forests to be raped.

The curator, a lean old man with close-cropped black hair, watched from behind a reception table as Carter studied the paintings. He hardly realized the man was there until he heard a quiet voice.

"Is this not what you expected?" he said.

Carter turned to find the old Indian standing right behind him. The man didn't blink. He spoke coldly, thumbs hooked in the pockets of his jeans and his eyes focused on Carter's face. He reached out and tapped two callused fingers on Carter's notebook, pointing at the paintings with his other hand.

"The father of your country did this. He wasn't there, but he gave the orders. Write that in your notebook. He killed thousands of our people."

Carter frowned and nodded. He stumbled for something to say. "Um, well, how many died?"

The man blinked at him.

"We are still dying."

## Saturday

THE STREET BELOW Carter's apartment was empty and quiet after midnight. He was so tired, he nearly did not see the piles of splintered wood where the vegetable tables had stood only hours before. The dirt roadside was slick with crushed tomatoes, bananas, onions, and mangoes. Tables lay in broken heaps, wet and stained, on the side of the road. He found two bicycles overturned, their wheel rims badly bent. Someone had taken the chains and gear works.

He stepped through the mess, touching the wood and shaking his head. "What the fuck happened?" he said, nearly shouting the words. Evidence lay everywhere and yet there was no evidence at all, no one to accuse. He knew that in the morning, with first light, flies would descend in clouds and remain until midday, when even they couldn't stand the heat.

In the darkness across the road he heard soft gasps, like sobbing, and walked toward the sound. A young woman squatted on the dirt, a cotton shawl pulled over her head and shoulders. She'd drawn her knees up so she could rest her forehead on them. Carter sat down on the ground a few feet away. He was too drunk to find the words to comfort her in any language, so he listened to her weeping, trying to imagine what had happened and who was responsible. Hired thugs? Or soldiers, a truckload dropped off to perform this specific treachery? Or was it the calculated work of the patrol he'd encountered earlier?

Carter watched as the woman raised her head and gazed quietly at the mess of vegetables and broken tables. He thought of how silent the city was at night. A light breeze picked up bits of paper in the street. His head swam. He was thirsty and sweaty and so tired, he felt as if he were part of the wreckage. Finally, he turned to the woman and spoke in French.

"Did you see what happened?"

She sat, unmoving, with her forehead on her knees again. He thought she might be asleep.

"Did you see it?"

She shook her head without looking up.

"Do you know what happened?"

She looked up and wiped her mouth with a corner of the cloth that was wrapped around her head. Carter saw that she was very young, with a soft, round face. She braced her body with her hands in the dirt and pushed herself to her feet, gathering the shawl about her head and shoulders. She turned and walked down the street, fading into the darkness. Carter listened to the flapping of her sandals.

He studied the many pieces of wood from the wreckage, flung about as if in some joyous frenzy of destruction. He squatted to touch the rough edges of a nearly round hole punched through a plywood tabletop. Someone, he thought, used a sledgehammer. The decayed food had begun to smell, and he decided to go. Even at this late hour, a few flies buzzed around his ears, arms, and neck, attracted to his sweat. For a few moments, as he climbed the stairs to his apartment, he thought he could hear each fly individually. He paused to listen, but the thought exhausted him and he hurried to his door, stumbling at the top of the stairway. He wanted to sleep and forget about the woman and her loss, about Salif and the city, about the heat. He undressed and bathed because sleep usually came easier when his body was cleansed of sweat and dust. Yet lying atop the sheets under mosquito netting and a ceiling fan, he couldn't close his eyes. His mind wandered through layers of questions about Salif. Then the electricity went out — an almost daily event. The fan stopped and silence ruled. The stillness of the desert beyond the city seemed to consume the night and the city itself, as if everything had died to be resurrected when the red sun came up again. He began to imagine where Salif had been taken and what terrible things might be happening to him.

After half an hour, Carter swung his feet under the netting to the floor. He sat on the edge of the bed with his head hung low, sleepless after a night of drinking. He went to his desk, picked up the hard wooden chair, and put it in the center of the floor. On his knees, he ran his fingers over the back and the seat to get a feel for the contours. Then he sat on the chair, his back straight, trying to form in his mind a picture of Salif's internment cell. In such a place, could Salif feel time moving, like a tangible, visual thing? Carter got up and closed the windows and shutters. (The building absorbed heat all day and radiated heat in the evening, so most nights he slept with all the windows open.) He looked for twine. Then, back in the chair, he tied his hands behind him in a loose, makeshift knot, lodging them in the small of his back to simulate the typical posture of a prisoner during interrogation. Then he tried to sleep, to think of anything besides being in that chair.

In a cell, Salif wouldn't be able to tell evening from morning or which he wanted more, a cigarette or water. Carter remembered a peculiar effect of intense dehydration that he'd learned about in training. When the body is deprived of water for a long time and the mouth becomes very, very dry, the tongue swells. After a couple of hours in that chair, half asleep at times, Carter spoke. "Hey there," he said. His tongue touched the roof of his mouth and stuck for an instant. When he moved his tongue, a hollow scraping sound echoed in his head. The alcohol had worsened his dehydration, and he was glad. He had to pee badly, his head throbbed, and he felt that somehow he deserved this. This little event, this little attempt at empathy, was like a memorial service. He mused on his friend.

*Salif is native to a continent whose humanity is spread like so many glass shards, large and small, each with its own shape. I could travel to Agadez, to Tuareg territory, and create a new misery for myself by searching for his people, the Bouzou, to learn more about him. But I'm ready to leave it at the fact that he's the offspring of slaves taken when, and from where, I don't know.*

*Here's what Salif has told me. When his father was sixteen, during the "Second Great War," he left his family and walked from Agadez to the river, a six-hundred-mile journey west. Because he was from a slave family, the French gave him a piece of farmland a few miles outside the village of Markala, where Salif grew up. But no village would accept his father because he was Bouzou, so he lived on the land he farmed. After a few years, he'd acquired more land and many camels. He married a Djerma woman, Salif's mother. His offer of marriage outraged the village and family, but he was able to pay a large dowry of animals. He later married a Fulani woman. His third wife is Hausa. Salif's father built separate houses in a compound for all three women.*

*Salif has many, many brothers and sisters, so there was always noise in the home, people talking in all those languages, Djerma, Fulani, Hausa, and French.*

*Salif's father liked to say, "My children belong to no tribe."*

*But there was a terrible fight between the Fulani and Hausa wives — Fatima, whose skin was lighter, and Aichatou. Salif was twelve and his memory of the event is clear — the two women rolling on the ground, the screams and sobs. They were clutching and scratching at each other. A neighbor entered the compound and separated them. More women came, and Salif's father and mother were summoned from the fields. The wives' faces were bloodied, and there were blood drops in the dirt. Women boiled water and treated their wounds. Salif remembers Fatima, the Fulani wife, sitting quietly with her hands in her lap. A strip of skin hung off her cheek.*

*Salif says the women had always been jealous of each other. They argued over how much work each did. They accused each other of stealing. They ridiculed each other's clothing, but they'd never before fought like that. Salif's mother explained to him what had caused the fight: Fatima told Aichatou that her dark skin made her ugly.*

In that chair, two hours into self-imprisonment, Carter imagined that a lieutenant in plainclothes entered Salif's cell. The man held a glass of water in his hand. At one point, he stood in front of Salif, sipping from the glass, which he took from a table just beyond Salif's reach. He said, "So, what do you teach your students?"

"French and mathematics," Salif replied. "You know that."

The lieutenant smiled, standing with a hand behind his back.

"Then we can share ideas on literature," he said. "Do you teach them Frantz Fanon, Aimé Césaire, or maybe Michel Foucault?" He studied Salif's face as he spoke. "You must know Foucault. He wrote that punishment in the twentieth century is the most hidden part of the penal process. Perhaps we should all pay more attention to him. Do you really think, Salif Moustapha, that there is anyone out there worrying about you? Your wife thinks you might be a traitor. We have spoken with her."

Carter pictured Salif looking at his inquisitor. Salif would say nothing at first. He would wait. He would smile.

The lieutenant continued with equal patience. "You are a rebel, yes? So I am sure you are familiar with Fanon and his idea that 'decolonization is always a violent phenomenon.' Would you not agree, Monsieur Salif?"

"Is that what you call this, what you are doing to me?" Salif said. "Decolonization?"

"You are a Tuareg, Salif. The French like the Tuaregs these days, more than they like our government." The lieutenant sipped his water. "You are a man of learning. I thought you might understand. Really, we are still fighting the French. Don't you agree?"

Carter knew Salif would have to speak slowly because his tongue would stick to the roof of his mouth. He'd say to the lieutenant, "Then you must know another passage from Fanon, that 'decolonization is quite simply the replacing of a certain "species" of men by another "species" of men.'"

"Oh, I quite agree with that."

"Did I pass that examination?" Salif said. "I am not a rebel. I do not know any rebels."

Carter imagined that now and then during this dialogue, the lieutenant would draw a deep breath. The man's eyes held a softness, as if he sympathized with Salif and was stalling for time, playing a role. Maybe, because of him, they didn't beat Salif much.

The lieutenant said, "We know little about your time in Germany. Four months, was it?"

Salif nodded.

"Tell us about your friends there. Europeans are fond of Tuaregs, you know. They must have asked you questions."

Despite that softness, the lieutenant behaved with subtle cruelty, taking small, lingering sips of water each time he raised the glass to his lips, like a man savoring good wine. Carter thought such an interrogator would be tall and young, a few years older than Carter's students. He might wear oval-shaped black-rimmed glasses. He would be curious and polite, but soft-spoken. The lieutenant would never become angry. The conversation went on inside Carter's head as he nodded off in that chair after three hours.

"People asked me about the river," Salif said. "They wanted to know about animals, you know, giraffes and lions and so on, and whether or not I traveled the river in a pirogue."

"What did you tell them?"

"I told them that I am the son of a farmer and that I did have a pirogue but that I did not fish. I charged villagers a few francs to take them back and forth across the river."

The lieutenant set the water glass on the table. "Salif, you are an opportunist," he said.

"We were poor, like everyone," Salif said. "The Germans always wanted to know about food and music and the drought. They asked what sort of home I have." He smiled, shaking his head. "Once a young man asked me, 'Who is president of Africa?'"

Carter liked to think that at the end of such a conversation, Salif would say something like this: "Perhaps you haven't noticed, lieutenant, that I don't look like a Tuareg. I look like you . . . Not that the color of our skin should matter."

After four hours in that chair, Carter opened his eyes. Drool dried on his chin and chest, and he was vaguely aware of a distant throbbing in his head. He tried to think again, but he could speculate on Salif's fate only so far. He was unable to ponder a more horrible outcome, one that didn't involve dialogue.

Dawn brought Carter fully awake, hunched over in the chair, stiff and sweaty. He felt nauseated from the beer and dehydration, but at least his head was not pounding. Dust made bright stripes across the room in the rays of sunlight that shot through the window shutters. He unbound his hands with difficulty and then he grabbed the pen and notebook on the table by his bed. He wrote one sentence: *Salif has not shown himself except in my pathetic dreaming.*

Carter opened the doors to the balcony and stepped outside for some air and sunshine. The street was choked with activity. Flies swarmed over the gooey wreckage of the vegetable tables; more swooped down on a cartload of fresh goat meat, which a young man pushed down the street. Carter shook his head, swallowed aspirin, and crawled onto his bed beneath the netting, where he again slept until he awoke hours later, as the sun was fading.

Carter dressed and went back to the bar. Brahima was out and had left the place in the care of two women, who worked as barmaids and prostitutes. They came from Brahima's village, and it was his duty to look after them. Carter flirted with the women, gingerly. He often brought them gifts of cloth or money as a way of endearing himself at the bar. Carter humored them. As he arrived that afternoon, he waved cheerfully. *"L'Américain est ici pour vous,"* he shouted. One woman halfheartedly chased him across the compound, laughing and waving a length of rope at him. Carter gave her five hundred francs, *"pour faire la paix."*

He spent the afternoon drinking and forcing himself through one of Salif's favorite novels, Zola's *Germinal,* in French, until he heard Brahima's old Peugeot pickup wheezing and coughing outside the wall. Brahima entered with a cardboard carton in his hands and wearing a flowing white cotton robe and new leather sandals. *"Ah, c'est mon ami l'Américain,"* he shouted as he disappeared inside the building where the beer was kept. He returned with a bottle, his stomach trouble apparently healed, and joined Carter, who tossed Zola aside, relieved to leave the dark and wet French coal mines and the men who knew they would die underground, like worms. *Germinal* was about a struggle against an unjust and unfeeling power structure. *Just the kind of story Salif would love,* Carter thought.

"I was in the country today, in my village," Brahima said. "My sister gave birth to a boy."

Carter raised his beer and they clinked bottles. He said, "Soldiers arrested the vegetable sellers in front of my building, Brahima. They smashed their tables and all of their vegetables. It's like glue on the roadside." He looked at Brahima. "What is happening in this country?"

For the first time that Carter could remember, Brahima looked worried. He slumped in his chair, hands folded, and stared wearily, over that great expanse of belly, down at his feet. He said nothing for a long time, occasionally sipping beer. Finally, he touched Carter on the knee. "You need to be careful, my friend. And so do I. Changes in this country are coming fast."

They drank together until after midnight, though they talked little. Carter awoke at dawn, lying on a filthy foam mattress thrown down for him on the dirt. He couldn't recall how he'd gotten there. The heat, the sunlight, and the flies opened his eyes and he rose immediately. His mouth tasted bitter and dry. The bar was empty. He picked up the mattress and leaned it against the wall. Carter walked home, where he took four aspirin, drank some water, and then slept.

## Sunday

IN THE MORNING, Carter felt foolish for drinking so much and resented the throbbing at his temples and in his joints. In bed, he propped himself up on his elbows, watching dust roll in the sunlight that came through the window shutters. He got up, made coffee, and decided to visit a couple of police stations to see what he could find out about Salif. He put on his sunglasses and his straw hat and walked down the stairs. He passed the rotting produce and splintered tables, where flies still swarmed heavily.

Carter went to the police commissariat closest to the checkpoint where he'd last seen Salif. His idea was to pretend someone had tried to rob him on the street, hoping that once inside the walled compound, he might catch a glimpse of prisoners or even develop a relationship with an informant. Tricky work. Making contacts among police officers was largely futile without a great deal of money. Inside a small office building, a policeman told Carter to "find your thief" and bring him in. Carter made a show of frustration, but thanked him. He stepped back into the compound grounds and wandered a bit, lingering beside a long concrete building with a row of corrugated iron doors. They were locked with wooden boards set in slots bolted to the walls. Above and beneath each door was a rectangular opening, a foot wide and about six inches high. He heard coughs, spitting, and moaning, a faint, steady, varied noise from behind each door. A hand protruded through the opening under one door, fingers flat on the concrete step. Carter realized a face was behind it, sucking in fresh air and daylight. He left, overwhelmed by the thought of dozens, maybe hundreds of people sleeping, eating, and defecating while packed in behind those cell doors.

On the street he thought again of that imaginary cell, or what Salif called "the very center of the eye," a quote from Foucault. Salif liked to use that phrase every time they passed a checkpoint together. "This is our life," he'd say. "We are objects of the 'disciplin-ary gaze,' residents of 'the perfect camp.'" Now Carter felt closer to grasping the outlines of Salif's prison, part of the broad geometry of surveillance and control, as if he held the map in his hands. The distribution of checkpoints formed the larger frame. The individ-ual detention cell was its intimate expression of control. In such a cell a man's imagination would become clear, his recollection pure, and his mind free to wander. No family, no friends. He could think. Maybe Salif imagined helping his father repair their house in Markala. They'd mix the sand and straw with water for fresh stucco to be spread on the mud-brick walls. Carter wondered what thoughts really filled Salif's hours in a cell, whether here in the city or far away in the desert. Carter believed these prisons served more to intimidate the population than to keep an eye on specific undesirables. Salif had called the whole system "the government's network of paranoia."

Carter supposed his search for Salif was largely an attempt at therapy, a way of coping with guilt. At a roadside table, he ordered a glass of tea and sat down on a wooden bench with his notebook. He made an evidence list, intending to present the U.S. Embassy with a persuasive case for investigating Salif's plight. He started with the checkpoint incident he'd witnessed, when Salif was briefly detained, and added the dates of his other disappearances. He de-scribed the wounds to his face, the broken fingers, Salif's fatigue. Carter included notes about his conversations with the headmas-ter and his statement about "sedition charges" against Salif. He also described the disappearances of two of his students, young men he didn't know well. He also had records of his conversations with Salif, which, unfortunately, did not constitute hard evidence. Really, he had no substantive leads, just suspicious circumstances and guesswork that seemed convincing only to Carter himself. *In Africa,* he wrote in his notebook, *evidence is a fairy tale.*

That afternoon, Carter went to report his worries about Salif to a UN official, a Belgian woman he'd met in passing. He caught her on the way out of the UN office compound and introduced himself. As he began talking, a light-blue Chevrolet Suburban with the UN insignia pulled up beside them, with an African driver behind the wheel. The woman smiled at the driver and raised her hand to signal him to wait. Carter sensed he had only a few seconds to make his case. He blurted out his worries about a "missing African friend" and told her about Salif's disappearances and injuries, and about the police jails he'd seen.

Her face clouded over. She shook her head. "This is not your affair. If you dig into this, it will get us all in trouble, especially you."

"But this man is my friend and colleague at the school. We work together. He may die if we don't do something for him."

She studied Carter coldly. She said, "I don't make those kinds of friends and you shouldn't either, especially here."

Carter stared at her. He said, "What you mean is you don't *make friends.*"

## July

"YOU SPEAK SO MANY languages, Salif. Which one is yours? Which is the language of your people?"

"In Africa, Daveed, to survive we live across layers of language. Knowing many languages is a way of reaching outside the village, of surviving the journey from one village to another. Why is my language important to you?"

Carter felt his face flush red. He finished his glass of tea. "I'm sorry, I only meant—"

"You know, sometimes I wish we all spoke a single language and that the whole world could not see with the eyes." Salif raised his index finger to his eye. "The Germans have a proverb, *'Bei Nacht sind alle Katzen grau,'* which means 'At night all cats are gray.'"

# WEEK TWO

## Monday

EIGHT DAYS AFTER Carter watched soldiers take Salif at a checkpoint — after someone destroyed the vegetable market outside his apartment, and after he betrayed a student to the minister of education — he stood at his desk in the classroom, preparing for a reading exercise with his students. The air was thick and moist, tinged by the salty odor of roasted goat meat that boys sold from open grills alongside the campus. Carter wiped sweat from his face and neck with a handkerchief.

He looked up at his students, suddenly aware of the distant sound of engines and a rush of voices moving closer. He felt thirsty. The muscles in his neck tightened, and he found it difficult to breathe as he listened, under the gaze of his students. He told them to take out their reading books; he sat down to compose himself. Outside, shouts in French and Hausa mixed with frightened voices in two more languages — Fulani and Djerma. Pickup trucks racing too fast in low gear made a strained whine. Somehow the tangle of voices and engines sounded much louder and more urgent than those of past visits from soldiers. It occurred to Carter that he should tell his students to run, but the thought came too late.

Four soldiers entered through the door and more by the open

windows. They wore the lime green berets of the *gendarmerie na-tionale*. The students turned at their desks. A few boys rose half-way, as if preparing to run. Carter stood just as the first soldier busted an empty plywood desk in half with a steel pipe. Carter stepped forward automatically, not out of bravery or the will to take action. He shouted, first in French, *"Qu'est-ce qu'il y a?"* and then in English, "What the fuck is this?"

Carter tried to make his way forward between the rows of desks, but a soldier blocked his path, putting a hand on Carter's chest and gripping him by the shoulder. He shoved him hard against a wall, and Carter felt a sharp pain in his shoulder blades. The soldier stayed with him, holding him against the wall. Others worked the room with pipes and rifle butts. They took up posts by the windows to block escapes. Carter gripped the soldier's arms to push him away, but the soldier was much stronger and knocked his hands aside, jamming his forearm under Carter's chin and against his throat. He lodged his knee between Carter's thighs. Some students tried to rush to the windows, only to be clubbed down.

The soldiers worked quickly. Carter had a sense of the rising and falling of rifle butts, like the motion women made when crushing millet in a mortar. Some boys fought back. One knocked a soldier down with his fist, but three soldiers responded and beat the boy to the floor, pummeling him with their rifles. Blood pooled around his head. The air filled with grunts and screams, blows on flesh, and the crack of splintering desks. Later, Carter would remember a girl standing in the middle of the room, her fists clenched, screaming words he couldn't understand, as if determined to stop the violence with the force of her voice. A soldier grabbed her by the back of the neck and hustled her out the door.

To see young people suffer and even die this way, like a cattle drive of souls. To hear the beating and the cries, like rhythms from some desperate dance. And to see the effects strewn across the floor, on desks: blood, teeth, a torn skullcap, a headscarf, sandals. Carter screamed in rage, "Why are you doing this?"

The soldier guarding him kept turning his head to the scene and then back to Carter. He smiled. "Don't worry," he said. "This is not your problem."

In English, Carter said, "Bastard!" and knocked the hand away from his chest. He tried to slip to the side, out of his grasp, but the man pushed him back against the wall even harder. Carter's skull hit the concrete, and he was aware of a sound like a sharp knock and pain at his temples. He raised his hands and cuffed the soldier's ears with weak blows. The man was tall and muscular and seemed a little surprised. His eyes widened and he punched Carter in the stomach, putting his other hand around his throat and thrusting his knee hard into his groin. Carter gasped and grunted, overwhelmed by nausea. With the soldier's hand at this throat, he could see the ceiling, and he pressed his hands back against the wall, gagging. Spittle mixed with vomit leaked down his chin and over the soldier's fingers. The soldier still had one hand free. He unsnapped his brown leather holster and drew his pistol, holding it up for Carter to see before dropping it to his side. He glanced around, first at one side of the room, then the other, and back at Carter, relaxing the grip on his throat. Soldiers had crowded students against the opposite wall of the classroom and had begun pushing them out the door. The beating dissolved into sobbing and moaning. The soldier was breathing hard, his breaths alternating with Carter's. His face shone with sweat.

"What's the matter," Carter said snidely. His voice was muffled and hoarse, his mouth felt sticky, and he had trouble forming the words in French. "You're afraid of children? Big, brave soldier." But the man didn't seem to hear.

Carter witnessed everything as if he were suspended under water. Then, in a moment of lucid panic, he gripped the wrist of the hand against his throat and put his other hand against the soldier's collarbone. The soldier turned and placed the barrel of his pistol against Carter's ear. He put his face close to Carter's.

"*Calme-toi*," he said.

Carter wanted to spit on the soldier. He smacked his lips, but he couldn't gather the saliva to do it. So he mocked him. "Big, brave soldier," he said again, though his words sounded like gasps. He tried to smile. But the soldier jammed the pistol barrel into his throat. Carter gagged.

He was conscious later, when it was all over, that he remembered little of what happened; only a few details were clear in his mind. Like the girl on her knees, hands covering her head, screaming. Carter saw a soldier kick her in the stomach so she fell, on her side, hugging herself tightly. He kicked her again and moved on. And what he'd said to the soldier holding him, or the strand of hair that tickled his forehead. And that pistol. He figured that he and the soldier must have stood together, locked in physical intimacy, the whole time. Carter could still hear him breathe, hear his neck brush against the collar of his uniform tunic as he turned his head, and smell the tang of his sweat. He had a dim recollection of his own shouting, but the words were difficult to recall, as if they had been confiscated, sucked from his brain. He thought of soldiers in a strange dance with their victims. He thought of Markala, Salif's village of birth. The image of a dance brought that memory to mind.

## August

DURING THE SUMMER BREAK, Salif had invited Carter to visit his natal home on the river, one of the few times Carter ever left Niamey. Salif had called it "Daveed's exploration of the broader territories in the cause of American diplomacy."

They traveled on a road of graded clay and gravel in a minibus that took seven hours to cover the sixty miles to Markala. Some thirty people crowded the vehicle, along with a couple of goats and all kinds of luggage. Eight large sacks of grain were piled on top. Before boarding, Carter took a long look up at the grain sacks, convinced the bus would roll over and burn. As if to taunt his foreign passenger, the driver pushed his machine at fifty miles an hour, too fast for the load they carried. A front tire blew. Carter heard the pop, and the bus leaned hard to the right. The driver shouted to the passengers to shift their weight to the left. That saved them, and the minibus came to a rumbling halt. Carter counted seventeen wrecks along the road that day, including a Peugeot sedan that had flipped over and was still smoking. He couldn't see anyone in or around the car, but neither did they stop to check.

They arrived in late afternoon. Sunlight stained mud homes a striking orange against the green of thick stands of mango trees and the gardens and sorghum fields that grew along the chocolate Niger River. The heat was close and heavy, so dense with moisture that it seemed to Carter that all the earth's gravity was pulling him down, focused on him alone. The air smelled sulfurous from discarded fish innards, mud, and decaying vegetation.

The bus left them on the edge of the village, where Salif attracted a crowd. Even with his vices, he remained the "king" in the eyes of the boys who had gathered there, and also the young women, who smiled and looked away as Salif met their eyes. He wore fine leather sandals and had exchanged his cotton tunic and leggings for European clothes, the garb of a man who had gone to the capital and made a life for himself. In his dark cotton pants and collared white shirt, Salif attracted a string of boys in ragged shorts. The younger ones carried Carter's and Salif's luggage, while others kicked a makeshift ball made of paper and bits of cloth stuffed into a brown sock. Salif was as relaxed as Carter had ever seen him, briefly joining soccer games in the streets, laughing, and giving a few francs to people who greeted him.

The sound of drumming and shouting drew them to a wide, dusty street near the river's edge, where a crowd had gathered around a group of dancers. The onlookers, men and women, watched with their arms folded across their chests, wearing the impassive expressions of people who did not want their thoughts to be interpreted. They did not clap and shout as Carter had seen people do at marriages, baptisms, and gleeful impromptu drumming events. The dancers, a dozen women and men, strutted and posed, using carved wooden guns as props. Two men wore gourds on their heads, like helmets. They shouted in guttural French that Carter couldn't make out and saluted each other in European mil-

itary style, palms out and fingertips to the temple, at stiff attention. Then they broke into convulsive steps, moving their arms
back and forth like pendulums before bounding across the open
space encircled by villagers. Then the dancers turned, raised their
knees, and stomped the earth in a furious march, stirring up a
thin fog of dust.

The boys around Salif had joined the onlookers, leaving the
luggage at the feet of Carter and Salif, who remained on the edge
of the crowd. Salif took a cigarette from his shirt pocket and lit it
with a small plastic lighter.

"Isn't this what you came to Africa to see? Our traditional culture? I think you said something once about wanting to broaden
your — what was it — your *horizons?*" Salif hunched over, smoking.
He put the cigarette between his lips and breathed deeply. Carter
said nothing.

"These are Hauka. They are spirit eaters. They speak with the
ghosts of French officers who ruled us. Some call this possession,
the very expression of the spirits of these men through the bodies
of our people. The Hauka believe they can draw on the power of
the colonials to make our lives better."

Carter's eyes were fixed on the scene. He knew he looked awkward in his floppy hat and sunglasses, hands jammed in his trouser pockets.

Salif continued. "I know some of these people. I grew up with
them. We have a saying here in the villages along the river: 'The
path of the sorcerer is a path on which the most able practitioners
are relentless seekers of power.'"

A woman in the troupe dropped her wooden gun and whirled
to face the crowd, her eyebrows furrowed as she glared, with her
hands on her hips and her feet spaced apart. She surveyed her audience with the stern gaze of a noncommissioned officer. Then
she stepped forward and squinted intently at them before breaking into a frenzied high-step.

The villagers looked on. Another woman dancer, face shiny
with sweat, turned and gave an awkward salute to the crowd,
then lowered her hand to slap her thigh. She shouted in French,
"You are all lazy! Work is what you need! Work is power!" She ap-

proached a farmer who wore a dust-stained robe, and she raised her hand as if to hit him. He stumbled backward.

Carter spoke quietly. "Is this a show of respect for the colonials, or are the dancers mocking the French?"

Salif didn't answer.

Carter felt uneasy. Many people kept looking at him, no doubt wondering what he was doing in this place. Yet, like them, he wanted to be there. Something about this spectacle, he thought, illuminated the country's struggle with power, with the outside world, and with the complexity of governing itself. He had so many questions.

Salif put his hand on Carter's shoulder. "Let's go, my friend. If we stay, we invite trouble."

Away from the crowd, Carter pulled out his notebook as they walked.

Salif frowned. "The Hauka have been around for a century, Daveed. You can write that down later."

Carter put the notebook back in his bag.

They carried their luggage through narrow byways to one of the largest compounds in Markala, a dusty courtyard with three mud buildings, a space that housed an extended family of three wives and many children. Two of the smaller buildings were sturdy wood-framed mud structures, whitewashed to reflect the sun. This was where Fatima and Aichatou lived, the younger wives of Salif's father, the ones who earlier did not get along. The largest building, where his father and the oldest wife (Salif's mother) lived, was three stories high, with a dozen window openings and pointed minarets rising from each corner. Fatima and Aichatou were peeling yams beneath a tree and greeted the men, as several small children tugged at the women's *pagnes* and stared at the visitors.

Salif pointed to a spread of grass mats in the shade of a mango tree and told Carter to sit down. He sent a boy off with money to buy hot charcoal while he went inside the main building to fetch a box of tea, a kettle, and a metal tray with two glasses. He returned to find Carter sitting cross-legged and studying the compound. Holding the tea things, Salif raised his eyes to the buildings, smiling. "I slept in all three of these houses as a child. A different room every night. I used to roam from mother to mother, teasing them."

Salif set up his tea things, and the men sat across from each other on the mats.

"I am the oldest. I have three brothers and two sisters in the civil service. They are all at posts in the east. One of my other brothers is a soldier. He is in Agadez. They employ him to interpret in Tamachek."

"Do you worry about him?"

"No, I have not heard from him in years. These other children are from the village."

Boys in dirty shorts and T-shirts surrounded them. One returned with a hubcap full of hot charcoal. The children laughed and touched Carter's arms and neck. Salif made halfhearted attempts to shoo them off. His mother and father had gone away for a couple of days to buy seed, but Fatima and Aichatou glanced over at the men. They whispered and giggled as they worked, these two women who had fought savagely over an ethnic slur, on speaking terms again.

"Tell me more about the Hauka."

Salif was making tea, and Carter was admiring how his hands moved, as if he were playing a harp.

"I don't know much, Daveed. The French banned the dances in the 1920s and imprisoned anyone who practiced them. They feared an uprising. For a time they actually outlawed our holy men, the marabouts."

"Do you fear the Hauka?"

Salif left the water to boil and lit another cigarette. He took a few moments to smoke, as if considering his words carefully. He lifted his head and exhaled. "People here talk about the Zima, the cult of seers who read the future and communicate with spirits and the world of the past, and they speak of black Zima, or 'soul eaters,' powerful magicians who express themselves through spirit possession."

Salif paused.

"And I do not question those beliefs."

Carter nodded and folded his arms. "It's like a confluence of spirit and body, Salif. What you're saying is that through this possession ritual, the victims' descendants are now forcing the murderers to testify against themselves."

Salif pulled on the cigarette. "Really, you should just go and travel by yourself, Daveed, see things on your own."

There was a long silence. Carter drank from his water bottle.

Salif stubbed out the cigarette in the dirt and spoke again. "Perhaps you should begin your travels with a visit to that boy's village. What was his name? Hamza?"

Carter shook his head and his face clouded over.

## Monday

OUTSIDE CARTER'S classroom someone blew long blasts on a whistle. The soldiers began to leave, dragging students with them. Others they pushed along in front of them. The men at the windows jumped to the ground outside. The soldier guarding Carter put the pistol back in its holster and took his hand off him. He looked at Carter as if to determine what to do with him. He smiled. *"Monsieur l'Américain,"* he said, drawing out the words in an odd nasal voice. He walked away.

Carter didn't rush forward right away to help the wounded. He stared, blinking through sweat and tears, unable to come to terms with the scene. He learned more details later. The soldiers in fact killed two students in his classroom, but certainly a room full of souls died that day. Cisse—the quick one, the footballer with an edge, not a hooligan, not even a dissident, really, but just a boy—Carter hoped he got away. He saw him leap out a window. That was one positive note in the memories that would remain vivid for Carter always: the pistol, the screams, and the image of a terrible dance.

## November

AT TEA, Salif liked to lecture. "You know, I have my own role model for rebellion."

Carter looked up at him. "Rebellion?"

"Yes, Daveed, rebellion."

Salif said his "patron saint" was a European traitor, a German named Claus Schenk Graf von Stauffenberg (Carter could see that Salif loved to pronounce that name, each word and syllable like a manifesto), an army colonel and decorated veteran who in 1944 nearly succeeded in killing Hitler with a briefcase bomb. Stauffenberg and a few associates were executed soon after their arrests. But the Nazis tried most of the conspirators before a so-called People's Court, whose "evidence" consisted of verbal abuse, charges of homosexual behavior, and suggestions that racial impurity, "the blood of Jews and Africans," had driven the men insane. The judges called them "dirty dogs." The defendants weren't allowed to wear belts, so they had to clutch at the waist of their pants when standing before the court. Salif had read the trial transcripts—in German, of course. Hitler, he believed, was obsessed with the notion that certain people, officers like Stauffenberg, said bad things about him. So the need to humiliate them was as great as the need to kill them.

"I read all the biographies on the colonel and everything about the trial. All the histories talk about Hitler's paranoia, but I really think that Hitler believed you must develop a strong sense of paranoia to survive. That was the kind of man he was. Paranoia was a tool. By humiliating his enemies, he could erase their bad words about him." Salif flicked the cigarette away.

"Are you sure, Salif? Did Hitler really believe that?"

"What he believed is obvious from his actions. In a sense, his fear of other people's words makes him like a true African military leader. That's the point, Daveed. Words live forever. Words are like wandering spirits that return home now and again, sometimes welcome and often not. In Africa, a word kills as sure as a bullet."

Carter nodded. "I'd never thought of Hitler that way.

Salif smiled. "You're not African."

## Monday

A SOLDIER ASKED, *"Qui êtes-vous?"*

Carter squinted. "What?"

"Who are you? What are you doing here?"

Students and teachers commandeered taxis to carry the injured to the central hospital. The wounded lay crumpled in the sandy byways between the campus buildings. Carter helped load them into taxis as soldiers watched from positions throughout the campus. A soldier pushed Carter and another teacher aside. He crawled into the backseat of a taxi and went through the pockets of two unconscious young men covered with blood. Carter watched, his head throbbing where his skull had hit the classroom wall.

"Mister David, Mister David!"

Carter turned around and saw Ibrahim Moctar, his student. The boy was shirtless and his face tear-stained, but he was composed. His arm was in a dirty sling, which Carter realized was made from the boy's own shirt. "Ibrahim," he said. "Are you okay?"

"They killed Mariatou, Mr. David. They broke my arm, and she was trying to help me. They beat her, Mr. David."

Carter clutched his head. "Mariatou?" he said.

But Ibrahim did not hear him. He walked by Carter and across the school grounds. "Wait a minute," Carter shouted. "Ibrahim —"

At that very moment the soldier challenged Carter — "*Qui êtes-vous?*"

Carter handed over his identity card, slipping it from his breast pocket as he watched Ibrahim walk away.

"I'm a teacher," he said to the soldier. "This is where I work. What are you doing here?"

He looked past the soldier. A few yards away a market girl, thin and frail in a dirty green cloth wrap and T-shirt, sold hard-boiled eggs to two other soldiers from a tray she carried on her head. The soldiers picked them over with their fingers.

The soldier handed Carter the card. "You should go," he said. There was softness in his face, evident in eyes that were wide and nervous. His gaze darted here and there, never resting more than a moment.

Carter walked away. He went to the headmaster's office, which he found empty, so he kept on walking, circling the campus. Hospital workers in light-blue coats tended to the injured under the gaze of soldiers, now looking relaxed and calm, as if the attack had been merely some sort of exercise. Because Carter didn't know what else to do or where to go, he lent a hand, carrying injured students to a classroom converted into an aid station.

Early in the afternoon, Carter left the campus and lost himself in the market crowds in the city center at a time of day when heat dominated, the fierce heat of the West African spring. As he walked, the high temperature sapped his ease of movement and even his mental awareness. There was no breeze to whip up dust, yet somehow he tasted grit on his teeth.

Carter needed a grip on reality, if that was the word. A better frame of reference. He needed to get away from soldiers.

He needed contrast.

Reassurance.

That's what Salif had said to him, again and again. "Daveed, get out of the city. See the reality."

The reality. In the capital city, civil service salaries hadn't been paid in six months. Soldiers got paid first, but even their wages were three months behind. The reality. The government had issued a standing order for Republican Guard troops to open fire on any vehicle that merely slowed down in front of the presidential palace on the Boulevard of the Republic. Salif and his family lived on food and money from his parents' farm. Another reality. The only people getting regular paychecks in the country were foreign workers, like Carter, a few cabinet ministers, and, more or less, the soldiers.

Always the soldiers.

## November

CARTER REMEMBERED the soldiers the night he and Salif traveled in a taxi in the city. They'd gone to visit a sister of Salif's wife, who'd given birth to a boy. Salif didn't bring his family for the visit — they would go later. He and Carter went to eat and offer gifts of candy, kola nuts, and money, and when it was all done, late at night, the two men got into an old, decaying minivan taxi to return to the lycée. They'd walk home from there.

The van had no doors and no seats, except for the driver's. It had one working headlight and no taillights. Passengers paid a few francs and packed in on the floor, in the dark—mostly men, sweaty and silent. In this country, no one talked among strangers in close quarters, especially strangers that couldn't be seen. The driver sped across a crowded city, slowing for no person, no camel or donkey, no pothole. Salif and Carter sat beside each other in the dark. They did not talk. Carter could see flashes of faces, bits of clothing, lives and personalities hanging in flickers of light from passing cars.

The bus stopped abruptly, throwing the passengers forward and against one another. The back of a man's head pressed against Carter's lips, and he tasted salty, bitter sweat. Through the front windshield Carter could see flashlight beams like two-by-fours of light stabbing through the front and side windows. Then lights flashed all around, blinding and immobilizing the passengers. No one moved until someone outside said, "*Sortez, sortez.*" Carter and the others tumbled out.

He could see more clearly in the pools of electric light outside. Soldiers moved about, snapping their fingers and shouting, "*Carte d'identité!*" Salif huddled with one soldier who held a flashlight to his identity card. A crowd of soldiers stood around three Tuareg men who wore white robes and light gray turbans that covered their faces. One soldier pulled the cloth down from one man's face, a centuries-old impulse toward revenge enacted in a new context, with a new balance of power. Debts had to be paid.

The soldier baited the Tuareg. "*Vous êtes bandit, non?*"

With relief, Carter could see the soldiers paid Salif no special attention. Salif took his card and stepped to the side, out of the way, into the darkness. Sounds were clearer than visual images—voices taut with emotion, footsteps, car doors opening and closing. Everything beyond the flashlight beams was dipped in black, unknowable, like some science-fiction outpost in space, guarded by beings Carter could not clearly see and whose objectives he did not understand.

Leaving a checkpoint with your papers approved and validated, Salif once told Carter, is like being reborn. You are alive once again, a valid citizen of your country until you arrive at the next checkpoint, where everything about your life is questioned again, as if for the first time. But now Carter could no longer see Salif. He waited in the shadows, unsure of what had happened to his friend and afraid to go searching just yet. He recognized no one in the flashes of electric light and could see only vague shapes in the darkness. He listened to voices without faces, different voices, different questions and answers in French, Hausa, Tamachek, Bambara, and Djerma.

"Where are you going?"

"I am going home."

"Where is that?"

"I live in Koni District, near the water tower."

"Why are you out so late?"

"I am a mechanic. I often work late."

"A mechanic? But your identity card says you are a farmer."

"Yes, when the rains come, I am a farmer. After the harvest, I am a mechanic."

"This is an infraction. You must add your other work to your identity card. Are you carrying a weapon?"

"No, I am not."

"If you are a mechanic, where is your garage?"

"In the marketplace. I fix bicycles and motor scooters. You can find me there anytime, next to the Dosso taxi station."

"You speak Hausa with an accent. Are you a foreigner?"

"No, I am Djerma. I was born in this country, along the river. Hausa is not my language."

"No, you cannot be a mechanic. Djerma men are not good mechanics."

The questions flew like random blows. Carter was fascinated and had to remind himself not to take out his notebook. He felt a hand on his shoulder and turned to see a soldier smiling politely. He raised his hand in Carter's face and snapped his fingers. Carter handed over his card. The soldier gave it a glance and handed it back.

"Don't be nervous, monsieur. There is much insecurity in the country now, but you needn't worry."

Out of the corner of his eye, Carter saw two soldiers push the three Tuareg men into a line, back to front, forcing each man to place both hands on the shoulders of the man in front. Another soldier looped rope around their waists, linking them in a human chain. A soldier with a rubber hose struck the third man on his back and shouted at them to begin walking. The Tuaregs shuffled down the street, with the soldiers following. The one with the rubber hose struck the prisoners repeatedly about the head and shoulders.

Salif tugged at Carter's arm.

"Daveed, Daveed, *on va à pied,* let's go."

They left quickly, putting the night between the soldiers and themselves.

"That was no place to be, Daveed."

They walked the rest of the way across the city, more than an hour's journey, detouring around checkpoints. Salif slept in Carter's apartment that night.

## Monday

LATE IN THE AFTERNOON, Carter walked to Brahima's bar, where he could at last relax among friends and drink himself into a stupor. But the bar was locked up. Carter shouted over the wall and pounded on the metal door. When no one answered, he decided he couldn't go home and spend the evening alone. He kept walking, hoping to clear his head. On impulse, based on what he'd heard about the beautiful landscape upcountry to the east, far from the river and the capital, he decided to take a few days to see the land, alone. Carter was sure the army would close the schools. He took a taxi back to the market, where he could buy a bus ticket to somewhere.

He badly wanted to believe in something more positive about Africa than the city he'd come to know—something pleasant about village life and about forests and plains teeming with wild animals. But he couldn't. Perhaps he hadn't looked hard enough. As Salif said to him once, "Daveed, if you want to, as you say, 'broaden yourself,' then you must work harder. You must take more risks."

Carter's few trips outside the capital had weakened his sense of adventure. He rationalized the hesitation in his notebook:

> Death lives along the roads everywhere outside the city. Skeletons of large trucks and smaller cars stick to the road as if to pinesap, sandblasted by desert winds. Villagers strip away all the parts to use or sell, and what is left of the wrecks looks like giant decomposing locusts. There is enough evidence of this roadside death inside the capital, but at least in the city the crowded streets slow drivers down. Outside the city the few roads run narrow and straight. There is little room for maneuver or error. Some survive, some don't.

None of that concerned Carter now. He wanted only to be as far away from the city as he could travel.


## March

AT TEA ONE AFTERNOON, Carter was distracted by Salif's still-swollen eye. Ahmed the groundskeeper had joined them, fingering his prayer beads and sitting quietly on a mat. As they drank, Carter considered how cuts got infected so quickly in the heat and healed so slowly. Salif kept the wound clean and bandaged, and at times it seemed to heal, but then it would open and swell again. Each time the wound got worse, Carter became nervous and now he could not keep his mouth shut. He raised a finger, pointing at Salif's face.

"What happened?"

Ahmed frowned and shook his head.

Salif smiled as if he'd seen the question coming. "It's not your fight."

Ahmed kept his head down.

Carter had heard American friends say the generals and colonels were arresting "troublemakers." People were vanishing. Some, like Salif, reappeared as if swallowed up and spit back out by the air itself. Mariatou, the young woman who'd challenged Carter so pointedly in class, the one who'd asked if he was a "crazy man," had been absent for over a month. Carter had asked around; people shrugged.

Salif gave Carter an honest response only after Ahmed had finished his tea and left. He spoke softly, and Carter saw now that he was angry. "You know what is happening in this country. You know the danger. Keep your mouth shut, even if I cannot. I have heard you asking around the school about your student, Mariatou. She is safe. She has gone to her family in her village not far from here. Now stop with your questions."

Carter studied his hands. "I'm sorry, Salif."

They sat for a few minutes in silence while Salif washed the tea things.

"You know, Salif, it's not just Mariatou. Three more of my students are gone now. I survey their faces every day like I'm keeping score."

Salif kept working. "So do I, Daveed. So do I."

Salif spoke again, more calmly. "My neighbors tell me that a white man has come looking for me in my absences. They say that he asks about how to find my wife. That must be you."

Carter nodded. "You're a difficult man to track down, Salif. You disappear a lot. I was concerned, and I thought your wife might be able to explain. You never want to explain."

"Please, it would be best if you do not do that again. My wife and children must be left alone."

## Monday

WITH THE NOON SUN directly overhead, Carter walked into the market in the city center. Seemingly everything was for sale here, including passage in compact sedans, station wagons, and minivans traveling in all directions. The odor of dung and roasted meat mixed in the air as if the market were alive with its own hot breath. Dried tomatoes and slabs of jerky lay across wooden tables. Raw goat meat hung from wires strung between the stalls. Blood pocked and matted the sand where men had butchered animals. And everywhere, a bitter smell pervaded the air as people shouted, debated, bartered, played cards, and ran about.

The market represented the Africa Carter had hoped to find, a surreal and sensuous place. He walked by a man selling the Koran; stacks of copies in Arabic, English, French, and Spanish were spread on a blanket. Beside him, a woman sold medicine; a dozen small pyramids of colorful pills offered a remedy for every health problem. The orange pills were stamped with the word SEX in black letters. A woman and a man sat cross-legged behind a waist-high pile of dead locusts, each one as long as a man's index finger. The woman was frying some in peanut oil over a fire while rice steamed in another pot. She spooned locusts into a bowl of rice, and with a toothy smile she offered it to Carter. He smiled and passed on the offer.

The woman laughed, her body gently rocking. She called out, "*Annnnaaaaassssaraaaa.*"

Carter kept walking, weaving among travelers and market goers, past rows of Peugeot sedans painted green, the color of vehicles going east. Nearby waited a line of sheds with metal roofs, each with a destination sign nailed to a wooden post. Ticket agents sat at tables, and Carter chose one with a sign for ZINDER, a city in the east, near the border with Nigeria. He waited to buy a ticket behind a woman who wore a bright yellow-and-red *pagne*. She glanced at him, adjusting the position of the baby strapped to her back in a cloth. As Carter waited, he heard a government news broadcast in French, blaring from a market stall. The announcer said that the president had closed the university and all secondary schools across the country.

A few feet away, a boy in a dust-stained T-shirt and shorts sat in the dirt, eating bits of boiled yam from a tin bowl attached to a cord around his neck. He scooped soft morsels out of dark sauce with four fingers and shoved food and fingers into his mouth. Another boy walked up from behind and slapped the first boy hard on the side of the head, knocking him over so his meal scattered in clumps and driblets over the ground. The thief scooped up some of the yam in his hands and ran, but the other boy was on his feet fast. With the bowl bouncing off his back and scattering the rest of the food, he tackled the thief, straddling his shoulders, and began yelling and beating him wildly about the head with his fists.

Behind Carter an older man in a flowing white robe and skull-cap noticed how Carter watched the fight. He nodded toward the struggling boys and frowned. "It is a hard life we live," he said.

"Yes, it is," Carter said, without looking at the man. He lowered his head and shoved his hands in his pockets.

"Are you Dutch?"

"No, American."

"Ah, American . . . Amereeeecaa."

The woman in front of him completed her business and walked away. Now Carter stood at the table. The ticket agent, a man in a gray cotton tunic and trousers, was writing in a book of accounts. Sweat stained his tunic where it buttoned in the front. Stacks of ticket books and coins cluttered the table beside piles of paper currency. The bills bore the likeness of the president in an olive green uniform against a faded leafy landscape of greens, reds, and browns.

Carter said, *"Bonjour."* He could hear the yam thief whimpering as he lay alone in the dirt, curled up, with his hands on his head. The agent looked up glumly, as if he'd just awakened from sleep. "Three thousand francs for one ticket," he said.

Carter drew a nylon pouch from inside his shirt. He opened it and handed over three bills, the equivalent of nine dollars. The agent wrote a receipt. Sweat from his wrist stained the paper and smeared the ink. Then he snapped his fingers.

"Identity card," he said, holding out his hand. The man took Carter's card and copied information in his account book. *"Améreeecain,"* he said.

Carter asked, "When will the bus leave?"

"Tomorrow." The agent did not look at him.

"Yes, but when?"

The agent blinked in response to Carter's urgent tone. He tapped a finger on the table. "Early," he said. "You come here early in the morning."

"There is no set time?"

"The bus will leave when it is full." The agent lowered his eyes to his account book, leaving Carter to look at the top of his head.

"Which bus?" He glared down at the man. Then, in an act that surprised Carter even as he was doing it, he put both hands on the table and leaned into the man's face, plucking the pencil from his hand. "Which bus?" he hissed. "What time?"

The agent looked at him for several seconds, as if too tired and hot to express anything more. He shrugged and folded his arms. "Be here at dawn," he said. "We will show you which bus."

A man and a woman behind him watched Carter with disapproving looks, and he knew he'd gone too far. He dropped the pencil on the table, stuffed the receipt in his pocket, and walked away.

And indeed, more momentous events were unfolding. Schools had closed, and soldiers shot to death several university students who were protesting on campus. They opened fire on civil servants rallying outside the Ministry of Finance to protest unpaid salaries, and the gunfire killed a seven-year-old girl who was riding the shoulders of her father, a postal clerk. She was shot through the abdomen. Soldiers also killed a Belgian aid worker, his wife, and their two children in their car, when the family slowed down to photograph the presidential palace. Several soldiers fired at once, and the car caught fire. Then an army battalion in the city imprisoned its commanding officer, a captain, demanding the government make up unpaid salaries. Loyal troops armed with rifles and fixed bayonets stormed the barracks. The battalion surrendered, with no shots fired. The president declared martial law, imposing a sundown-to-sunup curfew in the capital and placing more soldiers in the streets. The national radio reported that Tuaregs ambushed an army patrol in the desert and killed twelve soldiers. Rumors flew that they had killed many more and were asking millions of French francs in exchange for prisoners.

Carter left the motor park at the marketplace, not really thinking about where he was going or what he would do until the bus left the next day. It must have been just after noon because the midday call to prayer was sounding from the city's mosques. He loved the cry of the muezzins — the lyrical certainty of their voices and their power to call forth the masses. Carter counted on the muezzins to lift his spirits when the heat and the crowds suffocated his patience and reason. People milled about everywhere. Here, any desire to be alone was considered unnatural, a sign of mental illness. People lived outdoors, among others. They ate and slept and did business outside, relaxed and told stories outside.

Carter felt hungry and sorely wanted to take refuge at Brahima's bar. Vaguely, he wondered if Brahima, too, had been forced to pay for his excesses. His mind drifted with the smell of roasting meat. Butchers worked with slabs of goat or dog, which were turning on spits or lying atop grills. People passed by, occasionally shouting to him, but he ignored them. He looked for a place where he could eat and rest.

A small, barefoot boy ran up and grabbed his wrist, shouting, "*Le blanc, le blanc,*" and rubbing his hands over Carter's arm. Laughing, he ran off, and Carter exploded in rage, not so much at the boy as at Africa itself. Carter ran after him, weaving between market goers and cars, just barely keeping the child in sight. He pursued him across the market for a half-mile, his shoulder bag bouncing off his hip as he ran. Carter heard people laughing. Someone shouted, "*Kai! Anasara!*" and laughed, as if cheering him on. The chase reached a neighborhood of mud buildings separated from the market by a high cinderblock wall, with openings here and there. He pursued the boy through one doorway and up a narrow side street, where he saw him disappear through a corrugated metal gateway. Carter followed him, bursting into a wide, sandy clearing where an old woman was pounding grain in a wooden mortar, a baby strapped to her back. Hiding behind her, the boy clutched at her wrap. The baby began screaming at the sudden appearance of an unfamiliar white man.

The woman was thin, with wisps of gray hair fanning out from the blue cloth wrapped around her head. She straightened up and looked at Carter, her hand at her mouth. Then she dropped her pestle, raised her hands, palms out, and asked in Hausa, "*Anasara mineni?*" — Stranger, what is it?

Carter gasped for air, looking from the woman to the boy. He'd never thought of what he'd do if he caught the boy—he wasn't even sure why he was chasing him. Two men in long brown tunics and another boy emerged from a mud building. They smiled at Carter and one asked, *"Oui? Qu'est-ce que vous voulez?"*

He realized, as if for the first time, where he was, standing in someone's home uninvited, in a country that was not his own, in a situation of his own making. He coughed and shook his head. He looked at the woman and the boy, who was still clutching at her wrap. Carter smiled and began backing away. *"Ahh, pardon, il, il faut m'excuser,"* he said, stammering and tapping his fingers on his chest to show his remorse. He could see from their expressions that they spoke little French, but he continued his apology anyway. *"Je, je, je me suis trompé."* They gawked at one another, the family and Carter. *"Il doit y avoir erreur. C'est de ma faute."* Then he hurried out.

Carter walked back to the market nearly in tears, his shirt wet with sweat and streaked with dust stains. *My God,* he thought. *I'm losing my mind.*

He stopped in front of the cinderblock wall through which he'd chased the boy. The whole incident had happened so fast that he couldn't recall how it started. He leaned against the wall. He couldn't even remember what he was doing in the market. Tears mixed with sweat stung his cheeks and fell cool and salty on his lips. He sat against the wall, drawing his knees to his chest, and sobbed. With a handkerchief from his bag he wiped his face until the cloth was full of grime. He folded his arms over his knees and buried his face there, no longer caring what happened except that somehow he wanted to be alone when it did. After a while, when the tears stopped, he saw street urchins, four little children with dust-stained faces, standing around him in a tight half-circle. He closed his eyes, dropped his head, and tried to sleep.

## October

CARTER HAD A NEARLY two-year-old memory of Hamza Saidou that began with a rock. Carter was walking across campus one morning when he felt a sharp blow at the back of his head. Carter whirled around, holding his hand to the wound and wincing from pain. There he was, the thrower, a boy he recognized as a student, but whose name he didn't yet know.

Carter stood in the street, grimacing and gently touching the bump on his head, shocked by the blow and surprised that the boy who inflicted it still remained there, his face devoid of expression. Carter picked up the stone and walked up to him, his hand still on his head. He raised the rock as if preparing to throw it back at him. He shouted at the boy in French. *"Imbécile. C'est quoi ça?"*

He couldn't remember whether he dropped the rock or threw it in the sand to show his anger. But in his mind he could clearly see the boy looking back at him. Hamza's eyes were wide open, and he cocked his head to the side, as if puzzling out the stranger's reaction. Carter yelled, gesturing with his hands, hoping for some sort of contrite response. Later, he had to smile at the thought of what he must have looked like, freaking out over a boy on a dusty street in an African city. Even as he was fuming, he'd realized that Hamza had reduced him to huffing and sputtering, which must have earned the boy a certain status among his mates. A small crowd of men and women watched in silence until there was a pause in Carter's rage.

An older man, the caretaker of a mosque near the school, walked up to him. The man was tall, with deep creases in his forehead. He wore a flowing pastel blue robe and white skullcap. Gently, he touched Carter's head where the rock hit. He spoke in a mixture of French and Hausa.

*"Il est petit garçon, monsieur. Sai hankuri"* — He's a small boy, sir. Be patient.

## Monday

CARTER OPENED HIS EYES. His vertebrae felt sore where they'd rubbed against the rough surface of the cinderblock wall. More children surrounded him now, whispering among themselves and staring at him. Only minutes had passed, but he felt good enough to get back on his feet.

Carter put the chase out of his mind and walked, to cleanse

his mind. The sun needled his neck as he made his way across the market through throngs of people before stopping in front of a man who sold rat poison. The man squatted in the sand. Granular blue crystals made a tiny pyramid on one wooden board, and three dead rats with matted gray fur lay in a row on another. The man smiled brightly at Carter

"You see?" he said in Hausa, opening the palms of his hands and smiling. "Dead rats!"

In Hausa, Carter said, "I don't need it," pointing at the poison. He wandered on, trying to think of what to see in the east. Then he remembered he should go home and pack a few things, maybe get some sleep before catching his bus early in the morning. But the heat distracted him. He stopped at the remains of a small car, which was on fire, its twisted metal burning in the sand. The engine cavity was empty, its contents long since carried off. Flames punched through windows like unruly children. Such scenes had become familiar — garbage burning in the streets and flames and smoke rising from sewage gutters. Children and old men had made this abandoned shell a latrine and someone, maybe a trader sickened by the smell, had tossed kerosene and a match inside the wreck.

Carter bought a handful of goat meat from a man who was roasting an entire torso on a large grill. He chose the meat himself, pointing at the sections of flesh he wanted. The man sliced it into bite-sized morsels and wrapped it in layers of newspaper. A few feet away, with the package open in one hand, Carter ate, picking out chunks of meat with his fingers and stuffing them in his mouth as if he'd had no food in days. He licked the grease off his fingers, wondering whether it would be cooler in the east. He felt a little guilty about making the trip and told himself he'd get to Hamza's village as soon as he returned.

## June

"I LIKED GERMANY. I liked the people. They are honest about the past."

Carter looked up, startled to attention. He'd been fiddling absently with his empty tea glass.

"You think so? After the war, many Germans denied knowledge of the death camps. Many knew quite a lot and lied to save themselves."

Salif shrugged and sipped his tea. He gazed at the ground. "Well, I am sure you are right, Daveed, but the government is clear about responsibility. The German students I knew and some of the older people seemed at least more honest about their country's past than I sometimes think we Africans are about ours."

Salif smiled at Carter.

"And certainly more honest than the Americans. Did anyone from your government ever stand trial for your wars against the Indian tribes? How many did your army kill?"

Carter folded his arms and drew a breath. "Whose army? My army?" Carter knew what Salif meant, but he made a point to meet his friend's eyes. "If your point is about the United States Army, well then, yes, soldiers and settlers killed many tens of thousands of Indians across North America, maybe more. Whole tribes have disappeared. My country's shame is deep. So, Salif, you're right, but don't identify me with that army or those policies or that history just because I share a nationality and skin color."

Salif handed Carter a glass of tea. They sat silently for a few minutes. Salif changed the subject.

"You know, German mythology is full of evil creatures, but there is some justice in all that. The evil ones pay in terrible violence and sometimes the good ones, too. People's eyes are put out, or their bodies cut apart."

"What's your point?"

Salif held his glass. "Well, I very much like the tales of Grimm. I read them in German. There is great fear of the outside in those stories, fear of things and creatures in the forest. Like the story of Hansel and Gretel and the witch — do you know it?"

Carter smiled and nodded.

"They ventured too far into the unknown forest and there were consequences. They had to pay for their carelessness and curiosity, for their disrespect of tradition and the forest. I grew up with such stories. To us in Africa, the night is a terrifying place, full of spirits who dwell in rocks and trees by day and come out at night to do evil. When I was a child, my parents told me that if I ever saw a light by itself in the night, I should recognize it as a sign of evil, maybe even the devil himself, and run from it. Even the Koran teaches us that the devil can take any form he wants."

"Do you still believe in those things, Salif, the spirits in the night, dwelling in trees?"

Salif shrugged. "It's not good, maybe even dangerous, to deny the stories of your culture, even if they are strange and unbelievable. You know about the Nazi skinheads. They make me think of such evil in human form, but I didn't mind them so much. In Germany, they were easy for me to understand because they were honest about what they feared and hated, which was everything radically different from themselves. Everything they could not understand. I never had an encounter with them, but they were there on the fringes of the university, in the bars and coffeehouses."

Salif frowned and put his tea glass on the tray. "They murdered a Senegalese student in Baden-Baden when I was in Tübingen. They beat him to death. Awful people, yes, but at least I knew where I stood with them. I was the image of evil from the outside, which they feared so much."

## May

HAMZA STARTED A FIGHT once in class. Carter often thought of that, too. It must have been near the end of his first year on the job. The students never let Hamza forget. Carter had assigned an in-class exercise and was squatting beside a student's desk, answering a question, when out of the corner of his eye he saw Hamza half-stand at his desk and reach over the shoulder of the girl sitting in front of him. Her name was Miriam. In one swift move he plucked a pen from her hand. She squealed and slapped him, but Hamza kept the pen and laughed, raising it high above his head. She stepped into the aisle. She grabbed his right hand, which held the pen, and hit him hard on the head with her free hand. The class exploded in cheers and shouts; some students stood on their desks to get a better view of the fight. Miriam was a short, strong, fourteen-year-old farmer's daughter, wearing a white cotton headscarf with a matching blouse and cloth wrap. She continued hitting Hamza, using one hand to strike his head and the other to hold his tunic. Hamza was unprepared for her fury and only raised his hands in defense. Sobbing and screaming, Miriam yanked him from his desk, and he fell on the floor. She straddled him and rained windmill blows across his head and chest.

Carter approached them, pushing aside desks and students. He watched for a few seconds as Miriam beat Hamza bloody, letting her deliver her justice. Then he took the girl by the shoulders, pulled her off, and led her back to her desk. She sat there, gasping, her face wet with tears. Carter picked up the pen from the floor and gave it to her. The class had fallen silent. Another teacher and the headmaster, alarmed by the noise, entered the room at a run. But the fight was over. On the floor, Hamza propped himself up on one hand. His nose bled and a lip was cut. Later, one eye swelled shut.

Carter looked at the headmaster. "It's over. There's nothing to worry about."

The headmaster's eyes settled on Miriam. He looked back at Carter and left the room with the other teacher.

It wasn't over. Miriam was three or four months pregnant, which everyone knew and Carter thought must have fed the girl's rage — not just against Hamza, but against her situation in life. According to rumor, the child belonged to a teacher, who was married and had four children. Students had been teasing Miriam for weeks, telling her she could never return to her village. These scenes of torment probably motivated Hamza to steal her pen, so he could be part of the crowd. But the fact that Miriam, a pregnant girl, had beaten him so badly followed him ever after. Boys called him "woman face." Girls ran up to him and put up their fists, saying, "Hamza, want to fight?"

Miriam did return to her village, just days after the incident. The headmaster gave the official reason at a faculty meeting. She was a discipline problem, he said. Carter wondered at his own stupidity at letting the fight go on, knowing Hamza might have fought back and induced a miscarriage, perhaps even threatening Miriam's life. He was relieved when, months later, he learned she had given birth to a healthy girl.

## Monday

CARTER TRIED to push Hamza from his mind as he finished eating the meat. A man bumped his shoulder, and the oily paper holding the last two chunks of meat slid from his hand and onto the ground. The meat bounced in the dirt, and a boy dove for it, pinching the morsels between the fingers of each hand and sprinting away just as Carter felt something jam into his right front pocket. At once alert, he swung his arm in defense, striking the chest of a young man wearing ragged army shorts and a gray T-shirt. The man jumped backward and ran. Carter pointed at him, screaming, "*Voleur, voleur!*" He pursued him, repeating the accusation until the thief, or whatever he was, had to contend with a crowd.

"He robbed you?" shouted a well-dressed man, who grabbed the accused man's shoulder. But he again broke free, running headlong into another, larger man, who nearly fell. Four other men began pulling at the thief's clothes and limbs.

Someone said, "Thief, damned thief!" A man cuffed the accused on one ear with his open palm. The thief, though wiry and muscular, was surrounded now and struggling to escape, his face tight with fear. Twice he yanked his arms away from his keepers and tried to run, only to be grabbed by other men in the mob. Carter watched from a short distance, frightened. Six or seven men now pinned down the thief with their hands and feet, and many others formed a circle around him. Carter heard slaps and thuds and saw the thief fall to his knees, his arms flailing.

"I've stolen nothing," he shouted, "nothing!"

That was true. Carter never carried money in his pockets. Two men, one a soldier, now grasped the thief by the shoulders and arms. He gasped for air. Blood ran from his nose, down his lips and chin.

At the sight of blood, Carter finally walked to the edge of the crowd, shouting as loud as he could, "Leave him! He didn't take anything from me." But someone pushed him away.

An onlooker said, "Go. You shouldn't be here."

But Carter couldn't go. He was, after all, the accuser. The thief struggled to his feet, and the soldier tried to keep the crowd back. Someone held the thief's arms behind him while two men, whom Carter had seen selling vegetables, hit the writhing man in the face and on the head.

"Listen to him," the thief shouted, pointing at Carter. "I didn't steal anything!"

Carter felt a hand on his shoulder. "Monsieur!"

He turned to see a man in faded jeans, black leather shoes, white shirt, and jean jacket. The man gripped Carter's elbow and held up a leather wallet to show an identity card. Heavy black letters spelled out POLICE NATIONALE above his photograph and name, with the national tricolor embossed on the background.

"Come with me, please."

The policeman, holding his ID above his head, led Carter into the knot of people around the thief. Everyone but the soldier stepped back.

"You say this man robbed you?"

Carter shook his head. "He tried, but I never carry money in my pockets. You may as well let him go."

"I don't think so," the policeman said. "Don't move." He said something to the soldier and then walked over to a taxi, which was moving slowly through the market. He pounded on the roof and bent down to talk to the driver. After a few words, the driver got out and opened the rear door. The policeman and the soldier bundled the thief into the backseat between them. "Get in," the officer told Carter, nodding to the driver.

"Look," Carter said, raising his hands, palms out, "this is unnecessary. I didn't have any money in my pockets."

The policeman, out of breath, stepped out of the taxi. He was much shorter than Carter and grasped him by the arm, above the elbow. "Monsieur, this is a police matter now. If you refuse to come, I'll have to arrest you. Get in."

Carter threaded his fingers through his hair and wiped his face with his hands. He shrugged and got into the car. The taxi jolted forward, on police business, raising dust at fifteen miles an hour in the crowded market, weaving sharply and bouncing as people dodged the vehicle. Carter heard a squeal in the backseat. Over his shoulder he saw the thief struggling on the floor, wedged between the seats. The policeman put a hand on the thief's neck and another on his back, while the soldier knelt on the seat and held the man's wrists to the floor.

The thief gagged and spit. His voice made a muffled sound. "*Patron, patron, s'il vous plaît,* please, I didn't do anything." He was strong and pushed back for space to breathe. Carter could see his back muscles through his torn T-shirt. The policeman, one hand still on the thief's neck, pulled a pistol from his jean jacket and pressed it hard into the back of the man's head.

"Do you know who I am?" he shouted. "Do you know what this is?" He twisted the barrel into his neck.

"Why?" The thief wheezed. He squealed, "Why do you fuss over a white man?"

The officer shouted, "Shut up!"

Carter turned away from the scene. The thief grunted and gasped. Ahead the national tricolor flapped above the high concrete walls of a police station. The driver stopped the taxi just inside the station gate. The dusty compound contained several concrete buildings, one with broad steps leading to a wide doorway. The driver jumped out, ran inside, and returned with three men in khaki uniforms and black police berets. The thief made no trouble as the men pulled him from the taxi and hustled him, stumbling like a big doll, up the steps and inside. Carter followed, with another policeman, behind him.

Inside, an officer sat at a gray metal desk behind a waist-high concrete wall, whose once-white paint was chipped and faded. By a bench stood a few wooden chairs. The room was dim, lit only through open French windows on one side and the doorway. Brown stains streaked the walls where the roof had leaked during monsoon rains. The desk officer opened a small wooden gate, letting the policemen and the thief pass. A dirty ceiling fan overhead barely turned. The officer looked at the foreigner who'd just entered his station. He raised his hand and motioned Carter to a seat inside the gate.

Carter shook his head. *"Non, merci."* He wanted to remain on the other side of the wall, outside this affair that he'd touched off.

The policemen deposited the thief on a wooden bench along the wall. The man dropped to his knees, his hands on his thighs, pleading to the desk officer, who kept his back to him. *"Patron,* please, he is lying. Why believe this white man?" The officer rose, took two steps forward, and hit the thief on the side of his head. The young man's head jerked, but he didn't stop talking. *"Patron, s'il vous plaît!"*

Carter breathed deeply to calm himself. The plainclothes officer sat on a bench near the other policemen and the thief. Again, Carter tried to talk his way out. He raised his hands. "This is all so crazy. He didn't take anything from me."

"You mean he did not rob you?" the officer asked.

"Well, he tried, but—"

The officer wagged his finger. "No, it is clear, and he'll be punished. Now, you must tell me what happened. You are American?"

"Yes." Carter plucked his identity card from his shirt pocket and handed it over the low wall. The officer gave it a look and passed it back. Carter explained, as simply as he could, what happened in the market.

The officer frowned. "Why did you make the accusation if you knew you weren't carrying any money in your pockets?"

Carter bit his lip. "It was a reaction, something automatic," he said. "He put his hand in my pocket and I screamed, that's all."

"Yes, but you accused him, which means that you both now have to deal with the consequences. We cannot let him go. If we do, every thief out there will think we are soft." He raised his index finger. "This is a serious thing and you must be aware of what happens."

The officer nodded to a tall policeman in a crisply pressed uniform, who wore his hair neatly cropped. He'd been standing against a wall with his arms folded, and now he walked toward the thief, hooked a hand under the young man's armpit, and hoisted him up. The thief was sobbing as the policeman pushed him into a back room. Through the doorway, Carter saw the officer give the man a hard shove, and they disappeared behind a wall. Carter could hear the young man's body hit concrete and knock something over. There was a sharp thud, like wood hitting concrete. Carter heard blows and grunts. He began to pace desperately. The rhythmic thumping and occasional gasp sounded like some kind of business transaction, payments rendered behind closed doors. The fists and boots on flesh and bone changed to a repeated loud smacking, and Carter knew the officer was using a rubber hose on exposed flesh.

Carter's chest hurt, and his muscles tightened defensively, as if he'd been running hard and couldn't get enough air—or as if he too anticipated a beating. He stared at the wall that concealed the violence, wondering if the young man would die. More thuds, a measured punching, more gasps and grunts. But no more wailing or pleading.

He looked at the desk officer. "*Mon dieu, patron,* his crime wasn't serious." The officer sifted through papers and did not look up. Carter pushed both hands through his hair, wet and stringy from sweat. He felt as if he were party to murder. "You're killing him!" he shouted. "I don't want to be responsible for this." Carter closed his eyes and shook his head. "Jesus Christ," he said in English. Then he turned back to the officer and shouted, "Let him go!"

Carter paced again. He slapped the wall as he walked back and forth. "Please," he said, "this is crazy."

Finally, the desk officer turned toward the back room and shouted a few words. The beating stopped, and after a moment the policeman reappeared, dragging the thief by one arm. He positioned himself behind the thief with a hand under each armpit and pulled him onto the bench, propping him against the wall. In the dim light, Carter had trouble making out the young man's face, but could see fresh blood soaking the front of his T-shirt. The thief coughed and spit, his body swaying a little.

The officer studied Carter silently for a few seconds and then spoke. "This isn't America," he said quietly. "We have our own ways of dealing with thieves. And you walk in here and tell us how to enforce the law?" He paused, hands on his hips, and raised his voice. "You! You, sir, pointed your finger at a man in a crowded market and shouted, 'Thief!'"

Carter looked at the officer. He looked at the thief, who sat with his hands between his thighs and his head down. "I know," he said, "but I didn't mean for this to happen."

The officer shook his head in disgust. "All right, it's up to you. But if we let him go now, you understand he may try to find you. The outcome would be out of our hands. Leave here now, and we'll release him later." He laughed a little. "Maybe the market people will tear him to pieces." He nodded to Carter. "Go."

Carter's eyes lingered on the thief, who didn't look up. He seemed half-conscious.

"GO!"

Carter walked out as a police Land Rover drove through the gate and parked in front of the same building. He hesitated on the stairway, unwilling to leave without knowing for certain the thief's fate. Behind him, in the rear of the building, a metal door opened and closed. Carter heard groans and shuffling feet. Then someone shouted harshly in Hausa. Two policemen whom Carter had not seen before were supporting between them a large, barefoot man in a brightly colored shirt of yellow, blue, and orange; he also wore matching trousers. The man's heavy arms were draped over the officers' shoulders. A third policeman walked close behind them. Blood covered the front of the captive's shirt, and though he tried to hold his head up, it dropped and bobbed as the policemen struggled to support his weight. His head was shaven. His face was puffy and a cheek was badly swollen, yet he looked familiar to Carter. Blood trickled from an ear. The prisoner made a feeble attempt to move his thick legs, but he was being pulled too fast to keep up. The driver lowered the Land Rover's rear gate, and two of the policemen hopped in, hoisting their prisoner onto the rear-facing seat between them. The third policeman raised the man's legs and pushed, shoving him in against the seatback. He left the tailgate down.

As the Land Rover pulled out of the compound, the driver shifted gears and the car slowed down for a moment. Carter held his breath and stared hard at the prisoner in the back of the vehicle. He felt suddenly cold. The prisoner's head bounced off one shoulder; his arms and hands were folded behind his back. Carter blinked. It was Brahima. He could not be mistaken — he recognized that huge frame, the wide, fleshy face, and those clothes, all the colors. Carter stepped heavily down the steps and jogged after the Land Rover, which moved slowly down the rutted dirt road. Brahima and his guardians looked back at him. When he stopped to take a last hard look, Carter was certain that Brahima smiled at him.

## Sunday

THE NOTEBOOK lay open on a table in his apartment. Carter kept it that way as a reminder of how long his friend Salif had been missing. On Sunday he wrote, *Two weeks now and no word. Everything is very bad here. Believe Salif probably dead . . .*

Carter didn't leave the capital on a bus to the east. He couldn't. The army sealed off the city, blocking travelers from going and coming. Soldiers set up additional checkpoints on roads and footpaths and patrolled the land around the city, which struck Carter as funny. What did a few more checkpoints matter? The embassy point of view, the attitude from the air-conditioned office, was certainly different. After the shootings in front of the presidential palace, the European and American embassies feared a bloody free-for-all, with garrisons and commanders fighting one another while the rebels took the countryside. The end of his time in country, Carter learned, would come by evacuation in his twenty-fourth month there. An embassy courier delivered the news in a sealed envelope slipped beneath his door the day after the president had raided and closed the schools. Inside the envelope, on embassy stationery, was a photocopied note printed in capital letters, like a telegram, with the ambassador's signature. The French, German, British, Japanese, and Dutch governments, the message said, had already withdrawn their ambassadors to protest the shooting of students and the Belgian family. The American ambassador ordered aid workers and embassy dependents to leave the country. Carter had two days to prepare, and he was instructed not to leave his apartment, if at all possible, until an embassy car arrived to collect him. An American military transport would fly evacuees directly to the United States.

Late Sunday morning, Carter reread the embassy note while sitting on his balcony and listening to the news. The government radio was explaining that the city's main roads had been sealed off and the airport closed to commercial air traffic "for reasons of security." He dropped the note on the small writing table beside the crumpled bus ticket to the east. He leaned forward in his chair, elbows on his knees, studying the dense activity on the street. Occasional military trucks rumbled by, filled with soldiers. Someone had cleaned up the splintered wood at the roadside and probably salvaged it for firewood or furniture. A soldier bartered with a butcher who was roasting meat on a spit where the vegetable sellers had worked. With the bus ticket and note in his hands, Carter rose from his chair and stepped to the edge of the balcony. He let the pieces of paper flutter to the street.

# WEEK THREE

## Monday

CARTER ROSE at four in the morning. He filled two water bottles and put them in his shoulder bag, with nuts and four mangoes. He skipped coffee, picked up his bag, and pulled on his straw hat. He slid his sunglasses into his shirt pocket and walked out of his apartment into the cool darkness.

Before dawn, the heat was not quite unbearable as he reached the northern edge of the city and began the hike to the village of Mumbe, marching up and down a series of rocky slopes that rose gently northeast of the city. He wondered what Hamza's people would think of him, arriving at last more than a year after the boy's death. What would he say to them? He cursed himself aloud for not making the trip earlier, for not having the courage and physical strength to face the heat as Hamza had at this very hour, walking to school, every day.

"Coward," he said in a low voice, "you goddamned coward."

He followed a path that started from the top of La Colline, an old residential quarter of the capital that sat on a rocky butte a few hundred feet above the rest of the city. In his pocket, he carried directions to the village, which the nurse had given him at the dispensary where Hamza died. The pathway was straight and well worn. After two kilometers, Mumbe's mud homes, like golden brown blisters on the earth, came into view. At first light a thin veil of dust revealed only their silhouettes. Mumbe gazed down on the city, nearly invisible through the glare and the haze, slowly becoming more distinct as Carter got closer. Soon, even at that early hour, heat began to shimmer in the air just above ground, as if the soil were melting. Carter's white cotton shirt stuck to his chest, and beads of sweat rolled down his spine, a cool sensation that he savored. In two hours, the heat of the sun, combined with heat radiating from the ground, would evaporate sweat instantly. He still had two kilometers to cover and walked northeast, up and across the crumbling hardpan, stopping to drink on the half-hour. In rocky ravines, where sand collected, he saw where villagers grew meager crops of groundnut and tomato. Where the soil was deep enough, they planted potatoes.

A half-mile before he reached the village, Carter's approach was announced. Children tending goats or gardens followed him, laughing and shouting, *"Anasara, Anasara."* Even this close to Mumbe, he could hear the distant clamor of morning activity in the city. Wind carried the murmur of thousands of voices, the clatter of work, the whine of automobiles, and the honking protests of donkeys. After more than two hours of walking, he entered the hamlet's tiny courtyard, which was surrounded by a cluster of mud buildings. He clapped his hands. No one answered. A rooster pecked the ground at his feet.

The village was neatly kept. A few hoes leaned against a wall; they had wooden handles and metal blades probably made from automobile fenders. Through doorways Carter saw bedding. A copy of the Koran lay open on a white cloth spread over a wooden table. He heard faint shouts growing louder, accompanied by the snapping of sandals as someone approached at a run from outside the village.

A man in a muddy sleeveless blue tunic and brown leggings rolled above his knees turned a corner into the courtyard, breathing hard and smiling. He'd been shouting, *"Allahamdallalai,"* expressing his thanks for a visitor and bidding him welcome. *"Bienvenue,"* he said, raising his hands to show that they were muddy and that he couldn't shake hands. "I am Yaou. I am the village chief." An old woman in a bright green wrap, headscarf, and white T-shirt came out of a house, carrying a large enamel bowl of water. She must have been inside as Carter had clapped his arrival. Yaou said something to the old woman, and she set the bowl on the ground and went back inside, returning with a heavy steel lawn chair. She pulled it across the compound and underneath a leafy neem tree. She hurried away and returned again with a covered wooden bowl with two wooden ladles on top. She set them on the ground beside the chair and returned again with a smaller metal bowl of water. Carter smiled at her and she retreated to the house, returning again with a straw mat, which she unrolled on the sand opposite the chair. Yaou motioned to Carter, inviting him to sit in the chair. Then the chief set before Carter the larger water bowl so he could wash his feet and hands. Yaou knelt on the mat, resting back on his heels, and waited. When Carter was finished, he washed himself.

It was nearly 7 A.M., a late hour in a land where people rose before dawn to pray and work in relatively cool temperatures. To the southwest, Carter could see thousands of mud homes where the city spread beyond the first rocky slope he'd crossed.

After they finished washing, his host offered Carter the smaller bowl of water to drink from. Yaou was a French speaker who explained that he'd finished secondary school in the city before "the second great war." He'd spent eighteen years in the French army and had been working the fields ever since he quit being a soldier in 1957. He removed the cloth from the top of the wooden bowl and set it between him and Carter. Together, with the wooden ladles, they sipped thick, gray millet gruel from the bowl.

Yaou was a solemn old man, wiry and quick. A dirty white skullcap covered his head, and mud streaked his calves and clothes. He'd been mixing mud and straw in a shallow pit a few hundred yards above the village. Using a battered wheelbarrow, he brought the mud back to the village, where he was repairing the house he shared with his wife. He had broad shoulders, and the muscles on his forearms bulged like lengths of bark. Deep wrinkles fanned out from his eyes. He'd washed his hands but had forgotten his face, which was still covered in dust with patches of dried mud. As they talked, Yaou brushed his clothes off and apologized again and again for his appearance.

"I am so dirty. I was not expecting you."

"Please, it's nothing," Carter said. "You are very kind." He made a point of looking around him. "The village is empty today. Everyone must be out working, like you."

Yaou sipped gruel from the spoon, smacking his lips and wiping them with the back of his hand. "Yes," he said, "working, I hope. Everyone who is healthy has gone to the coast to find work. A few are still in the city." He raised his hand and gestured toward the capital; to Carter, it now seemed an impossibly different world. "I am old, so I must stay and watch over the village."

"Everyone has gone away? I don't understand."

"Oh yes, most everyone. That's true for all the villages around here. Every October after harvest, people travel south to work. A few go to the city, but there is less work there than on the coast." He took a sip of the gruel. "Many of our people have not come back in years. If there is no rain, there will be nothing to harvest."

Carter felt bitter that maybe he'd missed Hamza's family. He was also worrying about the purity of the well water used to mix the millet gruel. He sipped gingerly, making loud slurping noises without taking much into his mouth. The gruel was tasteless to him. Yaou read his face.

"You do not like it?" he asked.

Carter smiled. "It's good." He put the spoon in the bowl and wiped his mouth with his fingers.

Yaou said he was one of fifteen people left in Mumbe — old men and women and a few small children. Most villagers had traveled to the seaports of Nigeria, Benin, Togo, Ghana, and Ivory Coast to work on the docks or on the coffee and cocoa farms along the coast.

"Normally, there are two hundred of us here. We are farmers."

Carter looked around and nodded. "Can you really farm the land around here?"

"In the Birni Valley." Yaou pointed west. "Two days' walk from here. All the good land around the village is already taken by people who live in the city, and the rest is all rock now, you can see. The wind works against us." He paused and raised his ladle. "Please, have more gruel." He drank deeply and continued talking. "There's no work now. Not enough food. Years ago, we were well off. We had more than five hundred goats for our village. I used to have seven camels. I had to kill them because I could not feed them. The villagers who have traveled away send us money when they can. In July the rains will come, and many will be back for planting season."

"Why didn't you just sell your camels?"

Yaou squinted at Carter. "No one had the money to buy them. No one had food for their animals. We had to kill most of our goats, too." He leaned back on his heels and smacked his lips.

They were quiet for a few minutes while they had more gruel. Then Yaou said, "You know, when I was a young man, they were going to build a railroad from here" — he pointed at the city — "from the city, to the sea."

"Who?"

"The French. They were going to connect Senegal to Niger and then build the railroad south, through Benin." He shook his head. "They built some of it, you know, but then they made these borders. We are countries now and the whole thing stopped. The railroad never reached here."

Carter saw that Yaou was missing the fourth and fifth fingers of his right hand, which he still used to hold the ladle. Yaou caught the stare and held the hand up proudly. "*La guerre*," he said. "I served in the French army. I was in Europe and in Algeria. This is my life now." He raised his arms, hands out, and let them fall back in his lap.

"So you have traveled and you have seen war. You must know all about borders."

Yaou shook his head and spoke in a voice Carter could barely hear. "I know our lives should not be this hard. That is what I know."

Carter nodded and smiled. He was becoming nervous and

wanted to find a way to bring up Hamza Saidou. After half an hour of talking, Yaou hadn't asked why he'd come. So, abruptly, Carter began to explain that he knew the boy and that he'd been his teacher.

"I came to pay my respects to the family."

The old man smiled weakly. "Yes, we know of you. You are the American." He explained that Hamza's three brothers and two sisters and his parents had all gone to Abidjan, the Atlantic port city in Ivory Coast.

Carter closed his eyes for several seconds, dismayed.

"So, did he have family here? I mean, was there someone from his family here in the village when he died?"

Yaou shook his head. He smacked his lips. "No, they have not come back in a long time."

"Can I send them a telegram about Hamza?"

Yaou shrugged. "I do not know where they live. I'm not even sure they are still in Abidjan." He spooned the gruel with his ladle. "What would you want to say to them?"

Carter frowned and shook his head. "I have no idea."

Yaou nodded.

They sat together uneasily. After some silence, Carter said, "Um, did Hamza talk about me? Did he ever mention me?"

Yaou sipped his gruel loudly and licked his lips. "Well, yes, I think so. The boy told us an American taught him English. We all thought that was strange. Why do you come all the way here to teach English?"

Carter smiled. "So, he didn't say anything else then?"

Yaou shook his head. "No, I cannot remember anything." Then he looked at Carter sideways, his head slightly bowed. "Is there something he should have said?"

Carter almost laughed. "No, no, I was only curious."

The old woman reappeared with a small tray of sugar cubes and added them to the gruel. She was thin, and her face was so heavily wrinkled that Carter assumed she must have been about seventy years old. He watched her walk back to the house, her steps slow but certain.

"Is she your mother?"

Yaou wrinkled his brow and closed his mouth. "That is my wife," he said. "She is thirty years younger than I am." Carter nodded, embarrassed. Yaou mixed the sugar into the gruel. *"Ici la vie est dur*—life is hard. We live outside. We live in the sun."

They sat quietly for a minute. Then Carter asked where Hamza was buried.

"In the rocks." Yaou gestured to a rocky area up the slope, north of the hamlet. He put his ladle in the bowl. "Hamza was the only child from here to attend school in many years. He was never strong enough to go to the coast to work. He did not seem to have the stamina for the journey, so we sent him to the school. It takes many days by bus to get to the coast, you know. Sometimes, when there is no money, we walk part of the way. I have made the journey many times to Nigeria, Ghana, and Togo. I have not been to Ivory Coast, but my father made many trips there. Mostly I worked on coffee and cocoa plantations. We thought maybe Hamza would be a teacher or a clerk in some office and help support the village with his salary."

Carter looked at the ground as he listened. When Yaou was finished, he told him that Hamza had been a good boy, but as he spoke he heard Salif's voice in his head: "Tell them this boy mattered to you." Yet all Carter could think of as he spoke was the misery of the boy's life. He thought of his orange hair, the rock Hamza had thrown at Carter, and the fight with Miriam. Absently, Carter raised his hand and touched the back of his head. But he told Yaou nothing of those things. The old man smiled politely. The heat intensified, and beads of sweat cut the dust on his face.

"Hamza never did well in school," Yaou said.

Carter shook his head. "He was just a boy," he said. "He liked to tease people, even me." He paused and smiled. "He used to call me *Anasara.*" Carter laughed.

Yaou frowned. "That is disrespectful. I hope you punished him." He put the cover back on the bowl of gruel.

"School is not for everyone," Carter said, wanting to be empathetic.

The visit was not going well for Carter. He noticed a small boy and girl eyeing him from the doorway of one of the houses. He wasn't ready for Mumbe's emptiness and the fact that he seemed to be the only person mourning Hamza. He wanted to confess the truth of Hamza's last hours to someone, anyone who was close to the boy and who knew him well. He told Yaou about his last day in class, and about the malaria. Yaou listened, nodding, his eyes on the ground as he made sounds of affirmation. "Mmm," he said. "Mmm." He kept glancing up at the sun, and Carter understood he was growing impatient.

When Carter finished, Yaou said, "We all have the fever. But not you, I am sure. White people have medicine. Do you have medicine you can give us?"

This shut Carter up. He thought of what he must look like, in his clean khaki pants and white shirt, his wide hat and dark glasses, trying to relieve his conscience and fulfill his duty to Salif and doing a bad job of it. And here was this old farmer, wanting only to get back to work before the heat became too much. Carter, too, wanted to leave. He was angry, first with Yaou, who seemed to care nothing for the boy. Yet as he thought more, he became angry with himself, that only now had he learned of this reality — the slow starvation in the countryside and the exodus of so many people. Salif's frequent prodding — "You need to get out of the city" — echoed in his head, and he was ashamed. Carter shifted uncomfortably and smiled thinly at Yaou. He thought to himself, *What were you expecting? You thought these people would be waiting for you, and for what? To thank you?* Behind his thoughts, he heard Salif answer him: "Can't you see? Hamza Saidou failed them. Yes, he was just a boy, but he failed the people of his village. He died."

"I . . . I'm sorry," Carter said, glancing at Yaou and then at the ground. "I didn't bring any medicine with me." He bent over and reached for his bag. He took out the mangoes and the nuts and laid them on the mat. "Please accept these. You have been very kind."

Yaou picked up the bowl of gruel, removing the cover with one hand, and offered it to Carter. "Drink," he said.

## Monday

"FEVER KILLED HAMZA SAIDOU!" Carter was talking to himself in a loud voice as he hiked back to the city. "But I'll probably never know what happened to Salif Moustapha." Then he shouted, "Will I, Salif? I'll never know. You'll never let me know."

He began to cry a little, but he stopped. Crying was useless. It was nearly nine, and the heat pushed on him as he walked back to the city under the awful sun. He'd thanked Yaou and shaken his hand, promising to try to get some medicine to him. Carter felt the lie as he spoke it, unsure of where and how he'd find enough malaria pills for the fifteen people still in the village.

He hurried down the slope. The heat reflected off the ground and burned through the rubber soles of his shoes. Carter saw himself as a small creature crawling across a vast campfire pit burnt to ashen gray and dull brown. The air was so hot, it seared his throat; it hurt to breathe deeply. It occurred to him that he'd never really been out of the city on foot, alone, to see the country for himself and listen to people's stories. There was no escape except to keep walking. He pictured Hamza burning up on a bed in a cool room, with no escape from the heat of sickness, and Salif, perhaps in some desert camp out in the open, sweltering without shade or water. It seemed as if the spirits of both men were following Carter across the plain, back to the city. They would always be following him. They would never let him rest, never let him forget. He drank the rest of his water. He was lightheaded, but not in danger. More water would be available soon enough. For a few moments he savored the sensation that he was floating around in the boy's fever.

The nurse at the dispensary had said Hamza's temperature stayed at about 107 degrees for several hours before he died, cooking his brain and muscle tissue. Carter knew that when body temperature rose above 106 degrees for more than an hour, the internal cell structure broke down, forming skin lesions. The parasites, meanwhile, worked destruction in the liver and muscle tissue, producing spasms. Sometimes, in cases of very high fever, before reaching the critical temperature, the body released adrenaline in an attempt to cool off, producing more chills and contortions, which only heated the body more. Hamza's thermostat blew. The boiling point arrived. And death.

On the outskirts of the city, Carter stopped at a tea table in the shade of a eucalyptus tree, where an old man mixed coffee and tea drinks from a kettle of water over an open fire. Carter refilled his water bottle from the kettle and let the bottle cool under the table, as much as it could in the heat. He bought a glass of hot Nescafé. Carter remained standing and sipped his coffee, watching a tailor work inside the doorway of his shop across the way. He was an old man in a dark blue work coat, hunched over a pedal-powered sewing machine.

Carter turned to the tea maker and blurted out a question. "Where are all the young men and women in the villages?" He raised his arm and pointed toward the countryside.

Confused, the man frowned and shrugged, saying nothing.

Carter drank his coffee and collected his water bottle. He paid and walked on, down a narrow passage between high mud walls, descending the maze of sandy byways through the old quarter, among the mud buildings, until he emerged on the asphalt streets. Carter turned, taking a last look at the way he'd come. He felt he was peering back in time, into centuries of lives gouged directly from the ground, where he was now standing in the uncertain present, a place choked by cars, camels and donkeys, commerce and soldiers. He walked down the street, heading to Lycée Centrale, where there was nothing for him. No work, no students, no friends. But he didn't know where else to go.

## Monday

"WHY DID YOU COME BACK HERE?"

The headmaster stood in the classroom doorway, talking to Carter, who sat on the floor beneath the blackboard. Carter's shoulder bag lay open near his feet and he held his water bottle in his lap. He raised his head and faced his old boss, uncertain at first who spoke to him. The headmaster's face was puffy and covered with dark stubble. He was bareheaded now, dressed in sandals and a long dirty tunic that stretched over his belly. Sweat stained the front of his robe from his neck to the middle of his chest. Carter thought he looked out of place in unwashed clothes, a man of position who'd been stripped of rank. The shutters and windows were all flung open, and some of the glass panes were broken. The desks and chairs, mostly in pieces, lay in the dirt outside.

"I work here, remember?" Carter's reply was barely audible. Anyway, he was too tired to get angry. He took a sip of water and set the bottle on the floor beside him, stretching out his legs and resting his head against the wall. "I used to teach in this room."

The headmaster walked to the far wall, opposite Carter. Dried blood stained the floor. A few drops marked the wall. He looked down at the stains for several minutes, as if he could not comprehend what he was seeing. He waited as if anticipating Carter's questions. For some time the two men didn't speak.

The headmaster walked back to the doorway. "They have closed the school, monsieur. There is nothing here for you to do. All the foreigners are leaving the city now."

Carter opened his eyes. He drew his legs up, with his knees close to his chest, and wrapped his arms around them. "What are you doing here?" he asked.

The headmaster shrugged. He looked at Carter a moment as if to say something but then dropped his gaze to the ground.

Carter sighed and wiped his sweaty face with the shoulder sleeve of his shirt. "What news do you have of the students?"

The headmaster didn't answer right away. Carter looked at him. "Do you know what happened to Cisse or any of the others?" The headmaster still did not reply, and Carter leaned his head back against the wall, biting his lip. In a soft voice, he persisted. "Do I have to say the name? Have you heard anything about Salif?"

"No, nothing, I am sorry." The headmaster folded his arms. A few more seconds of silence passed. "Monsieur David, be glad you can leave here and return to your family." He spoke slowly. "Go home. Salif is gone, my brother is gone, many of our students are gone. We will never see them again. They have arrested several other teachers and they will probably arrest me. This is our life now."

Carter dropped his chin to his chest and closed his eyes. He wanted these last few moments alone in this room, his classroom.

"Please, go," Carter said.

The headmaster stared at him a full minute. Then he left.

When Carter could no longer hear the man's footsteps, he stuffed the water bottle in his sack and got to his feet. He walked around the room. He touched the bloodstains on the wall and ran his fingers over the blackboard. On the floor, near where his desk had been, he found a piece of chalk about the length of his index finger. On the blackboard, in capital letters and in both English and French, he wrote,

WHERE IS MY FRIEND, SALIF MOUSTAPHA? HE TAUGHT FRENCH AND MATH IN THIS SCHOOL. HE IS LOVED HERE. WHAT HAVE YOU DONE WITH HIM?

Carter broke the chalk in half and left a piece on the blackboard ledge. He put the other half in his bag. He took a step backward, rubbing chalk dust on his pants, and looked at the words he'd written. Then he turned and for a couple of minutes allowed himself another memory, an image of Salif sitting cross-legged on the floor, inviting David to sit, nodding his head and gesturing. He was talking and laughing as he worked the tea, pouring it, tasting it, adding sugar and tea leaves, hands moving furiously here and there. Carter thought, *Like a man never quite willing to accept the situation before him.*

Carter sucked in a breath of the air in that room and sat back down on the floor.

"What do they do with you when they take you away? What do they want from you, Salif?"

Salif poured the tea, raising the kettle high over his head. Carter frowned at Salif's face, his eyes resting on the bandaged fingers.

"It looks to me as if they beat you. Tell me why this is happening. What have you done?"

Salif sat with the kettle in his hand, staring at the ground, quite still. Carter tried to provoke him.

"*Tu es espion, n'est-ce pas,* working for the French or the CIA or the Tuareg rebellion?"

Salif jerked his head back and laughed. "No, no. I am not a spy, I am not a rebel."

Carter smiled and kept up the pressure. "What is it, then? They must think you're, well, doing something."

They waited together for the answer. Salif packed fresh sugar cubes into the teakettle.

"I do not know, really. I do not understand what they want from me. They just do not like who I am."

Abruptly, Salif looked up at Carter, as if to check whether or not Carter believed him, or perhaps whether his American friend had somehow betrayed him. Salif began to explain how they kept him, but not where.

"Don't ever come to find me. That would endanger you *and* me."

Salif's prison was a large room where a few other people were held — not one of the smaller, more crowded cells. There were often four or five other men with him.

"They are men like me. They are confused. We do not dare talk for fear of each other and of being overheard through the door. We sleep on mats and avoid eye contact. The room is big and square, with cracked concrete walls and long windows, which are kept closed and shuttered. They let us out twice a day to use the latrine."

Carter tried to picture Salif in a situation where he didn't control the conversation — where, in fact, speaking was forbidden. Salif was a traitor, they said. But Carter believed Salif was merely convenient, someone whose imprisonment satisfied the leaders, proving that the rebels were being dealt with. People were being rounded up: hundreds, maybe thousands like Salif.

Salif told him more.

"Three years ago, some months before you arrived here, Daveed, the headmaster came to my classroom with a slip of paper. It was an order for me to report for questioning. That was the first time. A few months ago, they came to my house. Three soldiers opened the compound gate. My wife was preparing dinner over a fire, and she stopped her work to greet them. My son, Oumarou, was only five months old and was strapped to her back. My daughters were playing nearby. As I came out of the house, I saw a soldier push my wife out of the way. He pushed her so hard, she fell to the ground, the wrap came undone, and my son rolled in the dirt."

Salif sat with his arms folded, his hands under his armpits.

"There was great commotion. Oumarou was crying. My wife was screaming at the soldiers as she tried to gather the baby in her arms. I ran to her, but a soldier stopped me. He bent my left arm behind my back and led me out. I struggled and managed to reach out and clutch my fingers on the doorjamb. They shut the door on my fingers."

Salif caressed his injured hand and continued. "That week they arrested my father and mother in Markala. Soldiers took them right from the house. They left the other wives, but took my mother, the first wife. I am fairly certain the arrests had nothing to do with me. It is just that we are Bouzou, so there is suspicion, you know."

He didn't speak for a while.

"They let my mother go the same day, but they held my father for a week. They beat him. He had bruises on his back and chest when they let him go, but he was okay. My father is strong."

Salif shook his head. "My father will not say a word. He is an old man. I have never understood what they fear from someone like him."

"That's an awful story."

Salif shrugged. "That is an African story."

# AMERICAN FOOD

PROFESSOR KEITA TRAORE is, according to the best authorities on West African ecology, *the man* on the soils of the Sahel region. He knows what should and shouldn't be grown there. He can talk dirt across six countries, which gives him certain marketability in a land wasting away under heat, wind, and too little water. Governments pay him to study the land where he grew up herding goats and planting yams with his family. He has advanced degrees in botany and geology from France and the United States. He can pick up an infrared satellite photograph of, say, the Madiama district in Mali and tell you what the soil depths are at a given longitude and latitude, what plants grow there, and how much carbon can be found at a depth of six centimeters. And he can do it fluently in four languages.

But Keita Traore can't cook goat head, his favorite food. The sheriff's deputy sees this clearly. Keita, who is six feet, five inches tall and thin as a twig, watches the deputy drop to one knee and poke a stick at the thing floating in a pot of steaming water on a dual-burner camping stove. The deputy, in a uniform of black short-sleeved shirt and trousers, is a muscular man with thin graying hair, his face a little sunburned behind wraparound bike racer's sunglasses. Keita squats beside him, wondering what he is doing.

The two men huddle like this, hidden in the lilac bushes a couple hundred yards behind Keita's apartment building. Keita hoped the bushes would provide cover so he could cook the goat head unseen by his neighbors and family. Now he looks up through the leaves and wonders who called the police. The building is part of a complex of clapboard townhouses on the edge of the eastern Oregon town where Keita and his family live. Each townhouse has its own burnt-out lawns, front and back, dense with thistles and morning glories.

Keita likes this part of Oregon — so much like home, a big land, dry and difficult. He walks to work at the state agricultural college where he has spent ten years, first as a graduate student and now as a professor. Rocky slopes of sagebrush and dwarf pines rise above town. For a century, cattle ranchers have barely hung on in these hills, complaining of wolves until they killed them all, and now of coyotes and, always, poor rains.

His children, a boy and a girl, are indifferent to the land where they live now, and to Africa, the land of their birth. They whine when Keita takes them on walks to show them plants like sagebrush, whose narrow, pale green leaves he likes to rub into their palms for them to smell. They moan and sigh impatiently when Keita and their mother, Aissa, try to teach them Bambara, their native tongue, or tell stories of life in the village. Often at dinner Aissa looks sternly at Keita while nodding to the children. Keita knows it is time to tell such a story. Nearly every day, out of earshot of the children, Aissa says to her husband, "You must talk to them about our home." So Keita tells them things like "Children, in the early morning my mother would take me to gather leaves for soup," and as he speaks the children fold their arms and roll their eyes. But he talks through their indifference, telling himself and Aissa that they are only children and they will change.

Aissa worries. She pleads carefully when she is alone with Keita and sometimes she sounds angry. "Keita," she says, "our children do not know the country where they were born. You travel back so often. You must take us with you."

Keita, too, is worried, but he lowers his head as if to blunt her annoyance and begs patience. "There isn't enough money," he says.

Yet Aissa *is* patient, and defiant. She savors heat, preferring bright cotton dresses and wraps in summer to celebrate the sun, and in winter a brilliant orange down parka, with boots. She tells people, "I dress to defy your rain." She is beautiful, shorter than her husband, with close-cropped black hair and cool green eyes. Aissa has known Keita since they were children in the village, and she is used to his absences, or at least Keita likes to believe that about her. From the village Aissa followed him to the capital where he went to university and she trained to be an accountant. When Keita went to Paris for a year of graduate studies in biology, she agreed to wait for him. She returned to their village, where she worked balancing the books for a government seed warehouse. She did not have the money to go to France, and he could not afford to return until he finished. Nor did she go with him when he took a job for a year studying soils on a wildlife preserve in Senegal. "I cannot support you on what they pay me," he told her. "I must put in my time. Things will get better."

But all that was before Oregon. Aissa knows how life would be at home on an $800 annual civil service salary. She reminds herself that at least now she is waiting with Keita and not apart from him. Still, her patience wears thin, which Keita cannot ignore. He worries.

The deputy squints, his head cocked to one side as he looks down at the pot, holding the stick at his side. Thin brown and white fur still covers the head. He pushes his sunglasses up on his head and squints at Keita. "What is this?" he says.

Keita hesitates. It is early afternoon in August and he and the deputy sweat under the sun. The head bobs and rolls a little as the water begins to boil.

"Well, you see," he says, "it's . . . goat head. We eat it." His voice is barely audible. He stands with his hands folded in the small of his back, expecting to be arrested, again. Suddenly, Keita thinks, *My God, the deputy cannot believe this is some person's head.* The shape is obviously not human, and there is the fur. He starts to wonder how he's going to explain this to the deputy, but that thought is quickly replaced by the worry of how this situation will play in the campus newspaper.

AFRICAN MAN ARRESTED
BOILING A SKULL IN HIS BACKYARD
POLICE SUSPECT HEADHUNTER CONNECTION

The deputy nods his head and smiles. He says, "Goat head, huh." He looks about forty, and the skin around his pale blue eyes is beginning to wrinkle. He glances over at Keita, whose long body is folded in a squat. Keita wants to tell this man that he inherited his great height from his mother, whose people come from the West African coast. But the deputy's face opens in a grin and he says, "Cool!"

Keita squints at the deputy, at once startled and relieved by the man's good humor. But he cannot quite trust the grin or the friendly word. Keita says nothing.

This would have been, Keita figures, his third food-related arrest in the United States. He was arrested or detained (he's never sure of the difference) a decade earlier at Chicago's O'Hare International Airport when he first came to the United States. He'd arrived on a connecting flight from Paris, while on his way to Oregon to begin graduate studies in soil science. He carried a suitcase full of Chinese green tea, dried carp from the Niger River, dried tomatoes, and dried goat meat, all of which he'd brought to make his meals more like those at home. He likes to tell people, particularly his undergraduate students, that he enjoys meals that are "robust." He likes to say it's important to understand the source — the very earth in which vegetables are grown and the animals from which the meat is cut.

"I'm not sure what you mean by that," a student once replied. "It sounds kind of gross."

"My friend," Keita said, "you might very well be in the wrong class."

Anyway, he'd wrapped the food items in clear plastic bags. This way there would be no questions from customs about what he was carrying.

"I still don't understand what I did wrong," he wrote to Aissa after he was freed from a federal immigration detention center a week later. At that time, Aissa was pregnant with their second child, a girl. She had stayed home in Africa with their two-year-old son until Keita could afford to bring the family across the Atlantic. "I declared everything as 'dried and processed foodstuffs,'" he continued in that letter,

> but they took nearly all of it and then they tried to charge me with smuggling drugs. They thought the tea was marijuana. I can tell you that one officer in the jail was a woman. She took me out of my cell one day, just me and no one else. We went to the cafeteria and she got me a cup of coffee. The coffee in the jail was awful, Aissa, the worst I have ever tasted in my life. I am sure it was not really coffee. I thought certainly I was in the most serious trouble, but what this woman wanted was to ask if any of the items in my luggage would help her husband during sex. I told her what I had told them at the airport many times — that it was all meat and vegetables prepared according to our Muslim traditions. I asked her if they do not value meat and vegetables in America. That made her angry. She said I was being "sarcastic." But I meant no offense. I tried to explain about food in our country, I wanted to tell her about our village and my mother, but she would not listen.

Indeed, when it comes to food, sarcasm has no place in Keita's life. He is passionate and particular and proud. He wanted to tell the jail guard many things about Africa. He wanted to tell her that when he was a boy, in 1973, he'd learned from his mother that he could eat the leaves straight off a balanite tree. Keita's mother pressed balanite nuts for cooking oil and boiled the leaves for soup. But he'd never seen anyone eat the leaves raw until one morning during planting season, when Keita went with his mother to sow sorghum seed after a rain. Their fields spread out on a sandy plain, a savanna marked by thin grasses and scattered acacia and balanite trees with narrow trunks and canopies shaped like mushrooms. Not so long ago, just years before Keita was born, grass had grown thick here and trees had thrived — not in great density, but a few meters apart in every direction. The acacia and balanite offered shade under canopies thick with green leaves. Now dust hung in layers over the land that he and his mother walked. Trees were few, like mere guests of the soil, and it was difficult to tell one field from another. Keita and his brothers marked the corners of the family fields with stones, or they cut a mark in a tree. Sometimes farmers from different villages fought over the fields — bloody, terrible clashes with hoes, fists, and knives. Keita had heard of such things, but never seen one, and his father forbade Keita and his brothers to fight anyone over land. "The Koran forbids violence between Muslims," the old man told his sons.

Keita's mother was then twenty-eight years old, a tall muscular woman with skin deeply wrinkled from a life of labor in the sun. She'd already borne seven children. Keita remembers she wore a long faded green cloth that morning, wrapped tightly around her waist, and a matching piece of cloth around her head, which she knotted to the side, above her ear. At the time, Keita had no idea how young his mother really was. To him, she was an old woman. She began working one row ahead of him, bending at the waist and sinking her hoe into the ground with her right hand, while plucking seeds with her left from a cloth pouch at her waist and pressing them into the hole with her thumb. She'd move sideways almost at a run. After a few minutes he was already several rows behind her, which was partly because he enjoyed watching her work. She moved on her toes, her feet in blue plastic sandals, kicking up wet sand while her hands moved up and down and around at the end of strong arms. He marveled at those legs and arms constantly in motion, never wasting a movement, as if she were an insect performing a dance across the earth. Her seed rows were straight. He tried to imitate her, tried to capture the rhythm and speed of her movements, but he fell in the wet dirt. Keita wondered if his mother had seen him stumble.

After a while she stood up straight, and he watched her walk across the field, grab hold of a branch of a balanite tree, and pull some leaves off. The nuts had long since been harvested. She ate the leaves right there, stuffing two or three into her mouth at a time. She sat in the sand, in the shade of the tree, chewing and staring at something in the distance. Keita didn't want her to think he wasn't working hard and he pretended not to see her, even though he thought her eating of the leaves very strange.

Later that day, when the work was done and he had a few minutes alone, Keita went into the bush to find a balanite tree. He had to climb up into the dense branches to reach what he sought. He took a fistful of the leaves, which were thick and colored a greenish gray from dust, and tasted one with his lips and tongue. Then he bit into it. The flavor was slightly bitter. He ate more, appreciating the easy food. Drought had killed many of the family's goats and there was little hope that this rain would be followed by enough water to make good on the seeds Keita and his mother had sown that morning. But at least the trees grew there.

The deputy looks at the head in the pot and laughs in a muted way, forcing air out his nostrils. He flings the stick into the bushes and studies Keita, looking up at this tall man with charcoal skin and bony frame in khaki pants, shiny loafers, and a white cotton short-sleeve shirt buttoned down at the collar — dressed as if he's just come from a semiformal business meeting. Keita always presents his best when he leaves the house. He wears similar clothes into the field in Africa, though with boots.

"People," Keita likes to tell colleagues in the field, "if I am to get dirty, at least I will be dirty and well dressed."

The deputy wipes his mouth with the back of his hand, trying to figure out what to say. "So you're over at the college?" he asks, making a conversational guess. Most foreigners in town were somehow connected to the college.

Keita tilts his head back impatiently and rolls his eyes, wishing the deputy would get to the point. He raises his arms in a little shrug and lets them fall to his sides. He says, more slowly and loudly, "Look, it is only the head of a goat."

The deputy purses his lips and glances down at the pot on the stove, which has not been turned off. "Yeah," he says, nodding his head in agreement. "Seems to me you should probably roast it first, you know? Throw it on the hot coals in a barbecue, or else you're gonna be boiling that thing all day long." He gives Keita a friendly tap on the shoulder with his open hand. "But wrap it in foil or something, will you? Your neighbor upstairs thinks you're some sort of cult freak."

He laughs in staccato and then stops himself and coughs when he sees Keita staring at him. "Sorry," he says, scratching the back of his neck. "I didn't mean any harm by that." He smiles weakly. "But we did get this phone call, ya know, and if you'd just cook right out in the open, on the lawn, you'd probably attract a lot less attention."

Keita wipes his brow with his shirtsleeve, more humiliated than relieved — not so much about the "cult freak" thing (he's used to overwrought American imaginations; for years, the botany department secretary wouldn't stand near him because she feared he carried the Ebola virus), but that he actually has to endure receiving cooking instructions from an American. From a common gendarme.

Once, in Africa, Keita had been obliged to travel with an American embassy official. The man had floppy red hair and worried about sunburn. He kept asking, "We won't spend much time in the sun, will we?" They were inspecting soil study sites funded by American money, and one day, driving a white Chevrolet Suburban on their way to a site, they stopped in a village to fix a flat tire. The village chief was an old man who, as a matter of traditional courtesy to travelers, insisted on feeding them with goat meat and rice. The chief's wife served the food hot, spread out on a large metal plate. She soaked the rice in a dark tomato sauce with bits of meat. Keita, the American, and the chief washed in a bucket of soapy water and sat on mats arranged around the plate, to eat with their hands. The American dug in with all ten fingers, spilling rice and meat in the dirt as he ate, while Keita and the chief ate cleanly with the right hand, rolling the food into balls with their fingers before sucking it off their fingertips and into their mouths. The chief smiled at the American and in his own language called for his wife to get a spoon. When she brought one, the American politely waved it away. "No, no," he said in English, "I'll eat like everyone else."

Keita laughed as the man continued spilling his food. "That's not like everyone else," he said. "Take the spoon."

The second food-related arrest—it really wasn't an arrest, but Keita thinks of it that way—happened four years after the Chicago airport incident, in the parking lot of a diner in Portland, Oregon, down the street from a hotel where Keita, against his better judgment, was attending a conference called African Food Systems: A Western Perspective. He was in his last year of studying for his Ph.D. and had gone to breakfast with two American students, whose work toward their master's degrees he oversaw at the college agricultural laboratories. Keita folded himself awkwardly into the booth, rising a full head above his companions even as he sat. The pair stared at him while he salted his three fried eggs, hash browns, and sausage, nearly emptying the saltshaker. But he had ordered only eggs and potatoes, and he pushed aside the sausage because, as a good Muslim, he could not eat meat prepared by a non-Muslim.

Keita looked up and caught his companions' eyes. "Salt," he said to them. "I need salt." Not knowing what to say, the two men looked back to their food. "It is an acquired taste," Keita continued. "I grew up in a place where one sweats a great deal."

"Yeah, well, be careful, man," said one of the students.

Keita looked at him a moment. Then, from the side of his plate, he picked up the little green parsley sprout that lay beside a razor-thin slice of melon and held it in front of them by the stem, twisting it between his thumb and forefinger. "Ameriiiican fooood," he said. "Very colorful, but there is really not much to it, is there?"

"Hey," said the same student, a skinny kid who sat beside Keita in a T-shirt and faded army fatigue pants. He had long, stringy brown hair and a mouth full of waffle. "It's a diner, man, give it a chance."

Keita nodded, and with his fork he speared a sausage and held it up in front of his face. With a deep frown of mock concentration, he poked at the surface of the impaled meat, where there appeared to be a blue substance oozing out. After a couple of minutes, during which his companions tried to ignore him, Keita finally determined that the substance was ink and that it formed a number.

"Hmmm," he said aloud, his eyebrows raised. "Did you know that this is sausage number three-seven-two?"

"Oh, don't worry," said the skinny kid. "That's just the FDA inspection mark. They do that with restaurant meat."

The other student at the table winced as he sipped his coffee. "I didn't know that," he said.

Keita left the sausage on his plate and worked carefully on the eggs and potatoes. Then, without thinking, Keita tossed a cup of lukewarm coffee over his shoulder and inadvertently doused a waitress as she walked by. He'd meant the coffee for the floor. Actually, for the dirt. The action was just a reflex. Keita put his face in his hands as his lunch companions looked on, stunned, and then burst out laughing. The waitress, in shock, looked at the coffee dripping off the hem of her uniform dress and down her calf. She glared at them all for a minute before quietly saying, "Jerks! You are real jerks." Keita was horrified and tried to explain.

"I am sorry," he said. "Where I come from we always eat outside . . . I . . . I . . . forgot myself."

Keita's companions apologized, too, but the waitress walked away without saying a word more. At the front counter she picked up the telephone.

"We gotta go," the Americans said, almost simultaneously. The two men dug in their pockets and tossed three tens and a couple of fives and ones on the table, to make up for the incident. They ushered Keita out of the restaurant, only to see a police cruiser pull into the parking lot, its strobe lights flashing. The cruiser must have been right in the neighborhood when the call came from dispatch, which had been alerted by the waitress. Two officers got out of the car.

"You the guys who can't mind your table manners?" asked one officer.

"We got a report of an assault on a waitress," said the other.

The police left fifteen minutes later, after Keita and his friends told them the story, frantically, explaining that what Keita had done had been a subconscious act, an accident, the simple tossing of coffee in the proverbial dirt, as if they had been at an outdoor restaurant. The skinny kid offered a run-on anthropology lecture about life, food, and eating habits in hot places like Africa.

"You see," he told the officers, "in Africa, the nutritional situation is much less complex and that means they eat differently than we do."

The officers looked on, with blank expressions. Keita, listening to the kid's explanation, screwed up his face in quizzical amazement. Then he heard himself do something he'd never done before, except to his children — he barked a command. "Mike," he said, "please shut up!" He rubbed a hand over his face and turned to the officers, looking down at them as he spoke. "It was an honest accident and I am very sorry," he said. "I will certainly pay to launder her dress."

By now Keita has turned off the camping stove. The years have added curly flecks of gray to his hair, but his lean build and face, unlined except for a permanent furrow of his brow, give him the same earnest look he had when he was a graduate student. He folds his arms and watches the deputy pluck a notebook and pen from his breast pocket.

"Look, you haven't done anything wrong," the man says to Keita, "but I still have to make out a report. Now, what did you say your name was?"

Keita gives his full name and tells the officer about his homeland in West Africa, his work at the university, and his wife, Aissa, and their two children, Ahmed and Fanta, who are all, at that moment, wandering around Wal-Mart, looking for lawn furniture. He doesn't tell the deputy that his son, Ahmed, his oldest at twelve, and his daughter, Fanta, who is not quite ten, were born in Africa but grew up here in Oregon. Nor does he explain how upset it makes him that they cannot speak their parents' language and how the children respond in English when he and Aissa speak to them in their tongue or in the colonial French.

"Speeeeak English," the children whine, children whose lives are as different from the lives of children in the village where Keita and Aissa grew up as to be, well, incomprehensible to African villagers. And Ahmed and Fanta likewise think of rural West Africa as foreign, bewildering. "They think you and I come from the moon," Keita often complains to Aissa.

Instead, Keita politely tells the deputy that he'll go up to the apartment and retrieve the family passports for him to inspect.

"Naaa," says the deputy, shaking his head. "I don't need those." He scribbles in the notebook. After a while, he stuffs the notebook and pen in his shirt pocket and folds his arms. "So," he says. "How do ya eat goat head?"

Keita, who has been staring down at the pot and mourning the futility of his effort, looks up at the deputy and smiles.

Keita had good reason to be boiling goat head in the bushes behind his apartment building. He'd planned to cook a meal as a surprise for Aissa, a taste of home, no matter what his children thought. It made him smile that Ahmed and Fanta would be horrified at the thought of eating a goat head. His idea was to prepare the head the way his mother had done it — on a bed of couscous soaked in the head's juices and dressed with onions, garlic, and tomatoes, with plenty of salt. The meal was to be a medicine for Aissa's resentment of Keita's frequent trips back to West Africa and the fact that she and the children had returned home only once since they arrived in the United States years earlier. Ahmed and Fanta had hated the visit and spent most of the time sick with stomach parasites.

"They'll get used to it," Keita and Aissa told each other. "They must give Africa more time. We must take them back." Keita would pause and add, "When we have money."

Keita had promised to take the family home that summer, but plane fare and expenses for the four of them were too much, not to mention the expectations of the extended family in the village, where most people work steadily only during the months of planting and the weeks of harvest. Keita is the only member of his family who has a steady income. Aissa's family depends on him, too. Every month he wires what he can — $100 here, $300 there — to pay for food and medicine, weddings, a uniform for his brother-in-law the policeman, schoolbooks for the children, and gifts for the newborns. All this on a research professor's salary. The bonuses for his consulting work are not enough. Sometimes Aissa does the books for small shops in town, but without a proper American university degree the pay is poor and infrequent. So she cleans motel rooms, does seamstress work, and watches other people's children while the bills mount.

Keita's work as a scientist brought a balance of pleasures and problems: lots of travel (some enjoyable, some not) and the contrast (which he loved) between his homeland and his adopted home. It took time to adapt to eastern Oregon's cold, sometimes snowy winters, but the dry climate in the high desert was familiar, and the dust storms and violent summer rains were curses of the land that he and Aissa understood well.

Once he'd taken Aissa and the kids on a picnic in the foothills of the Wallowa Mountains, where they walked in the woods and roasted meat and corn on the campground barbecue. Late that afternoon, as they were beginning the drive home, they watched the sky darken in the east as a line of thunderstorms gathered over a ridge densely forested with ponderosa pine. The sky cracked with bright lightning flashes and rain burst from the clouds. Soft thunder sounded in the distance. Ahmed and Fanta had fallen asleep in the backseat, and Keita pulled the car off the road so he and Aissa could watch the storm, "like at an American drive-in movie," he said to her. They watched the clouds move and smoke rise from lightning strikes, thick white columns of smoke, like rope connecting earth to sky. It was raining and the wind was blowing, but they kept their windows down because it was warm and the smell of sagebrush was strong.

"This is like home," Aissa said quietly.

"Yes," Keita said. "It is a very big place." Aissa looked at him and smiled. She squeezed his hand. Such a land made it possible for her — for both of them — to live far from home and still feel a certain familiar connection to the earth.

But Keita knew this wasn't enough. The landscape and the complexities of its soils were his own obsession, his work, not Aissa's. He wanted to make things up to her. A good meal was the best way he knew how. Yet it was not until he started cooking the goat head around noon — when he carried the camping stove and pot from the apartment while Aissa and the kids were at Wal-Mart, made the trip back to the car to retrieve the goat head, and then finally took the bloody thing, which had been slaughtered that morning and wrapped in wax paper, out of a plastic bag and set it in the pot — that Keita realized he had no clue what he was doing.

Early that morning he'd been standing outside a large barn, negotiating with the rancher from whom he would buy the goat. The rancher, in fact, was a friend, Sheryl Banks. She was a tall, sandy-haired, sunburned woman who taught veterinary science at the college and had an office one floor up from Keita's. Sheryl and her husband ran a clinic on a ranch where they raised sheep and goats, and a few horses. In the hallway outside her office a few days earlier, Sheryl and Keita made a deal to meet at the ranch early on Saturday morning. She greeted him at the barn in jeans and a T-shirt, steel-toed work boots, and a dirty khaki baseball cap pulled down over long, thick hair streaked with gray and tied back in a ponytail.

Keita showed up in his neat office clothes, wearing sneakers and carrying a leather shoulder bag. She took him to a small enclosure with wire-mesh fencing and wooden feed troughs. They fed their goats here, in the shadow of a large barn. "We give 'em feed grown without any chemical fertilizers," she said. "Best meat you'll ever have."

He quickly chose the fattest goat, one with a coat of white fur, except for its head, which was brown and white. They settled the price then disagreed, politely, about how to properly slaughter the animal. Sheryl offered to do it herself, but Keita wanted it done in accordance with Muslim ritual — the cutting of the animal's throat with the wound facing east, the direction of the Holy City of Mecca, where the Prophet Muhammad was born. This way the blood would spill on the earth, cleansing it and honoring Muhammad's very memory and work in the name of Islam. Muslim hands alone must handle the animal, Keita explained. As they talked, Keita stood a few feet from Sheryl, his hands folded behind his back in a posture of calm insistence.

Sheryl smiled at him, intrigued and unsure whether or not she should be annoyed. She said, "Don't you trust me?" Then she smiled, a little flirtatiously. Sheryl Banks had known Keita Traore for seven years, since he was a graduate student in her animal anatomy class, one of the sharpest students she'd ever worked with. He was quiet and efficient, detail oriented, and comfortable with animals, a good scientist. But she realized that morning that she really didn't know him at all. She said, a little playfully, "Keita, be honest. You won't let me touch the animal because I'm a woman, is that it?"

Keita politely told her a half-truth, and a half-lie. "I won't let you touch the animal because you are not a Muslim," he said. This was true, but it was also true that in Keita's experience women were not permitted to butcher meat. "I know you are skilled," he added, "but this is not a matter of trust. It is a matter of ritual. I am a Muslim, you see. A Muslim must eat only meat that is slaughtered by himself or by another Muslim."

As Keita spoke, Sheryl studied him and scraped the toe of her boot in the dirt and hay, rubbing her chin and smiling. Finally, she shrugged. "Suit yourself," she said. "I don't mean to sound stupid, but I don't know, does the Koran actually have instructions for butchering meat?"

"The fifth chapter," Keita said. "We call it a Sura, the term for chapter. They are not instructions, exactly; they are more like guidelines. In the third paragraph Allah warns us . . ." And he recited the deity's wishes, roughly, for the translation from Arabic on the spot was difficult for him: "You must not eat those animals which die of themselves, nor the blood of swine's flesh, and all that has been killed in any other name than that of Allah, and you must not eat the animals choked, or those animals killed by a blow, or fall, or a goring, or those killed by other animals, and you must make the animal clean by putting it to death by your own hand."

Keita looked at the ground awkwardly. He said, "Religion is not like science, I suppose."

American women, their directness and independence, particularly with men, made him nervous. But Sheryl's knowledge and her easy ability with animals impressed him. At the college horse stable he'd once watched her calm a horse that had become dangerously upset when somehow the hoof and ankle of a front leg became tangled in a strand of barbed wire carelessly left in an exercise corral. Sheryl entered the corral alone as the animal ran about frantically, at one point rearing on its hind legs to shake the wire off. She calmed the horse, talking to the animal until it stood still while she knelt on one knee and slowly removed the wire. Keita thought she must have special powers.

"I didn't mean to be rude," Sheryl said, suddenly.

"You weren't," Keita said. "We are both scientists. We are askers of questions."

She entered the pen and quickly put a rope around the goat's neck. She led Keita and the goat into the barn, to a corner where a large cement slab on the ground sloped into a drain. He carefully washed his hands at a large sink, using a bar of soap left by the drain. She grabbed a pair of oversize bloodstained jeans overalls from a hook and handed them to Keita. "You'd best wear these over your clothes," she said. Then she asked, "You don't mind if I watch?"

"Please," Keita said, "not at all." He looked away for a moment. Then he said, "I don't want to be trouble for you, but I must do this outside, on the dirt. It is important, you see, that I spill the blood on the soil in the open air in order to cleanse the earth."

She shrugged again, her hands thrust deep in her jeans pockets. "Sure," she said, "yeah, out back of the barn. There's plenty of room." They walked across the barn, Keita carrying the overalls over his arm. Sheryl pushed open a heavy wooden door and they emerged in an area of hard-packed dirt beside an empty horse corral.

"This will be fine," Keita said. He pulled the overalls on over his clothes.

Sheryl stood back and watched this very tall man take the animal by the head and rear, flip it on its side, press down on its head with one hand, and kneel on the torso, as if he'd been doing this all his life, which he had. Normally, another man would be holding down the goat's torso and legs, but Keita would not let

Sheryl touch the animal during the slaughter. Keita moved the goat so its head and throat faced east and yanked the head back to expose the throat. Then, with a freshly sharpened knife he'd brought from home in the leather bag, Keita made a long, deep cut across the throat, from left to right. He did it in one motion and carefully bled the animal as he leaned on its gasping and kicking body, uttering prayers in Arabic to honor both Islam and the animal for offering itself as food. *"Bismillahi . . . ,"* he began, in thanks to God.

Keita, breathing a little hard from the effort, took twine from the leather bag and a long screwdriver he'd bought just for the slaughter. Raising one of the goat's hind legs, he used the knife to cut and separate skin from bone just above the hoof, and then inserted the screwdriver beneath the skin, carefully working it up the leg, separating skin from bone, without piercing the skin. This way he scraped out an inch-wide tubular space between the skin and bone all the way up the leg. As a boy in Africa, he'd used a long, sharpened stick. Keita put down the screwdriver and again raising the hind leg, he put his mouth to the opening of the space he'd made and began to blow, and blow, and blow, for several minutes until the animal was bloated like a parade balloon, its skin tight with Keita's own breath. He picked up the twine and wrapped it around the leg above the hoof, cutting off the escaping air. He smiled at Sheryl and let the dead animal sit a few minutes, to give the air pressure time to separate the skin from bone and muscle.

"Now it will be easier to skin her," he said.

Sheryl nodded. She said, "That was beautiful, the way you did that."

After a while Keita went back to work. He cut through bone and cartilage to remove the head and handed it to Sheryl, who looked back at him, surprised. He smiled. "Now," he said, "you can touch the meat." She took the head with both hands and set it on the wax paper that she'd laid out on a table in the barn. Keita made a long incision from the throat along the belly, letting the animal's innards and some blood spill on the ground. He began cutting the skin away. It was almost as easy as peeling a large orange. Then he reached inside the animal to cut and scoop out the intestines and bladder and set them all in a bucket. He cut away the thighs, handing each to Sheryl, who wrapped the meat in the wax paper. Keita left the rest of the torso as it was. They wrapped it and stored it in a large freezer in the barn. Keita washed again at the sink and removed his overalls. He'd finished the whole job in less than an hour.

Keita and Sheryl walked back to his car, each carrying packages of meat in wax paper and wrapped again in plastic bags. "Someday soon you'll have to bring your family out to the ranch for dinner," she said. "We'll eat the rest of that goat meat. And if you want, I'll let you do all the work."

Keita and the deputy have moved the pot and the gas stove out of the lilac bushes and onto the lawn. They are standing and talking. Keita explains, "Goat head is my favorite food. In my country people eat it most often in the morning because a head offers a full meal for the whole day. But I like to take it in the evening. It is good to sleep on a full stomach." Then he pauses and frowns a little. "How did you know how to cook goat head?"

The deputy grins. "I'm a hunter," he says. "And my brother runs a restaurant in Seattle." He shrugs. "I've never eaten goat head, but I know animals and I can cook." He looks at his watch, which reads 2 P.M. "Get yourself a barbecue this afternoon and maybe you can have this ready in time for dinner tonight."

Keita hikes his pants up and squats. Using a handkerchief to keep from burning his hand, he turns the pot over to drain the water into the grass, letting the head tumble out on the lawn. The animal's face stares back at the men, its mouth shut and its eyes as blank in death as they'd been in life.

"My mother prepared this for us often from the time when I was a small boy," Keita says. "I learned only how to eat it. I did not learn to cook it." He smiles at this thought. The deputy drops to one knee, his forearms resting on his right thigh. Keita continues. "I remember now, she would boil the heads for some time, all at once, in a great pot, three or four at a time, and then throw them on a fire. She would prepare a whole pile of them once a week and then sell them at market." The deputy listens, his eyes on Keita's face. "But she always kept one or two for us. In the evening we would sit around the pot where my mother had set the heads in a hot salty sauce prepared from dried tomatoes, sometimes with rice or couscous. And we always used the same stone to crack open the skulls. We rinsed the stone in water, and my father hit the skulls on the forehead, just above the eyes." Keita laughs. "We would all, my brothers, my father, and I, reach in for a handful of the brains first and scoop it out like this." He puts the thumb and fingers of his right hand together and curves them. "The brain tastes like liver, you know, and is very high in protein. The brain and the liver are the most nutritious parts of a goat. Then we would dig for the eyes and the tongue. They are difficult to chew but good to eat."

Suddenly the distant sound of children's voices comes from the other side of the apartment building. Car doors slam and Keita looks at the deputy, a little resigned.

He stands up and sighs. "My family," he says.

At that moment, Keita's son, Ahmed, runs around the corner of the building, holding a new basketball in both hands. Aissa and Fanta are chasing him, laughing. The children are dressed similarly in shorts and T-shirts and sneakers. When they reach the lawn and the two men, the cook stove, and the goat head, Fanta screams, and Aissa puts her hand over her own mouth.

Ahmed looks at his father and then at the deputy, who smiles broadly and tries very hard to look as if nothing is wrong. The boy looks at the head in the grass and again from one man to the other and back to the head. His eyes grow wide and his mouth falls open.

"Dad," he shouts, "what is that?"

Fanta stares. Aissa drops her hand from her mouth and begins to laugh.

# DISTURBANCE-LOVING
## SPECIES

KATE TOLD ME it was like Africa hemorrhaging in front of her. On the road to Madaoua, a town near the French military hospital, they saw a body on the asphalt. A farmer in a dirty robe, lying face-down. Kate opened the car door to get out and help, but the nurse who was riding with her grabbed Kate by the shoulder. With a look close to panic, the nurse glanced up and down the asphalt, her eyes unblinking, her brow tightened, and pulled Kate back into the car. The man is dead, the nurse explained, and if Kate touched him she'd die, too.

They drove on. The nurse mumbled something about needing to get ready. "It's going to be awful at the hospital," she said. Then she crawled into the rear of the vehicle, a Land Cruiser, to find her scrubs and retrieve her medical bag. Kate watched her in the rearview mirror, this woman desperately pawing at baggage. Kate told me that scared her, as if the woman had lost the answer. The nurse sat in the backseat, took off her blouse, and pulled on a light-blue surgical shirt. She told Kate that the man lying on the road had been trying to get to the hospital.

"There will be others," she said.

"What do you mean?" Kate asked.

The nurse looked up while she wiggled into her scrub pants in the cramped backseat. "This is cholera," she said. "People get sick like this, they try to get to the hospital, they go to the road in large numbers. They die."

Cholera — set off by a comma-shaped microscopic beast called *Vibrio cholerae*. Kate told me that once she'd seen cholera, she had to know everything about it, as if the disease would reveal the logic of its wrath. Souley, her boyfriend, told me she was obsessed for weeks. She learned how people pick up cholera from water or food contaminated by others who carry the disease, and how the bacteria enter the intestines and release a toxin that causes organs to gush water and salt that can't be replaced quickly enough. The victims suffer severe diarrhea. People die within an hour of the first symptoms. Even minutes.

"They die of thirst," the nurse would say to Kate later, when the flow of bodies through the hospital had ebbed.

They kept on driving, Kate and this French nurse who had needed a lift to her work at the rural hospital the French army ran, out of the grace of colonial guilt. They passed bodies along the road, and small groups of people standing in the bush, gathered around loved ones lying in their own waste. Kate drove fast but couldn't get beyond the odor.

"I'd never known that smell," she told me. "Harsh and sweet. Like strawberry yogurt and gasoline."

People died minutes from that hospital. Some sprawled with their arms spread, reaching. Others lay curled up, clutching themselves. Kate had meant to drop off the nurse and go; instead, she spent two days lending a hand at the hospital. The nurse got Kate rubber gloves and a mask. She started by helping with a patient or two, holding a tube in a man's throat to feed him a rehydration solution of salt and sugar water or talking to a woman to keep her out of shock. Then she'd go outside and vomit, wash herself, and return. She helped carry people and bodies in and out of treatment rooms. The rooms were wet with waste, every surface. African orderlies in plastic gowns rushed about with mops and buckets of disinfectant.

"When two liters go out of a body," Kate said, "two liters have to go back in."

My name is Ben Quinn. I'm a botanist, a student of flora. Kate was my sister, and she told stories like the one about cholera. In chunks.

But this is my story. Not a report, if you will. I'm not sure what this story is — a sort of inheritance, maybe. What Kate left me. What I must talk about. My memory, my interpretation of events. I remember Kate as I knew her. In chunks.

I heard the cholera story after I got off the plane in the capital, when I went to visit her. Kate told it cold, launched in as if giving a briefing. She was on her way back to the city when that nurse, standing in the road beside a disabled vehicle, flagged her down.

Technically, a medical mistake killed Kate. But the cholera has a lot to do with how I remember her. And other things, too, like the way she handled a big Land Cruiser in a dust storm or her ability to stare down a hostile soldier. Kate attracted visceral experience, and everything that was most surreal about Africa — the drunken spread of the land, the arbitrary violence, and the bitter everyday mix of ancient Africa with more or less modern Europe — seemed to jell around her with this weird Kate-Africa synergy.

Anyway, we hadn't seen each other since high school. Ten years. Kate had been frozen in my mind as I'd always known her. A bundle of anecdotes, like habits. But I couldn't tell you who Kate was, what she believed, what she was like to talk to or spend time with. I had to follow her to Africa to find that out. And when I got there, I found Africa had simplified her. She'd cut her long brown hair, and she looked taller but not gaunt. Her shoulders seemed to fall more sharply into her arms. The tendons in her neck stood out, and the notch at the base seemed deeper by an inch. Her legs swam in khaki field pants. She wore flip-flops everywhere.

I spent my time with Kate in July. Monsoon season. Kate and I arranged the visit months in advance, though I was already in West Africa for my own reasons, working in Burkina Faso. I had a grant to study how grasses survive in different desert places where farmers graze animals, such as the Sonoran Desert in Arizona and the grasslands of the Sahel. Kate and I had never been close, but because we were geographically near and it seemed the thing to do, I went to see her, an eight-hundred-mile hop via Air Afrique. I'd only been in Africa a couple of months, and she was nearing the end of her second year.

She was a Peace Corps worker, managing village agriculture projects — gardens, tree planting, that sort of thing. We were eighteen months apart in age. I'm older. I failed first grade, which means we were in the same class all through school in Colorado — an adolescence spent in each other's way. Brother and sister, not twins, but reflections of each other: tall, gaunt creatures, like young trees, whose floppy limbs grew so fast that it took years into adulthood for muscle tone and metabolism to catch up. We fell into the habit, both conscious and not, of doing the opposite of the other in all situations as a way to preserve self-definition. Different friends, activities, different Saturday nights. Still, Mom called us "the twins," deepening our mutual resentment. Maybe at times it was hatred. Before Africa I can't recall ever having a complete conversation with Kate. We tried to make ghosts of each other. Out of high school it made sense that we left town in opposite directions, though we both went to college — I in biology on the East Coast and Kate in sociology on the West Coast. I liked plants, Kate liked people.

But, first things first.

I was not in the country when Kate died. I returned to handle things. To begin with, I had to meet the vice consul, who produced the paperwork, gave me a pen with blue ink, and asked me, politely, to sign my sister's death certificate.

I remember very little about the consul's office — institutional white — nor the man, really. Ivy League. I remember the cold air-conditioned room, insulated from the desert, as if in denial that the outside world existed.

He smiled. "I'm sorry."

"Yeah."

I put the document on the edge of his desk and read, "Kate Quinn, age twenty-eight, died of complications during surgery to remove her appendix at the French military hospital at Madaoua. Likely contributing factors: Hepatitis A."

Souley was the first to arrive at the hospital. Kate had been out of surgery about four hours and he saw her while she was unconscious but still breathing. It was Souley who explained the situation to me. Apparently, there'd been a mistake, he said. The surgery to remove Kate's appendix was accidental, a misdiagnosis by a young doctor.

Kate's appendix was fine. Her blood and liver were not. In the end the trauma was too much.

I like to be factual. These are the facts as I see them.

Kate's dead. Which is why I need to tell this story. She died in Africa, a fact that fits her profile. As if she'd planned it — to be consumed by a place she feared and loved. I thought of telling the vice consul about this. But how could I explain Kate to someone who lives and works in a climate-controlled world, freezing out the real environment that surrounds him?

I should know. I live by facts expressed in the language of science, which requires that subjects be stripped of character, deconstructed cell by cell, and organized by class, order, family, genus, and species. Common names are forbidden, and progress in research is attributed to no one.

For example, the alpine lupine — a favorite of mine, *Lupinus latifolius* — is what we call "a disturbance-loving species," or, as the guidebook says, "a nitrogen fixing legume, which is found above and below tree line and on disturbed sub-alpine terrain, such as along logging roads, on clear cut land, or in open areas vulnerable to landslides."

Those last words I wrote for *Graham's Flora of the American West*, a book with ten authors, each hired to contribute a specialty — plants of the alpine west, the arid west, rain forests of the Pacific Northwest, the prairie west, the wetland west, and so on. Each of us working in isolation, obsessed about proper credit, unwilling to surrender our "area of knowledge" to one another.

Disturbance-loving species.

The lupine is a plant that defies the neighborhood, which makes it a sort of kindred creature to me, the kind of personality I admire but do not possess. Once, on a collecting trip when I was an undergraduate, I found a lupine where it shouldn't have been—where no plant should have been—growing in a desert of blasted rubble on a slope inside the burnt-out core of Mount St. Helens, years after the eruption. The nearest vegetation grew miles away on pumice plains around the mountain. After the volcano blew, lupines were among the first plants to sprout on those plains, splashing purple and blue across soil the consistency of ground glass, which is what the volcano spit up: pumice—light, crumbly, and sharp. Lupines live where other plants cannot, breathing nutrients into torn-up soil so others might grow. But I was the first to find any plant where this particular lupine had taken root, this botanical commando showing off its brilliant purples near the lava cone steaming and growing inside the crater. A sort of "Fuck You!" from the plant world to the earth's most awesome power.

I snapped a picture of that lupine. I carry it in my wallet. Taped to the other side is a photo of Kate.

What I mean to say is that Kate was tough. The third day of my visit we were walking through the central marketplace in Madaoua, Kate and I, and Souley, her boyfriend from Senegal. We were in town for a few days because Kate worked with the villagers, planting trees. I'd just met Souley and liked him right away. He let her teach him how to play tennis and even how to drive. For an African man to let a woman lead in a physical contest seemed to me almost unheard of. Not that Souley had a choice. This is Kate we're talking about. She could handle herself with anyone, anywhere.

Like the Madaoua market. When I remember that place, I think of limnology, the science of freshwater lakes and streams. The market was densely compact and diverse, a big space like a great pond-based ecosystem, billowing with hierarchies of species and teeming with predators and parasites, opportunists and victims. A crazy maze of stalls and tables threaded through the market, contained by low concrete walls over a half-mile square. Butchers did their work in the dirt, mingling with vendors of electronics and plastics alongside tables piled high with bolts of cloth. Across the way, women sold vegetables, spices, and grains in great piles. Men traded in camels and goats as they had for a thousand years, but now they worked alongside a row of greasy wooden and metal shacks where other men fixed cars and scooters with parts of their own making. The smell of dung, spices, and engine oil needled my nose. Urchins ran in groups of three and four, picking pockets and stealing from one another; shoppers and merchants sometimes chased after them. The market was a place of evolution without chronology, full of items of custom and necessity from different times and places, all mixed up.

We were standing at a tailor's table, and Kate was running her hands over a piece of cloth, shaking her head and puckering her lips to make dissatisfied noises as she and the merchant argued the price. Souley stood beside her in a white cotton robe, like a long pajama top, and trousers. He was tall and muscled like a runner. He played soccer, though he looked distinguished, with the stately height and bearing of a grandfather clock and a face with pronounced cheekbones, soft eyes that narrowed when he smiled, and a wide mouth that complemented a strong, rounded chin. A face like a coat of arms, announcing a proud lineage. Beside him, the top of Kate's head was even with his shoulder.

Two soldiers in red berets were watching us. When Souley wandered off to buy a transistor radio, these guys surrounded him. They demanded papers. He fumbled with excuses, took his papers from his breast pocket, and dropped them — his identity card and a laminated letter of appointment to the government secondary school, where he taught history. This was not Souley's country. He was Senegalese — yes, an African, but still different. He was Woluf, six feet, six inches tall, with very dark skin. Around him, the soldiers looked like yapping dogs.

Americans roam the world with an enormous sense of entitlement that turns to rage when confronted by official injustice. Not Africans. They endure, they talk, they stall, they promise, they tell stories, they delay. Very effective, some of the time.

I stepped forward, but Kate put a hand on my arm. She watched carefully, as if gathering information. They backed Souley against the plywood wall of a stall. Then she walked over to Souley's side, so the men faced her as well.

Here's what happened. The soldiers laughed and one reached forward to push her away, but Kate caught the man's wrist and twisted it a full turn. The soldier cried out in pain, turning his body to face the other way, his wrist caught firmly in Kate's hand. She forced his arm up. A simple self-defense move.

I could see surprise and pain on the soldier's face. He'd just been handled by a woman. His comrade watched, too dumb-founded to act.

Souley gripped Kate's shoulder, and I could hear him speak to her in French. *"Kate, s'il te plaît, laisse-moi parler avec eux"*—Kate, please, let me talk with them. But she ignored him, and I could hear her speaking in Hausa, rapidly, with confident anger. The crowd had quickly thinned—fear of retribution, I suppose, just for being on the scene. A few traders stood with their hands over their mouths. There were soft cries of *"yaiyaiyai."*

Her hard brown eyes took in the soldier, one hand wrapped around his wrist and the other on his shoulder. Then she pushed him away. He stumbled off. The other soldier followed, and we left in the opposite direction.

Outside the market, Souley and I asked Kate, "What did you say to them?"

She wouldn't answer.

I was sitting with Souley at a tea table late the next afternoon on a roadside in Madaoua. Kate had gone off on an errand in the town, and we were eating fried millet biscuits with our tea. I guess Souley noticed I was eating heartily. He gave me a wide smile.

"You like our food," he said, speaking carefully enunciated English. Good English.

His words, not his English, made me smile in return. "I love food in general," I said. "Just ask my sister." There was a short silence and then I said, "That was quite a scene with the soldiers in the marketplace."

Souley said nothing at first. He finished his biscuits, and washed his hands in a plastic bowl of water on the ground beneath the table. I did the same.

He flicked his hands at the ground, spraying the dirt with drops of water, and started talking. "A few years ago I was a student in Dakar. University was not so easy. The only way to be admitted was on government scholarship to pay for books and food and for a dormitory room, but most of the time the money never came." He laughed. "We could stay in the dormitories, but we had nothing to eat. I was a taxi man for a while. In my third year I helped organize protests at the education ministry, and they arrested me." Souley faced me, his long legs straddling the bench. He folded his arms. "They didn't torture me, not horribly, anyway. They held us in this courtyard, day and night, for six months. Three times a day they made us do this walk under the hot sun." He slid off the bench and squatted, his hands clasped behind his head. "You know, like a duck. They would make us walk this way for an hour in a circle."

He took a few steps, bouncing on his toes in the dust. Some of the other men eating at the table turned and looked. I could see one reason why Souley survived. He was naturally lithe and flexible, and the squat-walk seemed painless to him. He stood up easily, his knees cracking, and sat back on the bench.

"The soldiers would hit us sometimes with belts or rope. They never hit hard enough to make blood. But a few students fainted and were taken away. Some I have never seen again." He shrugged. "One day they let us go."

"You're lucky, Souley."

He looked at me earnestly. "We were lucky those soldiers found us in a market yesterday. If we had not been in a public place, like on a road at night, Kate would have been beaten. She knows that. Whatever she told those soldiers, it was to shame them. She should have stayed out of it. I would have been okay. One day we might see them again." He shook his head.

Kate's form of hepatitis is easy to catch and not often fatal. A doctor at the Madaoua hospital said Kate might have had hepatitis even during my visit. But she never complained and I don't recall symptoms. Sometimes they take months to show up.

She spent a lot of time in the bush and might have gotten the disease from bad water and food, or an exposed cut. I don't know. It's not easy for me to focus on the straight facts of this disease.

The vice consul told me she might even have breathed it in. He said, "We tell all embassy staff not to go outside during the winter winds."

But hepatitis really wasn't her killer. The doctors thought she had appendicitis. Souley says she kept complaining about sharp pains in her abdomen. The abdomen. The liver is located behind the rib cage, above the stomach. The appendix sits far below, near the large intestine. It wasn't her appendix, but her liver! The two organs don't even live in the same neighborhood of the torso.

On the fifth day of my visit we were driving in Kate's Land Cruiser, just the two of us, about fifty miles north of Madaoua. We were a long distance from anywhere, making our way back from a village garden project across grumpy land rich with drifts of loose sand and sudden ravines carved by flash floods. It was late afternoon and across this plateau of gentle hills the sunlight threw long shadows. The car was bouncing hard, and wind gusts punched the windows and pushed sand over ground in foot-thick waves. The wind grew angrier, so the air around the car took on the texture of dirty milk. Scattered prickly prosopis bushes, what we Americans know as mesquite, and knee-high patches of elephant grass poked through the blowing sand. We passed occasional baobab trees with thick gray trunks and leafless twisted limbs. The roots of some stood high above ground where wind had eaten the soil away. Those trees looked like multi-legged creatures fleeing the land.

Then, with the suddenness of a mugging, something wide and black, big enough to block out everything in front of us, slammed into our windshield with a deafening crash. The glass spider-webbed. Kate slowed the car as this black creature struggled, wings slapping the glass, which was now concave. It cradled this bird in a kind of pocket, like a hammock. One leg had punctured the glass, so the bird was caught, its talons close to my face. Kate brought the car to a bumpy halt and the vulture—it was a vulture!—fell from the glass and flopped around on the hood.

I remember opening the door, jumping out to shake off the glass, brushing my clothes and cutting my hands, and then turning to see Kate coming around the back of the car with towels and two water bottles. Her face was bleeding from small cuts. Blood flecked her neck and white T-shirt. I stared at her, though I must have looked as bad.

"You okay?" she asked. She handed me a bottle and a towel. We sat in the sand and silently picked bits of glass out of our hands, our forearms, out of each other's faces and hair, and washed the blood away.

"Damn," Kate said. "Never seen *that* before."

I tried to think of what to say. "When'd you learn to drive?" In high school, driving had terrified her. Then I said, "Where did you learn to drive?"

She laughed a little. "Here."

Kate dabbed a bandanna over my face. She acted quickly and never seemed to waste a step or movement, as if she had perfect, instinctive self-awareness. I could see it in her driving and the way she performed first aid. She looked strong, as if she could get up and walk across the Sahara.

She caught my gaze.

"You learn stuff to get by here," she said. "You learn to roll with things, no matter how weird it gets."

I blushed and remembered something I'm not proud of. I was eight, maybe nine, walking home from school with Kate and two schoolmates, a boy and a girl. I don't recall exactly why, or what was happening between us, but for some reason I craved my sister's attention. Jealousy, probably. She was talking to the two other kids, and I couldn't get anyone to notice me. So I faked a fall, "tripping" on the sidewalk. But Kate and the others just looked at me and kept on walking. The boy and the girl followed Kate. I screamed that I was hurt, I cried and kicked at the cement, but Kate didn't stop.

She knew me. That hurt.

She still bore a faint egg-shaped scar on her forearm where a piece of metal had gone straight through after her school bus rolled off an icy road when she was seven. I'd stayed home sick that day. She always walked to school after that, and anywhere else she could, to avoid traveling in a car. I thought she'd never shake the fear.

The bird lay on the hood, which was smeared with blood and black and gray feathers. We noticed it was missing a leg and that its remaining leg still twitched. The gray, curved beak was still intact. I got up and grabbed a blanket from the Land Cruiser. I covered the vulture, which was now dead, and lifted the thing off the hood. The weight stunned me, and I staggered as the bird's wings pushed against my chest. I carried it a few yards and dumped it in the sand, blanket and all. Then I grabbed more water bottles from our luggage. Kate and I sat and stared at the half-covered bird, spitting dust out of our mouths and coughing. The wind was blowing harder. In the sky, dark clouds thickened, their bottom edges brightening as the sun faded behind the weather.

"Rain coming," Kate said.

We picked out more glass and washed dust and blood away again and again. We laughed a little. Then we smashed out the ruined windshield and collected the glass as best we could in a plastic bag. I found the vulture's other leg lying on the front seat of the car and held it up for Kate to see. She thrust out her hand. "Let me have that," she said, and plucked it from my fingers. She pulled a spare shoelace from her bag and tied the foot to the rearview mirror, so it dangled beneath.

"*Gri-gri*," she said, using a common word for talisman. "That bird will protect us now."

I said nothing.

We finished with the glass and sat to lick our wounds some more. Kate had a bottle of peroxide, and we dabbed the liquid on our faces, arms, and hands, wincing at the sting. Africa is the sort of place where a cut becomes infected in seconds, a factor of heat and humidity, the very dust in the air. We used the whole bottle, all sixteen ounces, and we finished the job with an eight-ounce bottle of my aftershave.

The wind picked up. We had maybe twenty minutes of good daylight left. Kate grabbed binoculars from the car, put one foot on a front tire, and stepped up onto the engine hood and then the roof. A dust storm was blowing in from the northeast; huge clouds were moving fast and swelling in a frenzy. The air felt cooler and I could smell the rain. Kate stood on the roof, pants flapping about her legs. She was staring through binoculars as if expecting to find something significant in all that wind-born fury.

That's when she shouted, "It's like the earth itself rising in rebellion."

I joined her on the roof. "What do you mean?" I asked.

Then, as if to shut me up, sand began to sting our faces as the dust clouds descended. We jumped, whooping and hollering, off the roof to get inside that car, which had seen so much sun and sand that its red finish had been blasted to weak pink.

We shut the doors and wiped dust from our lips. We gulped water and spit on the floor, though much of the water blew back in our faces. We started laughing.

"No windshield," I said.

But we were experienced desert travelers. I pulled lengths of green cotton cloth from our bags, and like nomads we wrapped them around our heads and mouths to make turbans. The world turned gray and the car rattled, creating the sensation that we were being lifted into the air.

Kate threw the Land Cruiser into gear, and we were off across terrain we could barely see, moving as fast as the rolls and dips in the road and Kate's nerve would let us. She was driving as if she could penetrate that storm, seeking some adventure at the heart of it that she hadn't yet experienced. At moments I loved it too, loved the feeling that we were riding high up into that wind. The vulture's foot danced below the mirror. Kate tied it loosely, I think, so its kick and sway would remind us of its presence.

I looked at her, this woman in a white T-shirt speckled with blood. I tried a joke. "Dorothy, Dorothy," I shouted. Kate didn't seem to hear. I stared out at the dust, thinking how in West Africa dust bleeds the horizon at both ends of the day, slowly turning the sky red, as if right there, on that line, Africa is bleeding again.

The rains came like a hydraulic blast, hitting ground stripped of topsoil. The water rushed over what was left — a craggy surface like the dried scab of a wound — gushing into gullies, cutting up roads, and washing away crops. Kate wrestled the Land Cruiser up an embankment to avoid the torrent. The wheels spun on the rain-slick rock, forcing her to drive up the slope in two switchbacks. At the top, she turned the engine off. We spoke little, silenced by the violence of the weather. In our turbans, only our eyes were exposed. Our windbreakers at least kept the sand off our burning skin. At moments when the wind and rain relaxed, I could hear the rush of water, a temporary river that we couldn't see for the dust and dim light.

Kate said, "If you don't count vultures and crazy fucking soldiers, dust storms are the only true form of wildlife left in West Africa."

I hadn't thought of it that way.

Kate said the "war out there" was already lost. "There" being the only regions of the world she knew firsthand. First, the American West, especially Colorado, where we'd grown up. And the "war" being, as she described it, "a struggle to protect the land itself."

"What do you mean?" I asked her. "Protect the land from what?"

She glared at me. "From us," she said. "What else? From our agriculture, from our mining and deforestation. Look around you. Look at this desert. This is our fault."

I am not so sure. But I didn't argue with her.

Reports from the "war" lay in her apartment in the capital, where I stayed my first night in country. Three filing cabinets held her project reports and field interviews, all her frustration in neat black ink. There were stacks of paper in dust-stained covers marked by seals of this or that agency. Problems according to the World Bank, the International Wildlife Fund, the Colorado Division of Wildlife, the African Development Bank, the U.S. Forest Service, the United Nations.

Off the floor I picked up one of her reports, which I'd noticed because she'd hand-titled it in blue-ink block letters — "CRAZIES."

She'd interviewed the survivors of a pitched battle between two villages, over farmland. Seven men fell on one another with hoes and machetes. Three died. Folded inside was a *Denver Post* story about a conflict between ranchers and homeowners furious about cows grazing their yards. A homeowner had shot several cows and then confronted the rancher with the weapon.

Paper lay all over the place. Ripped and wrinkled manila folders were stacked in messy piles. Old newspapers and magazines lay about like fallen leaves. West Africa and the American West according to *Africa Confidential, Audubon, Le Monde, Jeune Afrique, High Country News,* and *Earth Island Journal.*

I'd never been political. Life seemed safer in science.

I borrowed a book I saw on her desk. I still have it. A leather-bound edition of Rudyard Kipling's collected verse, published in 1927. In the table of contents Kate had checked off in pencil a favorite poem, *The Settler,* which Kipling wrote in 1903, a tribute to the end of the Boer War in South Africa.

Kate could recite it by heart. She did this, for example, after the vulture hit. We were sitting on the ground, with sand hitting so hard we couldn't tell the difference between its sting against our skin and the pain caused by shards of glass. She stared at the bird and began speaking, coughing but determined, as if offering the last rites. She shouted the lines above the wind.

> Here, in a large and sunlit land . . .
> I will lay my hand in my neighbor's hand,
> And together we will atone
> For the set folly and the red breach
> And the black waste of it all . . .

She recited them badly, emotion and meaning distorted by her raised voice.

"Kipling!" she shouted at me.

I stood up. "Kipling?" I shouted back at her. "He was a racist. What does Kipling have to do with it?"

She looked at me. "Maybe," she shouted, "but I like that poem. It smells of regret."

♦ ♦ ♦

People who suffer from hepatitis may have no symptoms or have all of them. That's the nature of disease: often there is a warning, but sometimes none. Hepatitis tends to show itself in ruthless ways: yellow skin, dark urine, and fatigue so intense that any movement is a labor. The sclera, what we call the "whites" around the iris of the eyes, turns yellow or a pale pea green. And then delirium arrives. I don't completely understand how hepatitis works, but I know enough. I think of Dutch elm disease, which works beneath the bark of its victim, slowly turning the milky white wood to a deep red-brown as it robs the tree of water until it wilts and dies, sometimes just falling over. I know there are five kinds of hepatitis. I know that Kate's liver was not removing enough bilge material from her kidneys. Doctors call it bilirubin, the stuff that causes skin to turn milky yellow, as if it is about to melt. Souley told me he saw "the color of death" in Kate's eyes. He begged her to see a doctor. He said she was difficult to talk to in those last weeks, unusually silent and not always coherent. She kept calling Souley "you," as if she couldn't remember his name. He could not get her out of bed some days. Souley said it was as if her spirit had been replaced by a different one.

They went to see a marabout. Kate's idea. She began wearing that vulture's claw around her neck. She paid a few thousand francs for more *gri-gri,* little leather amulets she wore around her neck and waist. The marabout wrote prayers in Arabic on tiny bits of paper and sewed them inside the amulets. Kate bought two powdered elixirs, herbs of some sort, which she mixed with water.

Jesus.

On my last night with Kate before I returned to my work in Burkina Faso, we were drinking beer on the dirt patio of this roadside bar on the edge of the capital. We'd been visiting village gardens all day. We were sweaty, and dust made my skin itch. Kate silently made notes on a dusty legal pad. That irritated me. I wanted conversation and a connection with her. I wanted attention. I said her report on the village machete war was hard to believe. She fixed her eyes on me and began describing the wounds and how men fought without hesitation, with the energy of rage and starvation.

"Half-starved men fighting half-starved men," she said.

Suddenly, we both looked up, alerted by the sound of screaming and shouting. A man in bare feet and torn, dust-stained pants and T-shirt sprinted out of the shadows down the street. He ran past the bar and into the open door of a cinderblock building under construction across the street. In the dark we could barely make out the walls and the outline of the open doorway. Three men, one carrying a pipe, followed him. We heard more shouting and screaming.

Kate was staring hard at the doorway. She rose from her seat and pushed her chair back. I stood and put a hand on her shoulder. "What are you thinking?" I said. "We can't go in there."

She sat down heavily. "Sorry. It's crazy. I'm compulsive sometimes."

"Who are they chasing?"

"Someone they think is a thief," she said in a whisper. "They'll catch him and kill him."

Kate admitted herself to the French hospital near Madaoua while on one of her working trips. Souley told me that. She'd called him at his school in the capital, using the phone at the Madaoua post office. She told him she was tired, very, very tired, and frightened, and that he'd find her at the hospital.

He traveled there by bush taxi, an old minivan. Two hundred miles in fifteen hours. It was dawn when he arrived. She died a few hours later. Souley called me in Burkina Faso from a phone at the hospital.

It took me three days to get a flight to the capital. Souley met me at the airport and told me the Peace Corps had already brought Kate's body to the city. That's when I met the vice consul, signed the death certificate, and arranged to have my sister flown back home. Souley and I took a few days to clean out her apartment. We didn't talk much. I suppose we were too confused and full of grief to know what to say. He said he would probably return to Senegal. When we finished, I thanked him and gave him a couple hundred dollars for plane fare or whatever. But he refused the cash, even when I tried to press it into his hands. We parted outside the door of the apartment. He said, "I loved Kate," and he was gone.

But I couldn't go just yet. I decided to travel upcountry and visit the hospital in Madaoua where Kate died. At the motor park in the city, I hired a Peugeot sedan in good repair, and a driver. The journey took most of a day. When I arrived in early evening, the hospital was crowded with people, a world of triage and pain, full of the smell of bitter chemicals and disease.

Strawberry yogurt and gasoline. Kate's words.

This was the only hospital in the country outside the capital, and three doctors worked there. The fourth, the man who operated on Kate, had been sent back to France. Three doctors for five hundred thousand square miles and ten million people. They were treating every type of disease there. Malaria, dysentery, yellow fever, cancer, meningitis, typhus, tuberculosis, AIDS, guinea worm, common wounds, the whole list. The French had built the hospital back in the 1920s. It stood behind a thick stone wall, off the main highway that crosses the country west to east. Four or five large buildings, stone and concrete, with metal roofs, made up the hospital. Patients slept in Quonset huts, those corrugated metal buildings that look like barrels cut in half. Staff and families lived in prefabricated aluminum houses, all nicely shaded by palm and acacia trees. There was a small stone chapel, too. You could hear the low roar of power generators inside an old metal shack. When I got there, I walked around first. No one gave me a second look.

African families camped in the courtyard outside the Quonset huts. Some had been there for months, providing food and comfort, waiting for loved ones to recover or die. Every hallway in every building was crammed with people. The day I was there, so full of righteous anger, a bus had gone off the road a few miles away. Bush taxi drivers brought the wounded and dead in creaky, ancient Peugeot station wagons. Maybe fifty people.

I got a few minutes with the senior doctor. He wore a blue smock dirty with blood and a cloth cap tied tight around his head. He seemed young and spoke good English. But his face was pale and sweaty, unshaven. The skin around his eyes was dark and puffy. He licked his lips a lot. There was shouting all around in

French and Hausa, and equipment and people being wheeled about. Bush taxi drivers argued with orderlies about payment for transporting accident victims.

He took me to his office, a tiny room full of supplies stacked in cardboard boxes. There was a metal desk crowded with paper and two simple wooden chairs. He remembered my sister from the cholera epidemic. She was a brave woman, he said, and he was sorry about what had happened. We talked for a few minutes about hepatitis. Then we were both silent. Finally, he said, "We make a lot of fast decisions here. We make mistakes. I suppose you can sue us."

He looked embarrassed for a moment, as if his words surprised him, as if he hadn't meant to say them. He was annoyed, I think, wanting to get back to more urgent matters. I sympathized. He offered to talk to me later. Then he turned and walked back into the suffering.

I swear I felt Kate standing there telling me to get the hell out — in those very words — to get out and let those people do their jobs.

# FREELANCING

## 1.

IT'S BEST TO START with hard details. Think of the props: fifty or so goats, a few cattle, and "the talent," so to speak — the inhabitants of a West African village, maybe one hundred people — elderly women and men, a few younger adults, and so many children. And there was Richard, the director. Richard Ward. In a way, it was fun to watch.

Think of "the set," the village of Tabotaki and its square mud homes, dusty footpaths winding among them. It was the kind of late afternoon when the sun blurred in dusty air, a soft light in waning desert heat. Good for taking photographs. Think of the "assignment," the "story." Think of drought — the "starving" animals, the "grim" elders in long brown tunics, and the "stars," the children. Richard selected seven, three boys and four girls, the dirtiest. ("I don't want smiles," Richard shouted, in his sharp Scottish twang. "Grim, I want grim.") To get the job they had to have extended bellies, the result of too much carbohydrate and no protein. ("We have to tell the story," he said.) Then — I remember this clearly — he said the children must change to rougher clothes or be photographed nude. He scooped up a handful of sand and rubbed it on a boy's face and T-shirt. He held the boy, who was about six years old, by the shoulder with one hand as he spread sand in his hair. The child screamed and broke away. Villagers laughed and pointed. Richard shrugged and turned his head from side to side as if looking for another child.

These things I saw.

Richard moved like a dirt devil — especially when he was nervous and trying to think — quick steps, this way and that, a camera in hand and another swinging from a strap around his neck. Short locks of red hair curled from beneath his khaki baseball cap, making him look younger than he was. The sun had turned his ears and neck pink. He wore high-top white sneakers and dirty khaki pants. A dust- and sweat-stained blue cotton T-shirt stuck to his bony frame.

He stopped pacing. With his left hand he plucked a plastic lighter and cigarette from his shirt pocket. To watch Richard smoke was to watch him reload. He lit the cigarette and sucked deeply on it, hunching over and raising his shoulders as he inhaled. Then he withdrew the cigarette, which was clipped between two fingers, and arched his lanky, thin body, head back, face to the sky, and hands at his sides, as he exhaled and took a deep breath. He took a couple more puffs and flicked the half-smoked butt away. A teenage boy picked the thing up and put it to his lips.

Richard turned to a group of older men standing a few yards away. With his hands raised, shaking them for emphasis, he pleaded in English, which no one spoke. "Look, people, we're reporting on disaster here. I need cooperation!"

The elders frowned and nodded respectfully, clucking their tongues. Our driver and translator, a young university student, watched silently from several yards away, with his arms folded. Richard clasped his hands behind his head. He paced for a minute and then let his hands fall to his thighs. He turned to face this young man. He pointed at him. "Do your fucking job," he said. "Translate!"

Richard and I were gathering material for newspaper stories on famine relief. That's our job. He takes pictures and I write. It was the young man's idea to bring us here. I don't recall his name, nor can I find it in my notes. He was twenty-two, tall, and muscular, and he strode forward with his head bowed. His feet, in leather sandals, touched the earth soundlessly, toes pointed forward. He wore a perfectly pressed light gray cotton tunic and trousers, and he translated Richard's English into Hausa in a toneless voice, which softened the words. But Richard began talking over the translation.

"Can't you see how important this is for your country?" Richard stared at the elders, dropped his hands to his sides, and squinted. "For your village?" The translator fell silent and walked away. Richard didn't notice.

The young man hiked up a slope that rose above the village. When I caught up to him, he did not acknowledge me. Together we walked on bare earth that felt like hard pavement under my feet. Farmers did some damage to this land, cutting forests to make room for crops, and the desert, too, was eating arable land under its own power. But no one knows precisely how such big expanses of African soil came to be so unforgiving. No one clearly deserves all the blame, no single group of people or specific natural event, and I've talked to everyone who would know — scientists and activists, old farmers, historians, and the leaders who make laws.

My companion looked up the slope, taking long steps on ground littered with fist-sized rocks. We stopped a quarter-mile above the village, clusters of sun-baked mud compounds whose arrangement looked accidental, as if they'd spilled off the slope and piled up at the bottom. The wind must have spared some sandy topsoil around Tabotaki. Here and there millet and sorghum plants grew in patches, like outsiders, in nervous little groups. Grass no longer survived, but on the plain beyond the village a few thorny bushes and acacia trees clung by their roots. A giant baobab, with a trunk as wide as a school bus and great gnarled limbs like massive hands, guarded Tabotaki on its southern edge.

I spoke in French. "How do you know Tabotaki?" I asked. The young man had a wide, fleshy face with deep-set, unblinking green eyes. He never smiled. Our trip had begun in the capital two days earlier, and from the start he'd kept a distance, answering questions bluntly.

He looked at me, hands folded behind his back. He said, "I

grew up in a village like this, near here." He nodded in the direction of Richard and the children. "I am one of those children. I herded animals; I planted manioc."

In the village below we could see Richard on his knees, trying to get a shot of children hitting goats with sticks. He held a camera in his left hand and gestured with his right, his shouting punctuated by the bleating of goats. Somehow, he'd lost his hat.

Impulsively, I said, "I'm sorry."

We were silent for a time. Then he spoke in a quiet voice. "You have your image of Africans, like we are animals. We've been working these lands a thousand years, and you portray us to the world like we can't think, as if you Europeans invented agriculture and government and soil conservation, while we Africans invented only misery."

He turned and walked down the slope. By morning we were back in the capital city. I never saw the young man again.

The visit to Tabotaki happened in 1989, which was a good year because it rained across many parts of inland West Africa. In places closer to the river and the capital, where the wind had not done its work on topsoil, fields of young millet and maize looked dark green at dawn, the leaves beginning to shrug in a breeze. Green spilled to the horizon, rippling over shallow ravines and hills. Across this land, farmers built egg-shaped silos of mud, with roofs of thatch layered in cones.

The storms that year brought life back to land the Sahara seemed to have annexed for good. In some places, the green appeared to suddenly erase the desert, or temporarily replace it, like a holographic image. Across the Sahel rain is fickle, though, blessing one village while ignoring another or falling with such violence that crops and homes are washed away. In early summer, the monsoon drives cool air heavy with moisture inland from the Atlantic Ocean. That air forces the drier, hotter air high into the atmosphere. But the heat of the Sahara pushes from the opposite direction, keeping the ground hot so the rising heat never really ceases. Often the heat shreds the monsoon, evaporating the moisture before it reaches ground. But in a fortunate year like this one, the rain overwhelms the desert. People welcomed the rains, but warily. They spoke of unrest among the spirits. "They are fleeing the land and sky," they said. "The rains cannot be trusted."

## 2.

WHEN VISITING AFRICA, I give people my office address in Paris. Never my home. That address is not auspicious.

My wife and I visited Paris in 1970. The city was cheap and lovely. We stayed, I as a freelance journalist and Karen as an English teacher. We have an apartment near the Boulevard St. Germaine on the rue du Colonel Moss, named after an infamous late-nineteenth-century explorer of West Africa, who dealt with resistance to French rule by forcing suspected rebels to shoot their own children. This is why, when I travel to Africa, I tell people only that I live near Lycée Louis Pasteur, where Karen works, rather than the truth, which is that I live on a road named for a psychopath.

Richard laughed at my deception and sometimes blew my secret. "He lives on a street that honors Colonel Moss," he once blurted out, when a government press officer in Mali asked me, by way of conversation, where I lived in Paris.

I don't know Richard well. I am sixty-three years old and he is a decade younger. In fact, I've rarely spent more than a few hours —and once just a couple of days—in his presence. But I've been around him dozens of times and crossed his tracks all over: at the trial of a former SS officer in Paris; in South Africa just after Nelson Mandela's release; in the former Zaire during Mobutu's last days, and in what replaced that bastard country, the new Democratic Republic of the Congo; and while covering the coronation of a king in Thailand. From one spot or another, I have written about tragedy and fortune and bumped into Richard.

I would tell Karen stories about him, that "brash" photographer I'd keep running into on assignment. Years ago, before the day that Richard and I visited Tabotaki, Karen was going through the mail over breakfast and handed me a copy of the *Columbia Journalism Review*. Richard looked out from the cover, with that

hard, blank look I'd come to know, his red hair still short and unruly as if it had not grown from the day I told him to get it cut.
His brow was furrowed, and his mouth was set, with his bottom
lip slightly tucked in under his teeth. Richard had deep blue eyes,
which an African farmer once told me are the mark of a man who
brings bad things. Blue is the color of the empty sky, "the color
of death," the farmer said. In the photograph, the veins on Richard's neck stood out and his chin seemed more prominent, making him seem even thinner. He wore a dirty khaki vest, like a fishing jacket, and held a camera in his hands. Another hung from a
strap around his neck. The headline, in black letters, ran down the
cover beside his face: "Photographer Chronicles the Soviets in Afghanistan and Wins a Pulitzer."

Karen said, "That's him, isn't it? He's that photographer you always talk about."

"Yeah, it is."

"He's good. I'd love to meet him someday."

## 3.

I LIKE TO THINK some of us in journalism are not voyeurs or
mere distributors of the pornography of poverty and decay, of
cultural destruction. I like to think that we deal in information
that provides people at home the energy and time to take up other
causes, what Richard likes to call "luxury activism." The campaign
against fur coats, for example, and the protection of the Yellow-
stone buffalo, or the work of people who take up residence for
years at a time in centuries-old redwoods. I like to think that what
I do is report the hard stuff, the life-and-death struggles unfolding
in countries where people cannot yet take for granted their own
survival. But the fact is I'm seldom able to spend the time to be
thorough. I'm never free to stay in a place long enough to understand the point of view of the people on the scene, like the nine-
year-olds holding automatic weapons at roadblocks or the people
trying to live on land that rain has forsaken for a hundred years. I
do not understand what that kind of survival is about. But I try.

Richard — he is the chief voyeur. The pornographer, though I am not without guilt. I went to Ivory Coast once to write about malaria. One day I sat for hours at the foot of a hospital bed watching a ten-year-old boy in a malarial coma. He lay on his back as if dead. His mouth and eyes stayed open, but his chest swelled with breath and his fingers and toes twitched. The parents, both teachers, knelt at their son's side, stroking his head and arms. We were waiting for him to die, the parents in grief and I in a quest for information. I wanted to describe what such death was like, but the parents became annoyed at my presence. The boy's mother got up and pulled me from my chair, tugging at my shirt. "*Allez,*" she said, "*allez.*" I left quietly. For all I know her son recovered.

This form of death doesn't interest Richard. "Malaria is intransitive death," he told me. "A mosquito bites a man. He lies down, he shivers and loses his head, and he dies. Who cares?"

Here is the kind of picture that does interest Richard Ward. In 1983, he captured that now-famous moment when a Russian soldier in Afghanistan emerged from a firefight with the *mujahideen* in a mountain village. In that picture, which captures one second in a man's life, fear and dirt etch lines of exhaustion on that soldier's face. He looks out from half a million magazine covers. The man, his head clean-shaven and smeared with grime, is coming down a rocky pathway, an automatic rifle in his hand and his uniform covered in gray dust. Dirt colors the hollows of his cheeks and the deep lines of his forehead, making them look as if they'd been carved into place. He squints at the camera with his mouth wide open, not to speak, but in fatigue and pain, as if he cannot control his jaw muscles. His lips are wet, and sweat or saliva drips from his chin. I love to believe that the soldier's face, with that squint around his eyes, also shows absolute annoyance, maybe even outrage. He was, after all, looking right at the camera. Right at Richard. That photograph got Richard on the cover of the issue of *Columbia Journalism Review* that Karen showed me at breakfast one morning.

When I was younger, like Richard, I did this job for the rush and the illusion that I was telling important stories. My work would unnerve people at home, causing them to put down their coffee and ponder what it would be like to experience the slow starvation of one's own family in a drought or the slaughter of that family at the hands of strangers — something that happened to a farmer I interviewed in Liberia.

I saw Richard first in the country in 1977, during another failed rainy season in West Africa, when he had no career and no name. He had just a camera and some savings to get him started. Early one morning, at a hotel called the Malam Daouda, I was returning to my room from breakfast, walking along the second-floor balcony, when I saw this man in the parking lot below, confronting Africa in his fashion, which is to say that he was screaming in a Scottish brogue and waving his arms. In a way, even then, it was fun to watch.

"What are you doing?" Richard shouted, as he paced the pavement in front of an old Peugeot sedan, apparently his car. A group of Africans had decided to camp at that spot, blocking his way. He stopped with his hands on his hips, this six-foot, four-inch-tall white man with wild red hair, looking down on the women, children, and men who were sitting on mats spread on the asphalt. He began pacing again, taking small steps this way and that and shouting with his head down, to no one in particular, as if practicing a grand speech. He had a camera bag slung over his shoulder, and it bounced off his hip as he walked. That uncombed red hair bobbed with every step. "This is a parking lot, a parking lot, you cocksuckers!" When he paced, he would run his hands through his hair, clasp them behind his head, and then let them fall to his thighs. (Over the years I've come to expect that gesture — the hands, the hair, the slap on the thighs — as a punctuation mark expressing Richard's frustration.) His hard-edged speech was the vocal equivalent of flying glass.

Several Fulani families had moved in and made the parking lot their encampment. There was plenty of room around the twenty or so cars parked there, mostly heavy four-wheel-drive agency vehicles belonging to the UN, Lutheran World Relief, and the like. The Fulani are nomads, cattle herders and warriors from the arid lands of the Sahel. They like to settle where they want and move on when they like. But the vast grasslands that supported that nomad life are gone, forcing the Fulani into conflict with settled farmers over dwindling arable ground. To survive, many have chosen to settle on farms and establish villages, while others still roam, often wandering into cities to sell what they can. Their appearance is unmistakable. Fulani men carry a long sword at the waist and wear a wide-brimmed conelike hat made of leather and tightly woven grass. The women dye their lips blue and keep their hair in tight buns on the top and sides of the head. They all have facial scars—short strikes cut into the skin high on the cheekbones and dyed blue, a sort of identification code in the African ethnic landscape, its permanence both beautiful and horrifying.

Why did they settle here? The capital city attracted refugees for all sorts of reasons. People fled land that could no longer feed them. Others wished to escape danger—rebel soldiers from a group angry with the government were recruiting in villages and shooting chiefs who didn't provide food or young men to fight. The rebels operated like the French before them, who punished villagers for failing to meet quotas for crops or raise the labor needed to build roads, sewer trenches, and whatever else they needed. Also, beyond the city, land mines killed farmers and herders in fields they had worked for generations. The city grew by the day. Mile upon mile of metal, wooden, and mud shanties spiraled outward from the city center, across sand and rock. When the rains came, the mud melted and shanties blew away.

I leaned against the wall in the hotel's arched entranceway and counted twenty-four people in the parking lot, which lay across the street from the city's densely crowded marketplace. A few men squatted around a teapot set on the coals of a fire built on the asphalt, their faces obscured by pointed leather hats with wide brims. Women, small children, and a dozen goats were gathered near them. They'd come to sell their handmade crafts, and by camping in that parking lot they'd redrawn the market's borders. No fence or wall surrounded the lot. Its only defense was the hotel guard, an old man who spent his days on a metal lawn chair set beside the hotel entrance. He likely didn't see a problem with people occupying such a large space. The Fulani spread out leather-bound jewelry boxes, sheaths for knives, and piles of dried meat and goatskins. They'd come to do business, and so had Richard.

The Fulani men looked at Richard as he sputtered and shook his head. They sipped their tea and stared at him glumly, swords across their laps, while the women softly laughed and talked among themselves. The children stared. I walked around the parking lot and threaded my way across the street, through cars, bicycles, and motor scooters, to the market, where the old hotel guard was drinking tea with friends. I told him about the problem in the parking lot. As we spoke, the din of voices and car horns rose as three camels appeared on the street, forcing traffic to the margins. The beasts walked with their heads raised high, moving with a deliberate and softly bobbing grace, as if walking on air. No one seemed to be leading them.

I looked back to the old man, who nodded and smiled. *"Ahh, oui,"* he said, *"Monsieur Ward."* I returned to the hotel and went up to my room. From my open window, just above the lot, I watched Richard plead with the women to move, as the guard spoke to the men. Finally, the men nodded, smiled, rose to their feet, and spoke to the women, while Richard paced. They all made room so he could move his car. They waved and smiled at him.

"About bloody time," Richard shouted.

I first met Richard in a hotel bar that same night. I made a point of meeting him. Richard had been in country only a few days. He was good; I saw that quickly. And young, twenty-seven, he later told me. He would sit at the bar with his photos splayed out, smoking and drinking beer from a glass, his work there for everyone to see. (He developed his photos in his hotel bathroom, with a red bulb fixed to a flashlight on a metal plate he screwed into the wall, and towels wadded beneath the door crack.) At first I thought that was the only point of his being in the bar — to advertise himself and pick up another job, or one of the women streaming through the hotel on various assignments.

I was wrong, at least in part. I watched a German woman, a journalist I knew, walk over and ask about his photographs. She smiled and said something I couldn't hear. She reached across the bar and picked up a photo. Her face changed to a studied frown as she held it, slanting it to catch light from behind the bar. Richard drew on his cigarette and stared at her.

Quietly, he said, "Fuck off." I didn't hear the words, but I read them on his lips. He took another drag on his cigarette and turned his head to blow smoke at the floor. The noise in the bar hushed, stifled by this sudden tension. The woman frowned. She dropped the photo in front of him, gave a kind of half laugh (what else could she do?), and walked away. Once Richard spit those words, he never seemed to notice the reaction.

Even then, as a young man, Richard had this sharp desert-rat look, which for some in the expatriate lifestyle is an affectation, an attempt to look rough. But in Richard it was genuine. He had long, oily hair that sprouted from his head in clumps, barely touching his shoulders. In those days he wore T-shirts and jeans everywhere he went. Photographers can get away with that, even at formal events. He seldom shaves, even now, and he doesn't seem to eat at all, which means he's rail thin, and his height accentuates his slimness. There are a lot of guys like him in this business, kind of crazy, kind of weird, with "field bravado," as we call it, but Richard is believable. He cares about the end product, the picture, nothing else.

Later, I would seek him out for assignments on stories I covered. It was never my idea. The editor of a magazine I wrote for in New York had spotted one of Richard's photographs in a newspaper — Richard had managed to get to the remote Saharan crash site of an Air France flight that had blown up in midair and killed 120 people — and told me to get in touch with him. Richard had gotten a shot of a Berber nomad picking through the wreckage. In the background a camel stood tethered to what remained of the tail fin, which was emblazoned with the French tricolor. Richard wired the photos unsolicited to agencies in New York and Paris. He won the notice he wanted. "Get him," the editor said. "He does good work."

But that night I'd never heard of him. I was drinking with a couple of acquaintances and watched as Richard leaned against the bar, smoking, with a cigarette held between two fingers. He cupped his chin with the other hand, a man unto himself, drinking glass after glass, drawing on smoke after smoke. He was fun to watch, though he didn't seem drunk. His fingers concealed half his face as if supporting a mask that wouldn't stay fixed. His fingers flitted over his bottom lip, picked at his teeth, and rubbed his nose. Occasionally he'd pick up his beer with his free hand and sip, smacking his lips as he set the glass down to take another drag on the cigarette, his shoulders hunched forward.

A few minutes after the German woman rejoined friends at another table, I walked up and peeked over Richard's shoulder at the photographs. He turned and looked at me, the hand with the cigarette a few inches from his face.

"What can I do for you?" he asked. He blew smoke out of the side of his mouth.

In front of him, on top of a messy sprawl of photographs, lay a black-and-white of an African woman screaming in rage. In the picture's slightly blurred background were a few cars and people, who paid no attention to the scene. The woman didn't appear to be injured, and she was looking directly at the camera, with both fists raised, framing her face. She was looking at Richard. I suppressed a smile. Think of her point of view. Being approached suddenly by this particular young man, with his camera and flaming hair, would make any strong emotional reaction, rage or whatever, completely understandable. A plate of lemon slices sat atop the photos on the bar. Richard sucked on one between sips of beer, letting the seeds linger in his mouth before spitting them into an empty glass. I studied the image of the woman for a few seconds and then tapped the photo with a pen drawn from my shirt pocket.

I told him, "Get close to your subject."

## 4.

RICHARD ALWAYS got close, but not the same way I did. He went fast, which is to say he never got involved; he followed the stories but never got caught up in details. I like details because they give me a sense of the big picture. I like knowing that in Hausaland women own cattle and crops and control the household money. But I hate human conflict, the stories of wars, massacres, and coups d'état, which generate the stuff that photo editors and people like Richard Ward call "sexy." It bothers me, for example, that tourism contributes $25 million a year to the economy of Rwanda, and that part of that profit comes from thirty-five "genocide sites" the government recently opened as tourist attractions.

"The trick is not to care," Richard said once.

I learned that about him.

Here's what I mean. I'm thinking of events surrounding a series of photos Richard made of an African woman mourning over the body of young girl, which happened just a few months after we met in the country. This was August 1977. The president, a certain general, invited the press and diplomatic corps to visit a farming village with him just north of the capital. I'd agreed to accept the American ambassador's offer of a ride there. The president wanted to make the point that the countryside was safe and that he cared about his people. I convinced the ambassador to let a photographer come along. That's when I told Richard to get his hair cut, "if you want to be taken seriously."

He said, "Whatever, boyo. Colleagues now, are we?"

He met me in the hotel lobby an hour before dawn, in boots, jeans, and a white collared shirt, his camera bag slung over his shoulder. His hair was freshly cut and his face clean-shaven. The morning was hot and breezeless, and his hair was wet and matted flat, highlighting a narrow face like that of a Roman general, with a prominent nose that announced ruddy cheeks and a wide chin. He stood there, in the middle of the open lobby area, with a cigarette clipped between two fingers of his left hand at his side, a few inches from his thigh.

I had to repress a laugh. For a moment he looked like a desk clerk, which is when I asked his age.

"I'm twenty-seven," he said, staring at the floor and exhaling, "just twenty-seven." He lifted his head and blew the rest of the smoke at the ceiling.

The ambassador arrived in a white Chevrolet Suburban with an American flag mounted on the front fender. We joined the president's motorcade at an appointed site on the outskirts of the city as the sun began to color the horizon. The heat wasn't yet awful, which is why the president timed his "visits with the people" so early in the day. The drive took half an hour, with six cars from various embassies, and eight Toyota Land Cruiser pickup trucks full of soldiers. The president's black Land Rover (a gift of the British) was wedged square in the middle. We drove to avoid ambush, moving at eighty miles an hour on a wonderfully straight asphalt road (a gift of the Canadians), just six meters wide and pointing north toward the Sahara, like a floating bridge across the vastness. After half an hour the motorcade slowed down as it approached the village, which the road bisected. Soldiers directed the embassy cars to pull off on the left shoulder. They surrounded the cars and pointed their weapons (gifts of the French) at us.

"They won't let us leave the car," the ambassador said to Richard and me, "until the president begins his tour ahead of us."

In cool bulletproof and soundproof isolation, we waited with the ambassador, his African driver, and two marines dressed in civilian clothes, one in front and one in the second seat beside the ambassador. Richard and I sat in the third seat. We watched through the thicket of gun barrels as the president walked down the road with his aides, waving and shaking hands with villagers, on his way to tour a garden project. Children lined the road through the village, shouting the president's name and clapping in time as their feet pounded a rhythm in the dust. They wore white T-shirts bearing a portrait of the general bedecked in a military tunic and cap. A light tank (another gift from the French) stood on watch on a hill above the village, its long gun aimed at the horizon.

The U.S. ambassador folded his arms. "Boys in uniforms," he mumbled. "God, I hate this place."

I didn't know this ambassador well. He was career Foreign Service, not a political appointee, which means I expected a cooler head. But he fidgeted during the drive out and now he rubbed his hands together nervously and leaned forward, with his elbows on his knees. He kept glancing from his watch, to the marine beside him, and then to the scene outside the window.

In a soft voice Richard corrected him. "These *boys* carry guns," he said. The ambassador appeared not to hear him. I looked at Richard. His bluntness made me like him, if only for that compulsive moment of truth.

The Chevy's air conditioner whirred. Outside, the president walked slowly, accompanied by a procession of aides in green field uniforms and blue and white pastel robes. He was a thin man, with a long face and slightly sunken cheeks. His uniform khaki tunic hung from his shoulders as if from a coat hanger. He wore a khaki peaked cap, with a green band around the stock, and shiny black leather shoes. A gentle wind tugged at his trousers, pulling the fabric against his thin legs. Long ago, he'd been a sergeant in the French army and had tended goal on the army football team. He was wounded in Indochina in 1951, taking a bullet through his shoulder. He walked gracefully now, gazing at some children who came up the road with a group of village men. The children danced and clapped, and the general looked on, his brow furrowed. Then he turned, with his entourage, up a pathway that led through the village to the fields. The president disappeared from sight.

The soldiers lowered their guns and followed him, while others spread out through the village. The ambassador said, "Let's go," and he opened his door. The heat descended on our skin instantly, like a heavy grip. The ambassador walked up the roadside, between the marines. I followed, making sure my notebook was tucked in my trousers, beneath my shirt, where it could not be seen. Richard, camera bag over his shoulder, was already several yards ahead. He turned and snapped a few pictures of the ambassador.

Then we heard shooting. At the sound of the first burst of fire, the marines bundled the ambassador right back to the Suburban, as if they'd expected the shots. They picked him up, hooking an arm under each shoulder, and ran to the car. Screaming villagers were running in the road, but I could still see Richard, that shock of short red hair weaving upstream through panicked people. I caught up to him, and we made our way carefully off the road and up the pathway the president had taken through the village. We hugged the mud walls of houses along the path and stopped now and then to listen. We passed the bodies of two children and a farmer, Richard snapping pictures as we walked. I do not know why, but in those minutes the sliding click of his camera seemed terribly loud. By the time we got to the fields, the shooting had dwindled to an occasional shot. There was shouting and wailing. Soldiers, we learned later, had hidden the president in one of the mud homes. He was unharmed. Villagers and soldiers ran about. Gunfire had killed a small girl, and her blood was sprayed across the leaves of the sorghum plants against which she fell. An older woman, her head wrapped in a bright green cloth, knelt on the ground beside the body and sobbed, her head on the girl's shoulder and her arms folded against her own stomach. I stared at this scene, feeling strangely calm, transfixed by how quickly and easily death had come. Richard and I looked around, and I began judging the risk of being seen taking a photograph or making notes, but Richard had already made his decision. He walked to the girl's body and knelt across from the sobbing woman. I was standing just a few feet away and could see that bullets had minced the child's torso. Blood covered the arms of the sobbing woman.

Richard took a light meter from his bag. He tapped it with his fingertips and held it over the girl's body, near the head of the woman, who was oblivious to his presence. A few feet away lay an overturned metal bowl, with its contents of dried tomatoes spilled on the ground. The woman buried her face in the dirt. Her fingers clutched at the girl's bloody clothing, a long one-piece dress with a floral pattern of bright yellows and greens. The girl's face was curiously unsoiled. Her mouth and eyes were still open, capturing the shock of the moment, but not the pain. There had been no time for pain. Flies had already begun to buzz around her face and form an odd gray outline along her lips, indifferent to the grieving woman. The girl's face had been recently scarred. Three-inch-long vertical strikes, deep and still pink, perhaps only days old, shone from the dark skin over her cheekbones.

Richard stood up, leaving his camera bag on the ground. He began snapping pictures from different standing angles. Then he dropped back to his knees, and then flat on his stomach, and then stood again, walking round and round the grieving woman

and the body. He went through several rolls of film, changing cartridges quickly. He gave two to me and put some in his pockets.

I've witnessed a few situations like this in my time and never
gotten used to it. In Africa, suffering and violence seem to be a
surreal and permanent part of the landscape, the offshoot of a
blurred cycle of political oppression and corruption, military up-
risings, and famine; in West Africa, death arrives, on average, at
age forty-three. Years ago in Benin a young soldier at a roadblock
put his pistol to my head when I hesitated to pay a "passage tax."
The weapon turned out to be a wooden toy, painted black and issued to this kid because the government could not afford to arm
most of its soldiers. He grinned and said, "Boom." In Nigeria, during the last days of the Biafran War in 1970, I watched an officer
shoot a rebel prisoner at a roadblock. The officer had stepped out
of a car and was speaking with the members of a patrol who had
brought the prisoner in. The man was sitting on the ground, bent
over, with his chin on his chest and his hands tied behind him.
The officer drew his pistol and shot the captive in the head, the
bullet punching his body backward onto the ground. I have never
forgotten the abruptness of this action: no events leading up to it,
no conclusion to it, no trace of any emotion. I carried a camera
back then, and the officer invited me to photograph him kneeling beside the body, with his pistol drawn. I obliged him. Then he
wanted me to photograph him as he cut off the dead man's penis.
I have not carried a camera since.

I looked back at the girl's body, trying to reconstruct the last
steps of the errand that ended here. Her arms and legs were
spread out. Her head was cocked slightly to the right, and her skin
had begun to gray. Flies covered her face now and buzzed thickly
about the head of the woman hunched over her body, her hands
clutching the cloth covering the girl's stomach. The woman buried
her face in that cloth, and when she lifted her head to breathe, her
face was shiny with blood. I was aware of my own breathing and
the woman's sobbing. After a few moments, I realized the woman
was murmuring, "Alllahhh, Alllahhh," over and over. All I could
do was watch.

Then Richard did something extraordinary. He was squat-

ting near the girl's feet, trying to get an angle on the body with
the sun behind him, but the woman was in his way, rocking back
and forth against the body as if her grief might call back the girl's
soul. Richard stood and walked over to the woman. He tapped her
on the shoulder. "Excuse me," he said, "excuse me, I need you to
move, please." He touched her again, jabbing her shoulder a little
with his fingertips. "Can't you move? I need a photo of her alone."

At that moment we heard loud voices behind us, and a soldier grabbed me roughly by the collar. Two soldiers took Richard by the shoulders and began leading us back toward the road.
One soldier yanked the camera from Richard's neck, snapping the
strap. Another grabbed his camera bag. Richard shouted, "What
the fuck?" and looked back at me. The soldiers seized the film inside the cameras. They searched Richard's bag but not his person,
nor mine. Crazy luck. Richard lost his cameras but got his pictures, five rolls' worth.

For days it wasn't clear who was responsible for the attempt to
assassinate the president. The soldiers captured four rebels and
shot them on the spot.

The government radio reported that much.

Richard and I were detained in an army barracks for two days,
film cartridges still in our pockets, and then escorted to the airport and deported to Paris. We sat apart on the plane.

My articles about the attempted assassination appeared in a few
American newspapers. They got little attention. The event was,
after all, just another blip in Africa's misery, a story that editors
cut to two or three paragraphs and buried on page nine. Standard African soup, no big deal. But Richard sold his photos to the
Associated Press in Paris, and a series of three images of that old
woman and the girl, the first pictures I ever saw him make on the
job, made page one around the world. Attempted coup in Africa,
dramatic images, story inside.

I eventually learned the president had everyone in the village
arrested and the homes bulldozed. I'm not sure what that means.

Here's an appendix to that story. Five years ago, on a visit to London, Karen and I went to see an exhibition of news photography

from all over Africa; it was sponsored by the Foreign Press Association. I'd written a short account of what happened in the village to be displayed with Richard's work. The organizers called the show "Africa: Land of Splendor and Agony." Karen and I got separated in the gallery, absorbed by our own interests. Eventually I wandered outside and found her on the museum steps, nursing a coffee.

Karen looked up and smiled. I sat down beside her.

She said, "Did you see Richard's work?"

I said, "I didn't look."

"Why?"

"Did they display the photograph of that little girl all shot up?"

She nodded.

"That's why," I said.

Karen squeezed my shoulder. She said, "I see what you mean."

## 5.

WHAT I FIND MYSELF returning to is that day in Tabotaki, the village Richard turned into a quasi film set, back in 1989.

But let me tell you this, first. By early summer of that year much of the Sahelian grasslands had turned to sand. The fresh rains meant little after twenty years of unwavering drought. The land had crashed. Half a dozen countries in the interior teetered on the edge, their governments bankrupt and their people moving to coastal countries by the tens of thousands every day, traveling on foot and crammed into buses and trucks. Richard Ward had published his fourth *National Geographic* cover, and I was back in the country with my notebook to do a series on drought relief. The president the rebels had tried to kill in 1977 died of a brain tumor, and a new man, a colonel, his cousin, ruled. This was also a time of coups d'état across West Africa, when young army officers attempted to govern a region that was in deep desperation, as if they—as if anyone—knew what to do.

Governments, relief agencies, and Western rock musicians were finding new opportunities to raise money for relief. Before every available camera lens, they were staging dramatic helicopter food

drops—mostly rice, flour, and dried milk. Once the relief workers flew away, soldiers and village chiefs seized the food and sold it
to their own people at two or three times the market price. Riots
broke out. The government banned helicopter drops and began
"distributing" food aid from truck convoys under heavy guard.

In Africa, I learned to smile a lot, as if time were my friend, to
make jokes easily and expect nothing. I learned that anger is the
worst emotion because it reveals everything—what you want and
how badly you want it.

The week before our visit to Tabotaki, I was at the Ministry of
Information early one morning, seeking a permit to travel with
a government food convoy, fifteen trucks loaded with rice, flour,
and high-protein soup packets for children. I sat in a wooden
school chair before an amiable man who sat at a large gray metal
desk, listening to him explain in French why it was not safe for me
to leave the capital. He wore a billowing white robe and a red fez.
Round wire-rimmed glasses balanced on the tip of his nose as he
talked, with his hands folded on the desk. The office was cramped
and chilly, besieged by piles of dusty papers on shelves, chairs, and
the floor. Dog-eared edges rustled under the breeze of an air conditioner that whirred from the window ledge. He said he himself
had not traveled out of the capital in five years.

"We can't guarantee your safety. As you know, there have been
troubles."

I shrugged. "That is kind," I said, "but you're not responsible for my well-being." My idea was to gently press him, perhaps
obliquely raise the possibility of a bribe, and if nothing worked,
to simply ignore him, rent a car, and take my chances. The phone
rang and he answered it.

"Yes, send him up," he said. "I have another American here." He
replaced the receiver and smiled. "One of your colleagues has arrived."

He walked in, a tall, thin man with short, unruly red hair, wearing khakis, a blue collared shirt, and sneakers. I hadn't seen Richard in a couple of years. Red-gray stubble claimed his chin and
cheeks, but his face was still thin and hollow. He frowned and

nodded to me; I frowned back. The official offered him a seat and began to explain in French the "difficulty of the situation." Dismayed and angry, I listened.

Richard put his elbows on the desk and leaned forward. "Look, I'd love to chat," he said in English, "but time is a serious issue. Can't you understand how important this story is to your people and your country?"

"Yes, of course," the official said, switching easily to English, "but—"

"What is this?" Richard was not yelling, exactly, but lecturing. "Why can't you just give us the permits? I represent one of the largest-circulation magazines in the world. A story like this can mean tremendous exposure and millions of dollars in food aid . . ." He went on.

The official's face froze, but he kept his composure. I clapped my hand on Richard's shoulder, tightening my fingers so that he turned and looked at me.

"Shut the fuck up," I whispered.

The official issued a joint permit, requiring that Richard and I travel together, but he forbade us to observe a food convoy and assigned us a government guide who would drive for us. Then he said to me, "Perhaps you can keep an eye on your friend."

I tried to focus on the story. We were speeding along a dirt road, three silent men in a white Land Rover. Richard sat up front with the guide who'd been assigned to us, the young university student who was also our driver and translator.

"I am pleased to be your driver," the young man said when we started the trip. "The ministry thought I might be of use."

I sat in back, studying my notes. The night before, a storm had brought dust and rain, dense sheets of muddy water carried by winds that ended as we left the city at dawn. Canadian engineers had elevated the road on layered tar and crushed granite brought from the mountains in the northeast. So the road worked like a dike and survived. The rains washed away young crops; instant lakes and ponds spotted the fields. Families were out planting their remaining seeds—millet, sorghum, corn, peanuts. People looked up as we passed. The men smiled and shook their fists in a gesture of greeting and respect. The driver lowered his window and waved.

Richard suddenly shouted at him to stop. We'd just passed a group of three men who were working a few yards from the road. He turned his head to look back at the farmers.

"Stop, stop right now," he shouted again. "Turn around." The driver and I were startled by the urgency in Richard's voice. We'd been traveling at high speed, and it took the man a hundred yards or so to stop the vehicle.

"What is it?" I asked.

Richard ignored the question.

"*Quoi?*" the driver kept asking. "*C'est quoi ça?*" The road was too narrow to accommodate a swift U-turn, so he had to make a series of furious forwards and reverses, gradually turning around while Richard rummaged in his camera bag and shouted, "What the hell, can't you drive?"

I looked at Richard as the car pulled up opposite the three farmers. He had the door open and was halfway out before the car had made a complete stop. Richard ran ahead and the young student at the wheel watched him in wonder and anger, raising his hands and looking at me.

Richard bounded down the embankment with his camera bag over his shoulder, a light meter in his hand, and a camera swinging from his neck. He shouted the traditional Muslim peace greeting as if he'd just learned it. "*Salamalekum, salamalekum!*" The farmers paused in their work, hoes in their hands, talking quizzically to one another and keeping an eye on this white man with so much gear hanging from his body.

"This is very bad," the student said to me. "Your friend is an imbecile. They don't know who he is or what he is doing. They could hurt him. He should have told me what he wanted."

The driver touched my arm and told me to stay with the car. Then he hurried down the embankment and into the field. To the farmers, muscular, barefoot men in torn T-shirts and shorts, this young man in pressed tunic and trousers, with white men in tow, must have looked like trouble, a tax collector or a police agent. The farmers had surrounded Richard, not quite in a menacing way, not close in, but more as a means to study him. They talked among themselves in low voices, eyeing the student and then me as I stood on the road.

Richard pleaded. "Please, go back to work," he said. "I want to photograph you while you work." He turned around and around, holding up his camera as a kind of explanation. One of the men said something to him in Hausa, and Richard, seeming not to hear, kept on talking. "Please, don't pay attention to me. Do your work."

Our young driver walked into the group while Richard looked on, hands clasped behind his head. The student began speaking to the men in Hausa. I don't know what he said exactly, but it took a while. He explained things. He made jokes. They all laughed. The men returned to work and let Richard take his pictures, but he had to keep his mouth shut. That afternoon we arrived in Tabotaki, where Richard performed his film-set routine.

I'm thinking now of my notes from the attempt on the president's life and the words I found recently, in my own rushed handwriting, large letters slanting down an otherwise empty page: *Girl sprawled on her back, much blood, all shot up, Richard circles with camera.* And these words: *They ought to shoot him.*

Those five words are barely legible, though clearly my own, and I'm not sure where I had the time and presence of mind to write them, standing there after shots had just rung out and as a woman cried over a girl's body. I don't remember writing anything, though I do remember stuffing my notebook in my pants under my shirt before a soldier grabbed me and hustled me along.

*They ought to shoot him.*

I don't remember having that thought. But from time to time I think of that sobbing woman and what might have happened, had the soldiers not taken us away. Would she have ignored Richard or moved aside as he asked? Would she have turned on him in an explosive rage?

Such a scene would have been fun to watch.

## 6.

KAREN AND I SAW Richard last year at a gallery show of his photographs on South Street in Philadelphia, near where we were visiting her parents. She'd read about the exhibit in the newspaper and told me that, after hearing all my stories about Richard over the years, she was curious and wanted to see "what he's like." I went along reluctantly, but I admit I was curious, too. I wanted to see how people reacted to Richard and his work.

When we arrived at the gallery Richard was sitting at a wooden table and signing prints. He waved at us and smiled. I nodded to him, but he was surrounded by admirers, so the two of us occupied ourselves with the pictures on the walls. I walked with Karen but kept my eye on Richard. The gallery consisted of just two rooms: a reception area, with a couch and a few chairs, and an exhibit room the size of a large hotel suite. Richard sat in the center, surrounded by his work. He wore a black suit with a dark green shirt and black tie and chatted amiably, signing prints with initials in the right-hand corner or scribbling a message in a copy of his book of landscape photography from Africa. I know the book. Richard had sent an e-mail message a while ago, asking if I would write the accompanying text. I never replied.

Karen and I stopped at a knot of people standing around the now-famous images from the assassination attempt. No one talked as they studied the pictures. When I turned to look at Karen, she was staring at Richard. People asked him questions here and there. The room was small, so we could hear most everything.

"He's so thin," Karen said in a hushed voice. "And cold. Look at him. People try to talk to him. He shrugs and he smiles, sort of, but he doesn't say much." She looked at me. "What a strange man."

A young man, college age, asked Richard for advice on how to get into photojournalism. Richard did not look him. He said, "Get a camera," and kept on signing pictures. I shook my head. Karen softly laughed.

A young woman, likely a photography or art student, bought prints of the elderly African woman and the girl. The woman was stylish and attractive, dressed in black—shoes, stockings, skirt—set off by a white sleeveless blouse. Before she paid for the prints, I watched her stand with her arms folded, studying the mounted display for several minutes. She stepped slowly along the wall and planted herself in front of the picture of the Russian soldier, her face a few inches from the photograph, scanning it as if she took note of details that we mere mortals, we non-artists, will never discern.

I went to get a glass of apple juice in the reception room. When I returned, the young woman was standing in front of Richard, with the prints in her hands. I walked over to Karen and nudged her, nodding at Richard. We were standing against the wall, several feet away from the side of his table. The crowd around him had thinned.

The young woman spoke in an even, matter-of-fact voice as she asked him to sign the photos. As he was making his initials I heard her say, "These people in your photographs—they must really hate you."

Richard did not hesitate. He looked right at her and said, "Yes, they probably do." He handed her the photographs with his initials and he added, "I bet people want to take your photograph all the time."

The young woman gazed down at Richard for a few seconds. She kept her eyes on him as she methodically ripped to pieces the photographs she'd just purchased. Then she dropped them on Richard's hand, still gripping its autograph pen, and walked out. Richard frowned and watched her as she left the room. Then he shuffled the torn-up prints into a neat pile and looked up at the next person in line.

I smiled and folded my arms. "Still want to meet him?" I asked Karen.

"Well, not especially," she said, "but that was fun to watch."

# TOUMANI OGUN

I N OREGON WE DON'T pump our own gas. The state won't let us, which is how I found Toumani Ogun. I ran into him at a Texaco station eight thousand miles from where we met twenty years ago. It wasn't an easy reunion. We faced each other from opposite sides of the gas pump, I in my pickup and Toumani standing in the rain beside another customer's car, his eyes on me a few seconds too long. For years I'd fantasized about meeting him in a place like this, where the balance of power between us had shifted and I could seek revenge by causing him pain and remorse. In fact, what often came to mind was something I'd read by Simon Wiesenthal, the Nazi hunter and death camp survivor, about a captured SS guard. The man "was trembling," he wrote, "just as we had trembled before him. His shoulders were hunched, and I noticed that he wiped the palms of his hands . . . he made me think of a trapped animal."

It didn't work that way with Toumani Ogun. I didn't encounter him in custody, for one thing. That September morning two years ago he tended my pickup, wearing shiny black leather shoes, dark trousers, and a white cotton business shirt, buttoned at the throat. He'd changed little — tall, around six feet, two inches, a thin and strong man but older now, fiftyish, balding, with gray hair in tiny curls on the sides of his oval-shaped head. He took my credit card for the gasoline and washed my windows, soaping the surface and wiping the water away with broad, even strokes of the rubber rake. His fingernails were finely manicured and his hands clean. He didn't smile, though he treated customers with crisp politeness. He called me "monsieur," as he had before, and said, after he filled the gas tank, "I am pleased to see you again, monsieur. Will there be anything else?" as if he'd been expecting me. In Africa we'd spoken French, and now he spoke English, accented and precise, highlighting syllables and consonants like someone who wanted to give every word its due respect.

Toumani Ogun owns the Texaco mini-mart on Broadway and Twelfth in Portland. He waits on motorists while Fatima, his wife, works the register in the cinderblock two-story building that is also their home. They keep an apartment upstairs. Toumani and Fatima — who is rotund and at least as tall as her husband — built their business on grace and efficiency. When my ex-wife, Ann, and I bought a house two blocks from the station, a few miles from the college where I teach political science, neighbors said we had to meet the African couple who ran the gas station down the street. That was two and a half years ago, just a couple of months before I realized who ran the place and a few more months before I figured out how to make myself known to him.

"And him, especially," said my neighbor, Katherine. "He's a character." She joked that he'd been president of some African country until he was forced to flee with his family in the middle of the night, or that maybe he'd commanded the secret police.

"He's a quiet one," she said, "so serious and straight, like an officer."

She was close.

A rifle fired from a few meters away is not at all loud. The shots sound more like soft, sharp claps — pa, pop — as if the gun is saying, "Pardon me, you're dead." Odd as well is the way a man looks when he's been shot in the chest. He jerks back a few steps, his knees bent, balancing himself for a few seconds, with his arms at his sides. Time has stalled in that moment. His face shows no shock, nor even pain, but is frozen in the look he had before the bullet struck. Or is it merely surprise on his face, his eyes wide open, alerted by some impoliteness? The rifle is old, low caliber, because he's not knocked off his feet. He falls to his knees, folding like a lawn chair, blood spreading across his white T-shirt, a hand in his lap and the other clutching at the wound. He sits back on his heels, his eyes and mouth wide open, and drops to his side to lie on the road in the shape of a limp zed. And I, standing there, caught between wanting to know who fired the shot and wanting to rush to the victim, between wanting to fight and wanting to help. The air is heavy. The only sound is the idling of engines, six heavy trucks in a line, painted United Nations blue — the team color of my employer at the time — loaded with medical supplies. Emergency aid. I did the logistics and led these convoys, which means the trucks were my responsibility, and so were the drivers and thousands of villagers we were trying to help.

The man who was shot drove the truck I rode in, and I remember his death as a consequence of my stubbornness. I was hesitating on payment of a bribe at an army checkpoint. An officer held our travel orders, telling us he was seizing two trucks and their cargo as tax. I offered money instead. Soldiers had surrounded us, guns in hand. But I'd focused on the fact that there'd been no threat in the officer's voice. He fell silent and nodded to a soldier, a kid, maybe nineteen, not much younger than the truck driver he was about to shoot on a nod. *My driver*, standing right beside me.

A minute or so on the other side of that nod, I knelt and rolled my man gently on his back, afraid of jostling the bullet in his chest. I had to see what I could do for him. I was frantic, shouting nonsense in English, "Jeesssuss, fucker, you shot 'im," looking from the driver's body to the officer, half expecting, half hoping that he would react in some way apologetically, to put things right. I sobbed, "Why, why, what for?"

It occurs to me now how odd thoughts come to mind under stress. As I was grieving, I also wondered how we must have looked out there, a bunch of people clumped together, connected by pathetic larceny on that sun- and dust-blasted road. I kept looking around, aware of my breathing and the hot breeze, thinking that beyond the trucks and soldiers, a land without trees and grass spread endlessly. A big sad place under a dusty wax-paper sky. And the silence of those moments, as if the heat had dissolved my words the moment I spoke them. I took a deep breath and leaned over my driver, gently tapping his cheeks to keep him awake.

His name was Harouna Ousmane. He was twenty-two years old. Sweat dripped from my chin onto his face as he gasped. His eyes blinked in the bright sun. He'd bitten his lip through, and a little blood ran down his chin and neck to his collarbone. I looked at the clean, roundish puncture the bullet made in his shirt. The cotton around the hole was blood-soaked but unfrayed.

"You're going to be fine," I kept saying. "You're going to be fine."

He mumbled words I couldn't understand, moving his head from side to side. I covered his wound with my hand, careful not to press too hard. His chest shuddered and pushed outward, and I could feel the knobby bone of his breastplate. Then he pronounced a single word twice, clearly, "*Hankuri, hankuri,*" the Hausa word for "patience." His body was still. His eyes and mouth remained open as if awed by some vision. For a few moments I was aware of every bit of the surface of my skin, the sweat and dust over every pore, and the flow of my own blood. I was aware of being inside another man's world. Through the blood on my hands, I felt his life swirl around me and slip away. I kept thinking that if only I could keep the blood inside him, press it back into the open wound, then I could stop Harouna from going away, and we'd have a chance to face down the men who had done this. His blood was warm on my hands, so alive, as if I was holding his soul. But his eyes were milky and cold. They did not move.

The soldier who'd fired the shot dropped his rifle. It clattered on the hard dirt surface of the road. He looked at me and my driver — his mouth open and his face a soupy mix of wonder and fear — and at the African drivers and aid workers, silent men and women who worked for me. They stood by the trucks, watching with deep-lined granite faces. They were hard people from the villages of that land. I'd recruited them myself. We watched the young soldier run into the bush, stumble in the sand, fall on all fours, and get back up. He lost his sandals. He was as much a victim as Harouna — I believe that.

I was still kneeling by Harouna, a body now, clad in bloody T-shirt, navy blue cargo shorts, and sandals. His bleeding had stopped. I breathed heavily, as if I, too, had been running. I looked from the officer's face to the blood on my hands. I didn't speak for a time, fearful he would nod again and someone else would fall. The officer smiled, his lips pressed together. He had clear brown eyes and he did not seem to blink at all. I was certain I'd seen his face before.

Finally, I said, "What is this?"

He stepped forward and thrust at me the travel orders I'd given him minutes earlier, three pages of government policy on foreigners transporting goods, with a letter from the Ministry of Defense, guaranteeing "free passage on all roads in the Takeita district." The pages fluttered in my face. He wore neatly pressed green fatigues, polished brown leather boots, and a red beret. He was tall, with a narrow, unlined face that appeared somehow patient and distinguished. Hair grew in dark curls around the sides of his oval-shaped head.

"You may go," he said. "But now you must drive the truck yourself." He pointed to Harouna's body. "There is your safe passage. You will put him in the seat next to you for all to see, and next time you will pay what we ask."

Still kneeling, I took the papers, smearing a little of Harouna's blood on them as the officer stood above me, very straight, feet a few inches apart, hands behind his back. He cast his eyes on me but didn't bend his head.

I said, "What's your name?"

He said, "I am Major Toumani Ogun, and you, sir, are in my country. Tell me your name."

I looked at Harouna's body. I drew his arms to his sides and wiped my face on the sleeve of my T-shirt. "John Heller," I said, turning to look up at him. "I'm a foreigner, but he was your countryman."

Toumani smiled with his lips pressed together. He didn't raise his voice.

"What makes you sure of that, monsieur? Is it that this man and I share the same skin color? Do you think it is that simple in Africa? You brought him here. He is no countryman of mine. Look at the marks on his face. He is a northerner, a goat herder."

I stared up at Toumani.

"Look at him," he said.

I obeyed, though I knew what was on Harouna's face — the scars of a northern tribe. Four long graceful strikes, narrow at the ends and wider in the middle, arced down each cheek. The scars remained darker than the skin around them, and now that Harouna's skin had paled in death, the contrast was more acute.

I stood up, my eyes on Toumani. "You killed a man for his scars?"

He put his fingertips together, as if he was praying. Those fingers, so clean, as if he never touched anything, and that strange smile on his face. He said, "Payment has been settled. You are free to pass, monsieur, but remember — this road belongs to me."

I drove three more hours that day, my truck leading the convoy. Harouna's body was slumped against the window in the seat beside me, his head covered by a T-shirt so I couldn't see his face and that open mouth frozen in the release of one last thought. We passed through more checkpoints. When soldiers saw the body and me, they waved us on. No questions. I had blood on my T-shirt, on my hands, and on my face. I never took my hands off the wheel. I never looked at the body beside me. And I've never been able to remember Harouna's face.

That was July 1984, when drought had dried up a part of Africa stretching from Senegal to the Horn. I was twenty-three, a year older than Harouna. Europe had disappointed me. Everything there seemed to have been fought over and worked out in a tidy arrangement. Blood had been spilled and cleaned up. They'd defined their borders. (Forgive me, it seemed that way back then.) I was looking for something to move me. Africa, with all its problems and mystery, looked like the place for a young man seeking clarity. My French was fluent, and after a year traveling in the former French West Africa—Mali, Burkina Faso, and Niger—I'd learned enough Hausa and bits of other languages to get by. So I stayed.

I started with small contract jobs, mostly translation work for foreign aid groups. When a shipment of, say, medical supplies arrived at the airport, I'd negotiate the stuff through customs, talk down the bribes, do the paperwork. I became a "fixer." I could talk to almost anyone, which was how I got into transport logistics, leading small convoys of aid trucks, six at a time, and negotiating our way through outposts of unpaid soldiers to relieve villages whose harvests had failed. Sometimes we paid the soldiers and they let us pass. Sometimes soldiers seized entire shipments. I once spent three days at a checkpoint, drinking tea and playing cards with soldiers. The trucks lined the roadside, and my drivers slept on mats beneath their vehicles, waiting for me to work some magic that would set them free.

We played *belotte*, a French card game of bluff and loud bluster. As I slapped my cards on the grass mat, making sure I lost the game, I said, "This food in our trucks, it's for your families, your brothers and sisters."

The soldiers laughed. "We are from the south," one said. "We have no family here."

They took half of everything. Sometimes, as you know, worse happened.

I did this kind of work in Africa for seven years until I decided I'd had enough.

At first I avoided the Texaco station, unsure of what to do. I considered notifying UN human rights investigators and the federal Office of Special Investigations, which hunts down war criminals. But my case was useless—twenty-year-old memories, emotions, and no willing witnesses. I have a few photographs that one of my other drivers had taken as he hid behind a truck. I have no idea where that man is today, and I'm sure he would be too afraid to testify. Besides, the pictures show no crime—just me, Toumani Ogun, and a man dying on the road, with a bullet in his chest.

Still, I sent an e-mail to a UN contact, detailing what I knew. She told me they had no jurisdiction without a formal government invitation and advised me to be sure of my evidence and then go to the Justice Department.

"John," she wrote, "let this one go. You'll probably never get him."

Good advice, which I ignored. Because of a chance meeting at a service station, emotions and memories were coming on hard and sharp. Revenge fantasies I'd been trying to bury now became real possibilities. I felt a responsibility to act, to force this man to confess and explain, even if there'd be no formal penalty. Toumani Ogun would answer to me. This has been my wish for two decades, alternating with dreams of courtroom justice, public humiliation, incarceration, and violence. I wanted to see Toumani Ogun on a street in Africa, in civilian clothes, walking alone. I'd follow him, ending up in some café or bar where I'd confront him in front of his countrymen, many of whom would have their own beefs with soldiers. Together, we'd force him to walk the streets, shouting a confession of his guilt and shame. Some fantasies are more visceral, such as following him home or into an alley (my God, an alley?), where I'd beat him senseless. Each fantasy has one constant: fear on Toumani's face, his eyes and mouth wide open, skin shiny with sweat. He was always mute in my fantasies. I couldn't imagine what he'd say in reality.

But to start, I kept things simple. I became a regular at the Texaco station.

On a wall of my living room hangs a traditional dagger in an intricately carved leather sheath, a gift from the chief of a Tuareg village that had been hit hard by famine. I bought other mementoes during my travels in Africa. I own two mud-cloth images of village scenes in Mali and a mask cut from a piece of eucalyptus in Sudan. A large photograph I took of a dust storm bearing down on a town in northern Senegal hangs in my bedroom, the first thing I see when I awake in the morning, a reminder of where I've been. They are all relics of another life, a time when I was younger and more engaged. I teach now. My academic work is in international affairs. But I'm not interested in theory or policy, in things like Marxist notions of government (I leave that to historians and English departments) or ways to "determine a language to co-address race in modern pedagogy and classroom ethics." As I tell my students, I teach "from the ground." This annoys some of my colleagues, who say I have no beliefs or that I'm shallow, not a scholar but "a storyteller." Some of that is true. I teach by anecdote and experience, which means, to quote one of my students, I "rant a lot."

Here's a rant. Every other year I offer a course in world health issues. I spout statistics, such as the fact that malaria kills a child every thirty seconds, mostly African children. I tell them how the disease overwhelms the blood with clouds of parasites, sucking oxygen from the white cells that course through the veins. The victim suffocates, a metaphor for what is happening across Africa — drought, war, disease, slow strangulation. No one can breathe. I tell my students that cerebral malaria begins as pain at the back of the head, where the neck meets the spine, and proceeds to a delicious delirium, which can be pleasant to live through if you don't fall into a coma. Because if that happens, you're dead.

On the other hand, my annual course on international human rights law begins with the essays of Hannah Arendt, who wrote, "The trouble with [Adolf] Eichmann was precisely that so many were like him and that the many were neither perverted nor sadistic, that they were, and still are, terribly and terrifyingly normal." Having raised the image of Eichmann, the soft-spoken technician behind Hitler's death camp program, I move on to case studies involving Africa and the notion that no one uses Africa and wins. The explorer Henry Stanley found that out. He perfected a method of lopping off the hands of uncooperative Africans and today his name is dipped in blood. Idi Amin Dada, the Ugandan dictator, psychopath, and would-be Scotsman, went insane; King Leopold's greed disgraced all of Europe; and the assassin Mobutu Sese Seko died in irrelevance after half a century of looting Zaire. The point is that these men, like Hitler, needed the help of legions to do their bidding, the rank and file of the "terribly and terrifyingly normal." In 1994, in eastern central Africa, bands of Hutu people, men and women alike, slaughtered 800,000 members of a rival tribe, the Tutsi. When the killing was finished, a Tutsi army in turn launched a war of revenge that has claimed as many innocent Hutus, maybe more.

At other times, not often, I tell my students about Harouna Ousmane. I tell them that he didn't speak English, but he could sing all the songs on *Bob Marley's Greatest Hits* nearly perfectly. I tell them that I taught Harouna how to drive and that despite my best efforts he loved to push those high-performance UN Land Cruisers as hard as they could go, but that he was a good driver at any speed, better than I was. I like to think he could drive well because he could read the land and feel it beneath us in a way I never could. After all, as Toumani said, Harouna was a goat herder. I also tell my students that every time we entered a village, Harouna knew some young woman, and while we were seeing to the unloading of supplies, he would disappear with her, hand in hand. I tell them he was fearless. He taught me about checkpoints. "The moment you show fear," he once told me, "you are lost." I'd notice Harouna's calm smile as he sat behind the wheel, with a soldier's gun pointing through the driver's window, the barrel just touching his ear. Soldiers liked to do that.

Here is a story about soldiers and Harouna. I like to tell my students this story because it involves adventure and because it makes me feel better, like a confession. I kicked open the metal door of a checkpoint guard hut one day. We were behind schedule and I was in a sour mood when, in open country, Harouna and I stopped behind an eighteen-wheel truck at a checkpoint eight kilometers from Takeita. Normally, a few soldiers sat on mats outside in the shade of the guard hut, but we saw no one.

"This is bad," Harouna said. "They have closed the door to the hut."

We waited a few minutes. Then I said, "What do you think we should do?"

"They are beating the driver," Harouna said. He looked at me. "We should wait. *Hankuri*, Monsieur John, *hankuri*."

As if to argue the point, a loud, anguished cry came from the hut. We heard grunts and blows. Shaking my head, I got out of the car, carrying our travel papers in a plastic sleeve. I looked back at Harouna. "Patience will kill the driver of that truck," I said.

I looked at the truck, which was full of onions in cloth sacks billowing from the top of the trailer — tens of thousands of onions — and began walking toward the shack. Behind me a door shut, and I turned to see Harouna leaning against the Peugeot, his arms folded and his face locked in a frown. He shook his head, but I smiled at him. The sounds from the hut grew louder, and someone was shouting harsh words in a language I didn't know. For a moment, I stood outside the door, which was a piece of corrugated metal on crude hinges. Then I kicked it open with the toe of my boot. The door clanged against a table.

Three soldiers huddled around a man who lay on the dirt floor, stripped to his shorts and curled in a fetal position. His forearms covered his face, and his hands clutched the top of his head. The soldiers looked at me. I smiled, holding up my papers, and shrugged, looking as innocent as I could. The door creaked, and I could still hear the thud of my foot against it. A soldier pushed me so hard that I stumbled, nearly falling.

"That's not very polite," I said, trying to keep my composure. A sharp clang rang out again as another soldier closed the door of the hut.

I was scared, but I smiled and raised my hands in a shrug of confusion to keep up the ruse. Harouna came running up behind me, but the soldier ignored him, grabbed me by the front of my shirt, and slammed me against the wall of the hut. He had a hand on my forehead as if he was taking my temperature, holding my head back against the wall while his other hand clutched a fistful of my shirt.

"You are a smuggler," he said.

Harouna shouted, "No, *patron*, please, we are not smugglers. Search the car; you can see we have nothing." He was standing so his face was between the soldier's and mine.

I shook my head. The voices of the two other soldiers could be heard from inside the hut.

"I work for a relief service." I gasped for breath. "This man is my driver."

With one hand the soldier pushed Harouna away, but Harouna stepped right back, shouting and pleading. "*Patron,* we have done nothing; we are not smugglers. We have only our clothes in the car and some water. Please, come and see."

The soldier clutched my jaw in his hand. "You are a smuggler. We will take your car and send you both to Takeita. The major will want to talk to you."

I'd never met the major and knew only his name, but when I saw that my papers in their plastic sleeve had dropped on the ground, I had an idea, a way to lie my way out of the situation. "I already have an appointment with your commandant," I said, gasping, as the man held my jaw. "Yes, with Major Toumani Ogun, in an hour. I have trucks coming, full of food for the villages."

He eased his grip on my jaw. I took in deep breaths.

"My travel orders are on the ground," I told him. "There is a letter from the major. He won't be happy about this." That, of course, was a lie.

And that was it. The soldier barely glanced through the papers and let us go. He even saluted as we drove away.

For several miles, Harouna gripped the wheel and wouldn't speak.

I said, "You're angry with me."

He looked at me, and for a moment I was startled. He seemed much older. I still can't remember Harouna Ousmane's face, but I remember that moment and the nauseated humiliation of being wrong, of feeling my righteousness fall away. I felt as if I wasn't the man of the picture and name on my passport, but someone else whom I didn't know.

"You are very stupid," he said. "The soldiers easily might have killed us both. And now there is the driver back there." He shook his head. "Things will be worse for him."

I stared at the road, trying to think of something to say. "I was hoping we might distract them," I said, "maybe free the driver." Harouna stayed quiet. I took a drink of water from a bottle between the seats. "Look, I took down the truck's license plate. Later on we can find him, check on how he is."

"He's dead," Harouna said. "The driver is dead."

We said nothing else to each other the rest of the day. That driver was one of Toumani's victims, and one of mine, like Harouna Ousmane.

There are other things I don't tell my students, things regarding Africa and the state of my soul, like the fact that I was married once. My first decision after Ann walked out (she let me keep the house) was to finish ripping out the lawn and replace it with mulch. I loved her, I still do, but once she was gone I didn't see the point in keeping grass that so uselessly soaked up water, which I hate to waste. Ann had never been to Africa, but she did grow up in Tucson, in the Arizona desert. Her parents were high school science teachers and passionate desert naturalists. "You have to understand," she said to me when we were dating. "I crave green. I was born in the desert, grew up in it, and played in it." Her eyes studied mine when she said this. "Our front and back yards were nice enough. We planted rock gardens with prickly pear cactus and yucca plants that shot straight for the sun. Beautiful green plants, yes, but painful to touch and always so dry. I love green, John. I love soft, lush, wet green."

Ann nurtured our lawn through Portland's dry summers. To placate me, she cut out patches of grass, replacing it with mulch and kinnikinnick, a native alpine ground cover that grows with thin, dense branches and tiny green leaves. When she was finished, we had a few meters of lawn left, but in summer she personally watered it every other morning at five for exactly ten minutes, and again late at night. Then she hoped for rain. "You'll see," she said, "we'll have a lawn and we won't waste water." Eventually we installed a watering system with an automatic timer. The first two weeks we had it, Ann got up at five to be sure the system worked. I loved that passion in her, even though I hated what lawn we had.

We met in the same graduate program at the University of Washington in Seattle in 1991, after I'd returned from Africa. A couple of years later we married and moved to Portland, where she entered law school. Four years after that we divorced. She couldn't relate to my obsessions, like my worries over lawns and water, like my identity card thing—I carry my passport everywhere I go—and the fact that I have trouble sleeping indoors, even during winter, because in those years of heat in Africa I slept out in the open, under a truck, on a roof, on a porch, or in a field, places where I'd wake to the sun grazing the desert.

In those years I didn't see much of tropical, rainy Africa. I spent more time in dry places, often sleeping in a hammock I fashioned to hang from the chassis of the aid truck I was driving. In Portland I bought an extra-warm, waterproof down sleeping bag and slept under the back-patio awning. At first, Ann thought it was cute and slept out there with me, but she drew the line on rainy winter nights. Here in Portland it rains from October to April. I can't blame her for leaving. Ann's a good person. We're still friends. She calls me often to check on me and say things like "You need more people in your life." And sometimes I'll call her for a reality check. She says I'm eccentric, which is nice, I guess. The neighbors loved Ann and think I'm a freak — alone, no wife, no children, and no lawn. But I couldn't handle putting water into grass, like rent. Good water, for what?

My neighbors, the older women anyway, take my hand when they see me in the street or at the grocery and ask, "How are things?" The Africans were like that — curious, concerned. "Don't you need a wife?" they'd ask. For years the questions made me panicky. But now I'm resigned to what I am, a refugee in my own way, with my own quirks defined by living on the road in the desert and by seeing Harouna Ousmane die.

I'm a nomad in suburbia.

Toumani Ogun commanded the third battalion for the northern region, charged with patrolling roads and regulating traffic. This meant he was a powerful smuggler — guns, drugs, auto parts, currency, medicines, firewood, clothing, and food, the highest-value commodity in time of drought. I had much to learn and Harouna's shooting was, so to speak, an important lesson. Toumani had carved out a piece of the country for himself and ruled it from the roads. We became intimates of a sort, not friends but business partners, which is how I phrased it at the time because I found it helpful, easier on the emotions, to look at our relationship that way. He, or his soldiers, welcomed us on every trip, extracting money or a few truckloads of food and medicine. Toumani needed us, and he and his people always knew we were coming. Sometimes an olive green Land Rover, accompanied by a truck full of soldiers, overtook my convoy, sirens blaring. Some days the man himself would step out of the vehicle, smiling, ready "to do business." Other days his soldiers would be waiting for us in a village, ready to "help" distribute the food and medicine we brought. That was the system after Harouna was shot. He was the sacrifice.

People rarely ask what I saw, about people starving to death by the tens of thousands. I get few questions even from my students, who study policy issues and theory and who rely on me to tell them what it's like on the ground in Africa. Occasionally someone will venture a question like "Why did you go into that work?" or "Why did you stay for so long?" I always ignore the last question. I haven't been back to West Africa in many years, and I don't know the answer anymore. Anyway, television has taken care of the visual details of disaster in Africa to the point that Americans are no longer moved by images of the barely living, the walking dead — however you want to put it. What else is there to say about a year-old girl so ravaged by thirst, diarrhea, and poor food that her body and face are no longer hers?

The worst was watching the stream of wretched humanity drain from the villages. The exodus was constant on roads and across the countryside, not crowds of people but a steady trickle, moving south, toward the coast. Barefoot young men and women walked with sacks slung over their shoulders, alone or followed by their families. Few animals remained, so men also pulled donkey carts on their own steam, loaded with belongings, with children, and with adults unable to walk. Women wore their brightest clothes, preserving a bit of dignity on a journey of humiliation. I remember two little boys and their mother sitting on a cart with a bundle of clothes and the enormous head of a bull, freshly butchered, its long tongue touching the wooden cart bed while their father pulled them along with a rope looped around his waist. Perhaps they'd sold the rest of the torso for truck fare to the coast, saving the head for themselves.

Toumani put it this way. "Why do you insist on feeding the

dead? Don't you see? It would be irresponsible of me not to seize much of what you bring, so it can be sold to people who still have lives to live."

That was the day after he'd had Harouna shot. I was angry, a little reckless, and went to see him at the army barracks in Takeita. I know now that if I'd been tougher, more experienced at the international aid game, more serious about "doing business," I'd have gone to "apologize" for the shooting and discuss future arrangements to prevent more "misunderstandings." Instead, I wanted to work off frustration. I wanted to tell Toumani about Harouna.

I'd hired Harouna from a village, a cluster of mud buildings called Dakah, where we delivered food. He'd been through high school but failed the exam to enter the national lycée. He spoke French, Fulani, and Hausa, as well as some Tamachek and Arabic. He asked me to find him Dick Francis novels in French. He had skin like coal and shaved his head because of the heat. The camels and cattle that had been Dakah's livelihood were gone, dead of disease or slaughtered because there was no grain to feed them, no grass for them to graze on, and no market at which to sell them. I met Harouna because the village chief used him as a translator. Harouna told me he couldn't find work and planned to join the army. So I hired him. I brought his body to back to Dakah the same day he was shot.

When I went to see Toumani, I showed my passport to the guards at the Takeita barracks, aware it might not be a good idea to confront the major with Harouna's story, that I might never leave the barracks, at least not as a whole person. Villagers talked of the barracks as if it were hell itself, a place people were taken to and never heard from again. I watched a guard wave his rifle while in conversation with another soldier. He saw me and grinned, raising his gun in one hand. "Does this scare you?" he said. I wasn't scared. I was pissed off. I'd known Harouna a few months. He'd been my responsibility, and he died because I wouldn't pay blood money.

Two soldiers escorted me to Major Ogun's office. He smiled as he stepped out from behind his desk. He sent his orderly to make us tea. His office was simple: a metal desk and leather chair for him, two wooden chairs for visitors, a light, a ceiling fan, and a picture of the president on the wall. No evidence of loot, no touches of luxury. When I mentioned Harouna, the major ignored me at first. The tea came, dark and sweet, wonderfully strong Chinese green tea. He waited for me to take my glass and raised his own. "To your driver," he said. "May he not have died in vain."

My intent was to reason with him and get a concession because of what had happened to Harouna — get the major to admit that his death had been unnecessary and then settle on the terms of our new relationship. But first I had to let him know how I felt. I wanted to kill Toumani, which I didn't have the guts to do. So I told him a story.

I raised my glass. "His name was Harouna Ousmane and you killed him." I drank, put the glass down, and spoke with my eyes on his. "I brought his body to his village. It was strange. Harouna's father was waiting for us just outside the village, on the road, as if he knew. He insisted on carrying his son from the truck all the way back to his house, nearly a kilometer." My gaze never wavered as I gave Toumani as vivid a picture as possible. "The old man put Harouna on a mat in the shade of a tree and washed the body with clean white cloth. He was singing something I didn't understand." I paused to watch Toumani's face. He'd tossed off his tea and sat with a hand on his desk, index finger tapping the tea glass as he looked at me. I said, "They buried Harouna last night, major. I watched that, too."

He studied me a few seconds. "You needn't worry about yourself, Monsieur Heller. As long as you use our roads, a tax must be paid." He paused. "So, are we going to do business?"

The door to the office opened, saving me from having to answer. A little boy entered, holding the hand of a soldier and taking small running steps between the desk and me. He must have been about three or four years old. When he saw Toumani, he smiled and shouted, "*Père, père*," raising his arms to his father. Toumani beamed and stepped out from behind his desk, squatting in front of the boy, who turned and stared at me, open-mouthed. He was curious, not frightened.

"Ahh, yes, this is Hassan," Toumani said, picking the boy up with his hands under his arms and pulling him to his chest. He rubbed his head. Then he held Hassan up above his head, his arms outstretched, appraising him and smiling broadly. "I have three boys and this is my youngest."

The boy squirmed in Toumani's arms, turning again to stare at me. He wore leather sandals, clean blue cotton shorts, and a collared shirt that buttoned up the front. His eyes were clear brown. Spittle had dried around his mouth, and he had not yet shed the slight chubbiness of a baby. Toumani kissed him on the forehead and handed him back to the soldier with a few words in Hausa. Hassan began to cry. The soldier left, holding the child in one arm and closing the door.

Toumani looked at me, the smile gone. "Your friend Harouna is gone from this life and this place. He is lucky. I would like to get out too, you see, but by different means."

I said nothing further about Harouna. I told myself he was spent currency. Bigger things were at stake in a land peopled by those who ruled and those who starved.

So we continued doing business, Toumani and I, until I left the country a year later for another assignment. All told, in the Takeita district I'd supervised seventeen shipments of foodstuffs and medicines, from which he or his men seized fourteen trucks, food and all. About $7 million worth of material. Often, I saw the food later in village markets, such as rice being scooped straight from blue United Nations sacks by some merchant client of the major. He had the trucks repainted in different ways. I'd see them everywhere, hauling people, animals, whatever they could hold, for a price. Sometimes I'd recognize one of his soldiers at the wheel, wearing civilian clothes.

I knew then it was time to leave Africa.

I got a certain satisfaction from watching patrons at the gas station tell the major what to do. I was tempted to walk up during a transaction with one of his customers and say, "Do you know who this man is? He's Major Ogun, ruler of roads in Africa, a celebrated thief and fine killer when he puts his mind to it." But I'd have only looked like a lunatic, or worse. I kept on watching him day after

day, an hour here and a few minutes there, trying to work myself
up to some kind of action but fearing also that I might do something stupid, something that would hurt others and me worse
than it would damage Toumani. I told Ann about Toumani and
my visits to the Texaco station. "You can't do this," she said. "The
obsession will ruin you." She was right, but that didn't stop me. I
had a vague fantasy of meeting another of Toumani's victims right
there at the gas pump, someone like me, a possible co-conspirator
with whom I could plan revenge.

I met no one like that, though the idea was not far-fetched.
Portland, like many American cities, hosts thousands of African
refugees from conflicted places such as Liberia and Sierra Leone,
Somalia and Sudan, or Ethiopia. They are mostly men and boys
— former soldiers, urchins, tailors, artisans, merchants, farmers —
with a few women. They come from refugee camps in nebulous
border regions, such as the undefined zone that separates Kenya
from Somalia. After time in the camps, some become soldiers
themselves, while others find work or enter resettlement programs
in Europe and the United States, exiled from homelands that civil
war has destroyed. Their families are gone, and they find themselves in, say, Omaha or Portland, alone, placed in schools and
with host families (or, if they're old enough, in their own apart-
ments), puzzling over the social oddities of an American high
school, breaking up corrugated cardboard for a living, or working
the drive-thru at Wendy's.

One of my political science students, a twenty-five-year-old So-
mali, lost his parents because government soldiers suspected they
supported the wrong side. His name is Faisal, and he won't tell me
how his parents died. He spent his childhood, from age eight to
age fifteen, with two younger brothers, in and out of the camps.
He learned English and he's been lucky.

I see a little of Harouna Ousmane in Faisal, though I can't recall Harouna's face — except for his scars — and it doesn't matter.
They'd be about the same age. Faisal, like Harouna, was a member of those who stood on the other side of the checkpoint line,
the side with no power and nothing to offer in exchange for a life.
Faisal is tall, strong, and handsome, very smart. He often comes

to my office to talk. I make him green tea and we talk about his course work and American life. He says things like "Americans like stories in little boxes. Each story must be the same." He tells me about raids that Arab bandits made on his village in Somalia and about his walk across the desert with his brothers, dodging bandits and guerrilla soldiers from different groups. At the refugee camps in Kenya, just inside the border, fresh bodies lay in the dusty streets every morning, victims of disease, starvation, and violence. Finally, when Faisal was fifteen, rebel soldiers kidnapped him one night and made him part of their army.

"They were black men like me, not Arabs," he said. "I carried a gun for almost a year and took part in raids on other camps. We stole food and money. We took children to be soldiers. One night I ran. They did not catch me. If they had, I would be dead."

"You helped kidnap other boys?" I said.

Faisal shrugged. He sat in a soft chair across from me, his hands clasped across his stomach, staring at the floor in leather shoes, dark socks, khaki pants, and a white collared shirt. He carries himself elegantly, moving in long deliberate strides, but with an earnestness that suggests he is aware of every moment in this new life. Faisal doesn't fidget. He rarely blinks in conversation. I have trouble imagining him in a dirty T-shirt, shorts, and sandals, lugging an AK-47 over his shoulder.

"Professor, I kidnapped boys. I have killed people. Even the camp was a violent place," he said. "A boy attacked me with a knife once for a piece of bread. I turned his knife on him." Faisal looked at me calmly. "Do you want to know more?"

"I'm sorry," I said. "But I want to know—what happened to your parents and your brothers?"

Faisal dropped his gaze to the floor. "Please, do not ask me such questions."

I sat in my office for a long time after Faisal left, wondering why I did not feel the same hatred for him that I did for Toumani. Faisal is, after all, a confessed killer of innocents, but during those years of killing he was a youth trying to survive and make sense of a world that took his family. No one can blame him for his choices any more that I can blame the young soldier who obeyed

Toumani's order to shoot Harouna, and then dropped his weapon and ran off into the desert, sobbing. Toumani Ogun is different. When I knew him in Africa, he was an adult who made cold-hearted choices and consciously used his power to enrich himself and spread misery and death.

Faisal put together a guest presentation once for my African affairs course, which is full of earnest and idealistic young people, mostly white. They talk of traveling, joining the Peace Corps and the Foreign Service, or working for Mercy Corps. Faisal gave them a slide show with a narrative about life in the camps, including newsmagazine shots of children playing pickup soccer, of tents and metal shacks, of children being treated for malnutrition and gunshot wounds, and bodies in the streets. He filled the report with facts and figures, and he offered one anecdote. "To prepare us for the American winter, they made us take turns standing inside a large refrigerator where they kept ice and medicines."

By the end, students were nervous, coughing and shifting in their seats.

"How did you survive?" one young woman asked.

Faisal didn't hesitate to answer. "I am lucky," he said.

I don't tell my students this, but I'm also relieved at the boredom and impatience—or is it queasiness?—we Americans feel in response to foreign news. In my line of work I'm surrounded by colleagues who wring their hands over "our national isolation" and indifference to geography that is not strictly our own. But I believe our detachment—ignorance, if you prefer—is a gift, a point of view we can afford for things that don't directly impact us. The rest of the world envies us this bliss, and some hate us for it. I read the foreign news and I pay attention to what's going on in Africa, but I also take comfort in this splendid isolation that I see in my neighbors who can't find Somalia on a map. One is a retired prison warden and his wife. Another owns a miniature golf course with his two sons and moonlights as a stonemason. The woman who lives across the street is divorced from a police officer and teaches high school physical education.

So, I don't mind that the news of Africa appears on, say, page fourteen, section A, of the *Oregonian,* where I recently found three paragraphs from the Associated Press about an African president's assassination. That lack of emphasis, the news buried deep, delivers the blow softly for me. The headline stacked over one column read, PRESIDENT OF WEST AFRICAN NATION SHOT TO DEATH. He died on the tarmac at the national airport, boarding a jet for a state visit to France. The head of the presidential guard shot him in the face.

I liked the cold justice of his death. He was an African military leader who died as he lived, in a country few have heard of. And I liked the idea of a picture of Toumani Ogun under a thick, black headline about his career as a killer. It occurred to me that I could perform an execution by media. I wrote the lead paragraph in my mind: "A professor at Portland College has accused the owner of a city gas station in a sordid murder and corruption conspiracy in Africa, involving international food aid . . ." Crime-scene tape would seal off the Texaco station while police searched Toumani's business records, as Fatima sobbed. She'd be deported before her husband's trial.

I seized on this scheme on the way to work one morning. From my office, I called an editor at the *Oregonian,* the mother of a former student of mine. I told her all about Toumani Ogun and the Texaco station. She listened carefully and asked a few questions.

"Do you have any evidence? Photographs, witnesses, documentation, anything?"

I thought of the photographs I had of Harouna's death. They lay in a drawer somewhere, useless. I felt the heat of embarrassment in my face. I said, "I have no evidence, but I *am* a witness."

"That's not enough, John. Without clear evidence it would be your word against his. He'd sue us right out of business."

I said nothing at first.

"I'm sorry, John."

"I can write an op-ed piece."

"John, we can't touch this."

One day at the Texaco station, I waited behind the wheel of my pickup and smiled at Toumani as he approached my window.

He said, "Can I help you, monsieur?"

"Fill it with premium."

"Yes, monsieur. Will that be all?"

"Clean the windshield, and don't top off the gas. I hate it when gasoline dribbles down the side of the car."

Fatima was on to me. I'd been dropping by the station daily, sometimes twice a day, for weeks. She was a large woman with heavy jowls. In contrast to Toumani's work dress, she wore colorful cotton wraps and shawls and kept her head covered with a white silk scarf. Every time I showed up, she'd come out from the little mini-mart and watch from the doorway, scowling at me with her arms folded. Sometimes she kept customers waiting at the register until I left.

Toumani shook his head at my instructions. He didn't shy from looking me in the eye. "Do not worry, monsieur."

"Spilled gasoline ruins the paint job. You should know that, major." I smiled at Fatima and gave a little wave. Her stare hardened.

"Yes, I know."

"You better know," I said. "You'll pay for it if you ruin my paint job."

I was baiting Toumani. A childish thing, certainly, and he knew what I was up to. His indifference surprised and hurt me, yet I knew that for him *to say nothing* was the logical way to cope with being recognized and challenged. Show no fear — this was the rule for surviving in Toumani Ogun's domain. And here, in my world, what else could he do? That exchange at the gas pump made me feel low and brutish. I've witnessed with shame how patrons often don't bother to look at him, or use polite address, such as "sir," or "please" and "thank you." He's unknowable to most. He's a black man in the United States doing a certain job. He's the help — though he owns the station — in a largely homogeneous white, middle-class city. He's invisible to most, an outrage to a few. Two blocks from Toumani's Texaco station in 1988, in a scuffle over a parking place, a teenage skinhead used a baseball bat to beat an Ethiopian man to death.

Not that I'm worried about Toumani. Believe me — he and the skinhead are fellow thugs, brothers in arms. But I was curious. I wanted him to explain a few things and I felt right in confronting Toumani Ogun. We were on my turf now. But I had to work up to the confrontation in my own time and on my own terms. So, for weeks I'd visit the gas station to "buy" something. I'd look into his face and smile, chat about the weather and the latest African football standings, and boss him around because I thought it would feel good. "Wash all the windows, will you, major, and hurry." I wanted to torture him slowly, believing that my presence alone would make him squirm and recall the things he knew that I knew. I wanted to torture him because of what, as far as I was concerned, he still was — a thief and murderer.

Yet he always greeted me smoothly. "Ah, my very best customer," he'd say, his face the same expressionless façade it was the day I caught up with him at the station. Unflappable.

One day, I decided to confront him directly. He'd filled my gas tank, and I was leaning against my car, arms folded because it was cold, watching him clean my windshield. A fine October mist was falling. He worked in a dark trench coat, brown knit gloves, and a gray wool driving cap. I'd gotten out of the car so we could talk on level ground.

"You remember Harouna Ousmane, don't you, Major Ogun?" I used his military title to remind him of our shared past and tip him off to my intentions.

He worked on the windshield without breaking his rhythm. "Yes, of course," he said.

"You toasted him with a glass of tea in your office the day after you had him shot to death in front of me. You must remember that. His blood was on my hands and clothes." I waited for him to speak, but Toumani finished with the windshield and retrieved my credit card receipt from the pump. As he handed me the paper, still holding the wiper, he looked right into my eyes and smiled.

He said, "There you are, monsieur."

My voice went up an octave. "Harouna was my friend."

"Really?" Toumani said. "I thought he was your driver." He dropped the wiper in its bucket, shaking his head and clucking his tongue. "Poor man. I didn't know he was your friend, monsieur. I am impressed. Friendship takes a long time to grow. Did you live with him in his village? Did you speak his language? Did you eat meals with his family?"

I stared at Toumani, my arms folded with my hands under my armpits, to hide their shaking. "I'm still in touch with his family in Dakah. I send them five hundred pounds of rice a year through the American embassy."

Toumani listened, hands folded behind his back. "How good of you. Are you sure the rice reaches the village?"

"It gets there, you bastard." I nearly spit on him. "The embassy makes sure of it. How can you smile, you murderous son of a bitch? This is my country you're in now."

Toumani looked at the ground. "This is America, monsieur. This country is for everyone, even for me. You know that. Fatima and I are citizens now. One of my sons has attended your military academy, the one that is called West Point." He licked his lips. "It is a pity that you are angry, monsieur. It must take a great deal of energy to be that angry for so long."

I thrust my hands in my jacket pockets as Fatima watched from the window of the mini-mart. I asked Toumani, "Are you in contact with anyone in the country?"

"Oh, yes," he said. "We go back every year. We see our families and we bring gifts. Yes, every year. Fatima wants to go back permanently, but that is not possible for me."

"Why not?"

Toumani turned his attention to a large four-by-four pickup that pulled up at another pump. The customers, two young men in paint-stained jeans, boots, baseball caps, and jean jackets, looked like the hardened types I could hire for a few hundred dollars to trash Toumani's gas station in the middle of the night. But the idea shamed me and I let it go. One shouted his gas order to Toumani, and they walked to the store, carrying plastic coffee cups.

"Major Ogun," I said. "We need to talk, only you and me, away from here."

He was holding the pump in the truck with one hand, the other hand folded behind his back, his head turned sideways, watching the fuel price scroll up on the pump housing. It had been two months since our reunion at the Texaco station.

"When?" he said.

"Tomorrow, 5 P.M. I'll pick you up."

"No," he said quietly. "Tell me the place. I will meet you there."

"Alone, please."

"Of course," he said. He finished and placed the pump back in its cradle.

I took a notebook from my back pocket and wrote the address of the House of Vishnu Teashop, a hangout of mine on the other side of the city, where he would not be recognized. I handed him the slip of paper.

"Yes, we will have tea," he said. "I know this place, the House of Vishnu."

"Don't be late," I said.

I saw that smile again, his lips pressed together.

"I am always on time, monsieur. That is how I do business. You know that."

The Portland rain soothes my nerves, so badly singed under the African sun. On the Pacific Northwest coast the sky comes in close and wet, in shades of deep gray and sometimes nearly black. Clouds form a ceiling of rounded, fuzzy edges that brush the city wet. Some days clouds kiss the tops of buildings, as if to bless them. The contrast blurs my memory of Africa. In the Sahel, in countries like Mali and Niger, the sky is always a distant blue or dim brown from dust, and when the sky does touch ground, it is with the violence of monsoon rains and the desert haboob, the dust storm of the photograph on my wall. Not a kiss, but a fist in the face.

That's not all. Even when I jog, I carry my passport in a nylon travel pouch that hangs from my neck beneath my shirt. I tense up at the sight of military and police uniforms, though here in my own country the anxiety passes quickly. I also cook with bottled water. I have trouble in grocery stores, weighed down by so many choices. I don't own a television. I subscribe to twelve newspapers and magazines.

Ann told me that sometimes I would gasp and sit up in my sleep. Nothing dramatic, just a sharp breathy sound and then an abrupt movement, and I was sitting, looking around the room. She'd touch me on the shoulder and gently shake me out of it. "You're sweating," she'd say. At first I denied the nightmares because I could never remember them. Ann gave me a notebook for the bedside. "Write it down as soon as you wake up," she said.

Here's what I found: I dream about bodies lying on dusty African streets, though I never see the killing, and the only body I recognize is Harouna's, with his bloody shirt front and open mouth. In another dream, I'm walking with Harouna across the desert as he's herding goats. We're looking for grass and water, but there isn't any, and the herd keeps getting smaller. I dream that someone taps me on the shoulder in my front yard, and I turn to encounter a soldier in a red beret, demanding my identity card.

While Ann and I were married, we slept outside most summer nights, though she sometimes coaxed me to sleep inside. I was asleep beside her in the house before dawn one July when I sputtered and sat up. I got out of bed and began pacing, clutching that notebook and a pen in my hands to calm myself by trying to recall the dream that awakened me. But I remembered nothing. Ann groaned and closed the bedroom door. Even with all the windows open, the house was still hot. It hadn't rained in a month, which is normal for a Portland summer. Outside I heard a spitting sound and a steady *ssssssss* as sprinklers came to life on the neighbor's lawn. Then our system switched on. The neighbor's yard was several times the size of ours, and they watered it two hours every day. Suddenly, I was angry. I couldn't tolerate throwing water on a lawn whose only purpose was to look nice. I shouted, "We don't fucking need a lawn. Water conservation is a human rights issue." (I don't remember saying those things, but that's what Ann told me I said.) I went to the garage, wearing only my boxer shorts and sandals, and got out the pickax and shovel and started ripping out what little grass we had. I didn't do it to spite Ann. I wasn't thinking of her at all. It was 6 A.M. when I realized what I was doing, and I stopped. I tried to put back the sod I'd ripped out, on my knees, patting it down with my hands. I was sobbing.

Ann left me that same day.

♦ ♦ ♦

I'd seen the major before the shooting, I was sure of it, and when he smiled during that meeting in his office at the Takeita barracks I remembered where — on the Takeita road two weeks earlier, the same road where Harouna would die. I was in a UN vehicle, a Peugeot station wagon, with Harouna behind the wheel, on a scouting mission to check out the roads and meet with army officials. The road, unpaved and badly rutted, ran north across a wide, rocky plateau, through Takeita and on into the Sahara. The road was hard-packed dirt and gravel, and it stretched, at a slight incline, across the plateau, a reddish stripe easy to make out as it turned gradually to the east and vanished over the horizon. We drove at seventy miles an hour, raising thick dust behind us.

We passed four women crossing fields, with brown clay pots of water balanced securely on their heads, steadied by one hand. They wore headscarves and wraps of bright green, blue, yellow, and orange, colors that splashed as they walked, challenging the drab land.

We traveled for two hours without seeing anyone else. In the afternoon, with the sun behind us, we could make out in the distance a tiny, dense plume of dust against the blue sky. I thought it a welcome break from the monotony, something to puzzle over. At first the dust resembled a feather, but as the distance closed it seemed to spurt from the earth. We watched until the source of the dust gleamed in the sunlight, before vanishing beneath a rise in the land. We guessed the vehicle was two or three miles away.

"He is moving fast," Harouna said, "very, very fast, probably police or army."

I slouched in my seat, bare feet on the dashboard. "Police or army? How do you know?"

Harouna smiled, and the scars on his face seemed to reach and spread. I never asked about them, though I wanted to. He sensed my curiosity.

He drew an index finger along the scars on his cheek. "This is my land. I know where to find grass and water. I know this road. People communicate something by the dust they put in the air." Harouna shrugged. "Like a signature."

"You can find grass and water here?"

"Yes, but we must walk many miles from the village to feed our animals. Sometimes we are gone with our animals for days and weeks. Every year we must walk farther from the village."

A glint in the distance caught our attention, probably as the sun caught a side-view mirror of the other car. Harouna leaned forward and I sat upright, squinting through the dusty windshield. He usually drove with his hands in his lap, thumbs on the bottom of the steering wheel. Now, gripping the wheel with both hands, he maneuvered to the right, and we leaned with the roll of the road grade toward a drainage ditch, slowing down, while up ahead the dust cloud swelled.

Then, as we drove over another rise and descended the other side, two figures, a man and a donkey, appeared, marching toward us up the road several hundred meters ahead, between us and the dust cloud. The approaching car bore down on them, its dust plume rising like the tail of a wild animal. As we drew closer, Harouna hunched forward and pointed at the man and his donkey, his index finger pressed against the windshield.

"Look, look, he's coming from the well."

Large plastic water jugs hung off the animal's flanks, like awkward wings, bouncing as the farmer jogged alongside. He wore a long white tunic that flapped in the wind, and a wide-brimmed straw hat. He must have heard the rumble behind him, but he still led his donkey at a trot.

"The fool thinks the car will go around him," I said. "Jesus, Harouna. The other driver is looking into the sun. He can't see them."

We were now within a mile of the other vehicle. Harouna jammed the heel of his hand into the horn, sounding long beeps.

The farmer's gray beast bolted, its long ears flattened, as it charged across the road to the east, bucking its hind legs viciously. The farmer started to run after the animal but then glanced behind him to see the car speeding toward him. He zigzagged a few steps and jumped to the side of the road, into the drainage ditch, and scrambled out of it onto a field of sand. He stumbled to his knees, the hat still on his head, and knelt there. The donkey bucked wildly, trying to shed the water jugs, moving farther and farther from the road. Harouna hugged the roadside at a crawl, as the other car roared past, blasting its horn and flashing its lights. It was a Toyota Land Cruiser, olive green, a color reserved for army vehicles. The man in the passenger seat turned to look at the farmer running across the field, and then at us, smiling. Our eyes met for a second or two, and his face was clearly visible. Eventually, I connected that smile to the major.

"The army," Harouna said, shaking his head. "Bastards."

The House of Vishnu Teashop is a storefront business in a concrete and steel office building. The top floors house two law firms, a dentist's practice, and an architect's office. The teashop takes up the ground floor between a haberdasher and a stationery store. Above the doorway, protected by a bright orange cloth awning, is a multicolored mural of Lord Vishnu — the Hindu preserver god, defender against evil — a muscular blue-skinned youthful figure, with four arms and long, thick black hair, astride a giant eagle. The artwork is kitschy tourist stuff from India, which makes Vishnu resemble a rock star, a specific one — George Harrison. I like that. This Vishnu is gaudy and accessible, uninhibited, surrounded by a swirl of lesser Hindu deities who look out from every space in the shop — plaster statuettes, posters, and post cards of gods mingle with pictures from India, and they're all for sale. I like as well the varied and shocking likenesses of Kali, the goddess of death and destruction, the goddess of thugs. Three hand-painted plaster Kali statues look down from a shelf behind the counter, each with a garland of human heads, whose faces express either terror or ecstasy, I can never tell. The eyes are wide open. Tongues, swollen and red, hang from the mouths, dripping blood.

Useful catalysts for my memory. I go to the House of Vishnu Teashop to think and make sense of my notes from Africa. The place is neutral, neither African nor American, which helps. I rewrite my notes, adding details between the lines and in the margins, eventually developing essays and chapters, as I sit in a place I've never shared with Ann or my friends. I wrote a book at a table in the House of Vishnu, using research from a few return trips to Africa. I called it *The New Colonials: Africa's Military Juntas*, and published it a few years ago. But I've got tenure now and my focus has changed. What bothers me about Africa is more personal. It's *all* personal. Often I go to the House of Vishnu in the evenings after dinner, or on Saturday mornings, and sit with old notebooks and photographs, pen and paper, searching for clarity. This is part of my pattern. It's not healthy. I know that.

So did Ann.

She challenged my insistence on sleeping outside, arguing that it underscored my compulsive nature and how separate we were, despite being married. Maybe there's also a connection to my negotiating a bribe with Toumani that day, in the presence of his soldiers' guns, and why in those days I'd occasionally pick fights with soldiers.

Before the meeting at the teashop, I went through my old notes. I retrieved the photos the driver had managed to take without being caught. I laid them on the table in their envelope, unable to look at them.

But I remembered that Toumani Ogun watched as I lifted Harouna's body from the road. I'd forgotten that part of the story, or more likely suppressed it. Toumani stood in the middle of the road, hands folded behind his back and his brow furrowed, as if curious to see how I would handle the situation. On one knee, I bent down and slipped a hand and forearm beneath the small of Harouna's back and my other arm just under his shoulder blades. My knuckles bled from friction with the road. When I tried to stand, the body rolled forward, almost out of my hands. I reacted by pulling the body up and jerking my head down, so my face pressed into Harouna's bloody shirt front. I tasted him on my lips and I tried to spit. On the second try, his spine cracked and his body bent in a bow over my arms when I stood up. He was still warm and not yet stiff, as if some breath of him remained. I don't recall having trouble carrying him but was startled when the fingertips of his right hand brushed my thigh, his arm jerking back and forth as I walked. One of the other truck drivers held open the passenger door of my truck, and together we laid Harouna on the seat. His eyes and mouth were still open. The driver took off his own shirt and carefully draped it over Harouna's face and head, arranging his hands on his lap. The driver shut the door and returned to his own truck. I ignored Toumani as I walked around the front of my truck, opened the driver's side door, and mounted the step to the seat. He remained in the middle of the road until I started the engine, and then he stepped out of the way. I shifted the truck into gear and eased forward. Harouna's body shifted so his head rested against the side window. He stayed like that until we arrived in Dakah a few hours later.

Toumani was right about one thing—it *does* take a lot of energy to stay angry. I'd thought of kidnapping him—in the name of Harouna and the villagers who'd never gotten food or medicine because of this man—and breaking a few of his bones, and, yes, even shooting him. But I couldn't convince myself that revenge would matter.

I wanted clarity. To get that, I thought I had to provoke him.

At the House of Vishnu, I sat at a table away from the windows, holding a newspaper in my hands and a file folder of papers and photographs on my lap, things I'd prepared for our meeting. When Toumani Ogun opened the door of the teashop, it was nearly dark. He was dressed in his work clothes and wore a white cloth Muslim skullcap. An old woman in a sari, with long gray braided hair, worked behind the counter, making biscuits. Out front, a teenage girl, the third daughter of the couple who owned the shop, cleared tables. She wore jeans, sandals, and a T-shirt with a drawing of Nehru stenciled on the front. The girl's name was Asha, a Hindi word for "hope," her mother told me. Asha was sullen and quiet, as teenagers can be, and wore her dark hair in a long braid. I spoke to her only to place my order. "Not much hope in that girl," her mother said. "She's lazy like an American teenager."

I stood to greet Toumani. "Thank you for coming," I said.

Toumani Ogun nodded and smiled as he pulled out the chair opposite me. I sat down. He removed his long coat and seated himself, folding the coat over his lap.

"She could be a rock star," I said, pointing to the Kali poster.

Toumani glanced at the poster and back at me, ignoring the

comment. "Mango juice," he said to Asha. He handed her his coat.
"Hang this for me, please. I do not want it touching the floor."

"I'm going to order tea," I said. "Would you like some?"

He shook his head and sighed, pursing his lips. "No, I cannot
drink this tea. If I drink tea, I must make it myself. The juice is
fine."

"I'd like to use a tape recorder," I said.

Toumani sighed. He pressed his fingertips together in a tent
against his lips. He smiled and nodded. "I will tell you everything,
my friend, everything I know, but I cannot allow you to use a tape
recorder. That would be silly, no?" He folded his hands on the table. "So, Monsieur Heller, you want to ask for my surrender?"

"No, that's not what I want."

Asha brought Toumani his juice. A few moments of silence
fell between us as I studied him, looking for signs of anxiety. He
drank his juice in careful, measured sips, noiseless, as if intent not
to leave a trace of himself, even a sound.

"What I want," I added, "is for you to tell me why."

Toumani laughed softly. "Is it not obvious, Monsieur Heller? I
wanted to get my family out. You know the life in that land. The
road provided the means for our escape. We are refugees. We are
survivors."

"Refugees? Really?"

"I had three sons. I sent two of them to school in France. They
still live there now. Our third son came here with Fatima and me.
I told you about him, perhaps? His name was Hassan. He was at
West Point."

I smiled. "Yes, I do know about him, Toumani. Another soldier
in the family. Have you told him about your career in Africa?"

Toumani looked at me, without expression.

"That's a lot to manage, Toumani, a family here and sons in
Europe. Lots of complexities, lots of paperwork, different embassies to deal with — yours, the French, the Americans. That takes a
lot of money."

He spread his hands on the table. "Yes, the will to survive is
very good motivation."

"That's true." I smiled. "But you say it was about survival. I don't believe you, Toumani."

"Monsieur, what you believe about me is unimportant."

"Then why did you agree to meet with me?"

"Business, Monsieur Heller. You have business with me."

I was nervous, slightly panicky. I felt as if I was losing my chance. I opened the folder on my lap and took out a photograph, which I pushed across the table against his fingertips. It was a picture of Harouna behind the wheel of a Land Cruiser. Just his profile. The picture was overexposed and it was impossible to make out the exact features of his face. I remember he looked serious in some way when I took the picture. The door was open. He had one hand on the wheel and a foot on the ground.

"I went to his funeral, you know. I had to return to his village and present his body to his family, but surely you remember that. I have something else for you." I kept my hands on my knees, so he couldn't see them trembling.

Toumani smiled. "You are going to take out a pistol and shoot me here, a bloody killing in a public place. How very American."

I shook my head. "I can't do that, but I have thought about it."

"I know."

From the folder, I took a stapled sheaf of papers printed with single-spaced text and handed it to him. "I know who your son is, Toumani, the one named Hassan. Third in his class at the Point, an impressive young man. You may recall that I met Hassan once when he was a small boy. It was in your office in Takeita, the day after you ordered Harouna to be shot. He must be a captain by now or maybe a major like you." I smiled. "I'm going to send him this letter. It's the story of Harouna's death. I wanted to send it to a newspaper, but they were afraid you'd go to court. As for me, I don't care what you do. Here's a copy if you'd like it."

Toumani's cheek twitched. His eyes were moist. I smiled in order to drive home a little cruelty of my own.

I said, "Don't you think it's appropriate that he know about you and me and Harouna and all those truckloads of food and medicine? I'm sure the army can help me find his address. I'll include a few photographs with the letter. Here are copies." I held up the envelope for him to see. "Proof is important, you know. You can keep these, too."

I still had not looked at the pictures, but from the envelope I handed them to him, one by one, color prints of Harouna's body on the road. I was a little surprised by the images, which I couldn't help but see as I passed them across the table. He glanced at them and set each one aside in a neat stack. I'm in the photos, leaning over the body. In one, Toumani is standing behind me, with his hands folded behind his back. His face is clearly visible, expressionless, looking down at me and my driver. Harouna's hands are flat on the ground, his knees are bent, and he is pushing his body up in an arch. His mouth is open. I didn't remember Harouna's body arching like that, in agony.

"Your son Hassan should find them interesting."

Toumani turned his hands over on the table and looked at his palms. I didn't know whether to feel anger or pity.

He said, "My son does know, monsieur. He already does know."

I glared at him. "I don't believe you, Toumani."

He looked at me steadily. "Your information is incomplete. Your research has failed you, monsieur. My son is dead."

I looked at Toumani Ogun. My mouth felt dry.

"What?"

Toumani folded and unfolded his hands on the table. "My son Hassan was killed in action. He was doing his duty. He died in an American war. And now, through the eyes of God, he knows everything."

Toumani stood up and called to Asha for his coat. The girl rolled her eyes and retrieved the coat from a wall hook. I said nothing at first. I offered no condolences, but not out of spite. I simply did not know what to think, sitting there, suddenly emptied of my anger. I felt calm, as if Toumani had reached forward and lifted a burden for me.

"Go ahead and say it," he said, looking down at me. Asha shoved the coat at him. Toumani took it without looking at her, folding the coat over a forearm. He clasped his hands in front of him and stood his ground, speaking in a steady voice. "Tell me how you know the feeling of loss. Tell me how I deserve this, to lose my son in the service of your country." He paused and repeated the last words slowly. "Your . . . country."

I shook my head and looked away from his face.

"I don't have to say those things," I said quietly. "I suppose what I came here for no longer matters." I looked back up at Toumani. He was hunched over and his head leaned to one side; his lips were barely parted. He blinked as if trying to remember who I was. I said, "I am very sorry."

But I don't think Toumani Ogun heard me. "Send your letters and photographs anywhere you like, monsieur," he said. "I will not run. I do not care anymore."

# ACKNOWLEDGMENTS

I am grateful for the people who helped me write this book. First among them is my friend and colleague Debbie Lee, who for years has patiently listened to my stories about Africa. She believed in this project from the start. Without her friendship, her penetrating questions, her selfless faith and interest in my writing, and her careful reading of many drafts, this book would not exist.

I am thankful to Lan Samantha Chang for finding merit in these stories and to the Katharine Bakeless Nason Prize of Middlebury College and the Bread Loaf Writers' Conference for their support.

Brandy Vickers, my editor at Mariner Books, asked thoughtful questions and offered insightful feedback and unflagging enthusiasm for these stories.

Henry Marchand and Paula Coomer offered valuable critiques. Cathie Chilson, my sister and onetime travel companion in Africa, is the model for Kate in the story "Disturbance-Loving Species." She is very much alive and read these stories to ensure accuracy on aspects of the expatriate experience in Africa.

Scott Olsen, editor of the literary journal *Ascent*, gave generous feedback on portions of the manuscript. *Ascent* also published parts of the novella, *Tea with Soldiers,* and the story "Freelancing."

The stories "Disturbance-Loving Species," "Toumani Ogun," and "American Food" were published in the *Clackamas Literary Review*, *The Long Story*, and *Gulf Coast*, respectively.

My friend, the late Joquim Keller, told me many tales of his adventures as an aid worker in Africa before he died in Niger of hepatitis. Some of his stories are in this book.

John Bishop and Jon Titus, two intrepid botanists, generously allowed me access to their research on Mount St. Helens and let me accompany them on numerous expeditions to the volcano.

Rich Wandschneider, director of Fishtrap, an institute for writers in Oregon, gave me a two-month residency and a cabin in the Wallowa Mountains, where I began writing this book.

The Idaho Commission on the Arts gave me a generous fellowship that paid for a return trip to West Africa to gather material.

My employer, Washington State University, along with the College of Liberal Arts and the Department of English, provided research grants, including a College Fellowship and a Buchanan Scholarship, to fund three more research trips to West Africa. Sue McLeod, Victor Villanueva, and George Kennedy—the department chairs I have worked under—were particularly helpful.

Baba Wague Diakite and his wife, Rona, also sheltered me in Bamako, Mali, at the Toguna Cultural Center, which is Wague's brainchild. The center provides housing and workspace for African and expatriate artisans. Thanks also to Wague's brother, Madou, a Bamako taxi driver who put his vehicle and himself at my disposal.

Laura Gephart has offered me shelter, a place to write, and unconditional love and encouragement. Her mother and father, David and Carolee Gephart, veterans of the international aid business in Africa and around the world, invited me into their home, hearts, and lives. I am forever thankful.

Ali Ongoiba, director of Mali's National Archives in Bamako, the capital city, gave me free access to the archives and to his own extensive knowledge of the colonial history of the Sahel.

Many books were important to my research, and I want to mention two. The first is *Veiled Men, Red Tents, and Black Mountains*, a personal account of field research in the Sahara in the 1920s by the late Alonzo Pond, an archaeologist and writer who wrote on the natural history and culture of the Sahara. Pond's descriptions of his meetings with Tuareg leaders were helpful to my understanding of Tuareg culture. Michael Tarabulski, research librarian at the University of Idaho and a friend of Pond's, turned my attention to *Veiled Men,* which Michael convinced The Narrative Press to reissue in paperback in 2003.

The anthropologist Paul Stoller's book *Embodying Colonial Memories: Spirit Possession, Power and the Hauka in West Africa* helped me understand spirit possession and the culture of the Hauka in Niger. It is in Stoller's book that I found the Songhai proverb "The path of the sorcerer is a path on which the most able practitioners are relentless seekers of power."

Finally, I must thank the two men to whom I have dedicated this book.

The late Abdoulaye Mamani — novelist and poet, activist, politician, political prisoner, and my friend in Niger until his death in a car accident in 1993 — is the inspiration for the novella, *Tea with Soldiers.* I spent many days listening to his accounts of political life in the early days of Niger's independence and of his experience resisting the rising military dictatorship.

Oumarou Badini, soils biologist and travel companion, told me stories that helped provide material for this book. He opened his life and home to me in both the United States and his native Burkina Faso. He has been answering my questions about science and Africa for a decade and has hosted me on several field trips to Mali and Burkina Faso.

## BREAD LOAF AND THE BAKELESS PRIZES

The Katharine Bakeless Nason Literary Publication Prizes were established in 1995 to expand Bread Loaf Writers' Conference's commitment to the support of emerging writers. Endowed by the LZ Francis Foundation, the prizes commemorate Middlebury College patron Katharine Bakeless Nason and launch the publication career of a poet, fiction writer, and creative nonfiction writer annually. Winning manuscripts are chosen in an open national competition by a distinguished judge in each genre. Winners are published by Houghton Mifflin Company in Mariner paperback original.

### 2006 JUDGES

*Mark Doty, poetry*

*Lan Samantha Chang, fiction*

*Susan Orlean, creative nonfiction*